K. D. Miller

ISBN: 979-8-9887609-6-2

For everyone who believes in second chances.

* * *

And to Warren Zeiders, whose music inspired this book.
...and also his abs. They're out here doing the Lord's work, y'all.

This book was inspired by the music of
Warren Zeiders. If you're an eagle-eyed fan, you might spot
some nods to his songs throughout this book, but I've added a
footnote to each one within the pages and listed them all
below. I think they give you a little extra insight into Bowen &
Laney's thoughts and feelings.

Give the songs a listen and check out all of Warren Zeiders'
stuff!
His songs are amazing...and his abs ain't half bad either 😉

1. PRETTY LITTLE POISON
2. SIN SO SWEET
3. WEEPING WILLOW
4. CAN A HEART TAKE
5. HAPPY HURTS
6. SOME WHISKEY
7. STONE'S THROW AWAY
8. LOVE IN LETTING GO
9. LIES
10. BETRAYAL
11. LOVING AND HATING YOU
12. FIGHT LIKE HELL

Contents

Chapter One

LANEY

BEING CALLED to someone's deathbed is strange. It's even worse when it's someone you don't particularly like. Worse still when that person is your own mother.

I stare at my suitcase, running the chain of my necklace across my lips over and over. I stare at the black cardigan, wondering if I should bring it after all and then groan. I've packed and repacked at least six times, putting the sweater in, then taking it back out, then throwing it in again, like it's the fucking hokey pokey.

"It doesn't matter," I mutter to myself, running my hands through my hair. The hospital told me to take as much time off as I needed—I mean, I haven't taken a single personal day in the past eight years, I volunteer to work every holiday so everyone else can spend time with their families, and do so many hours in the free clinic that they should probably name it after me at this point, so I guess I'm due—but I don't plan on staying in Riverbend any longer than I need to. I'll go, say my goodbyes, maybe get some tiny semblance of closure, put mom in the ground, and be back in Virginia by next week. At least that's what I'm telling myself to be able to do this at all. My feelings on all of this are complicated to say the least, but complicated doesn't at all equate ready to say goodbye.

"Are you all packed up?" my best friend, Beth, calls. I groan, throw the stupid sweater in again, and zip the suitcase up. *Done. The end.* I toss my phone charger and computer in my backpack, and lug it and my carryon out into the living room. She eyes the small bag, one red brow arching. "Your packing efficiency frightens me, you know that, right?"

I huff out a laugh and go to the fridge to grab a water. I'd offer Beth something like the proper southern host I was raised to be, but she practically lives here and helps herself to anything she wants. Sure enough, I spy a Pepsi sitting on the island already next to an open bag of chips.

I take a long sip of my water and lean my elbows on the counter.

"So, how are we feeling?" she asks, hopping up on one of the chairs opposite me and popping a chip into her mouth.

I shrug and sigh. "I don't know. Sad, I guess? That's how I'm supposed to feel, right?"

"You're supposed to feel however you're feeling, Lanes. There's no handbook for this stuff. You and your mom are…different than most mother-daughter duos I know. It's ok if you aren't a sobbing mess right now. From what you've told me…well, I honestly wouldn't blame you if you threw a fucking party afterwards." I can't help but laugh. I love her for not giving me the old *blood is thicker than water, forgiveness is divine* bullshit lines. She just gives it to me straight, no matter what. Good, bad, ugly, I can count on Beth to always be real, and it's one reason we became such fast friends when I moved in next door to her.

She takes another chip and looks thoughtful. "Well, either way, at least it gives you an excuse to take a break from work."

"I don't need a break," I argue, though we both know it's a lie. I've been…I don't know, in a rut, I guess? I love being a doctor…in theory. I'm a good one. I like helping people. I worked my ass off to get where I am. But…being a doctor, especially a surgeon, should be a calling and I don't hear it in my heart. I honestly don't know if I ever have. *One more thing to blame mom for…but that's a whole other conversation.*

I've tried to work myself into submission, like if I just do it enough, I'll learn to truly love it eventually, but it hasn't happened yet. I'm starting to think it never will, and I'm not sure what to do with that information. It's on the *Deal With It Later List* for now.

Beth rolls her eyes and pops another chip in her mouth.

"Gimme one of those," I say reaching for the bag, but she yanks it away and peers inside, searching. I roll my eyes. "You can't always have *all* of the ones with the best seasoning. You have to share the cool ranch goodness, you little gremlin. Plus, they're *my* fucking chips."

She shrugs. "Right now, they're in my hands, and possession is nine-tenths of the law, my friend. Trust me, I'm an attorney." She frowns. "Ok, *almost* an attorney. But see, this is why I need the chips! I'm stress eating while I study for the Bar."

"Objection!" I yell, pointing an accusatory finger her way. "I know for a fact you're a stress *cleaner*, not a stress eater—you just like stealing my food. So, gimme." I snatch at the bag, but she dances away to the living room with it, her long coppery-red ponytail swaying behind her. I've been jealous of the color since the day I met her, and even toyed with trying it out myself, but Beth, in her brutal honesty, had assured me I couldn't pull it off. She was probably right, so I settled for putting some auburn highlights in my own dark brown tresses instead. This, she assures me every time I get it colored, is a definite win.

She grabs up the remote and turns the TV on.

"Overruled!" she calls and I laugh, glancing to clock on the stove. We have about an hour before we need to leave for the airport. I take a deep, settling breath. It'll be fine. I'll go and she'll tell me whatever it is she needs to tell me—probably some parting remark about how I'm a disappointment or how she hates the way I've cut my hair—and...it'll be done. Simple. I inwardly scoff at how fucking stupid that sounds.

"Oh! I love him!!" Beth cries and turns the volume up.

"And here to sing his brand new single, let's give it up for Bowen Wright!" some talk-show host says and I clench my jaw. It's not like I haven't gotten used to seeing him or hearing his name since his career has blown up...and ok, maybe I've even checked up on him on social media once or twice because I'm a glutton for punishment apparently (especially when he posts those workout selfies...), but there's still always that split second any time I see his face or hear his voice or his name where my chest twists and the memories flare. You'd think after all this time, it wouldn't affect me, but apparently this is a wound that time simply refuses to heal.

Beth turns to me.

"I know you don't like him, I'm sorry. But the new song is *so* good, Lanes. You gotta give it a chance. Plus, good lawd, *look at him.*"

Beth is my best friend, but it's still a newish friendship and there's plenty she doesn't know about me. Like my dating history.

"Anyway, just listen," she begs.

I sigh and stand there, not sticking my fingers in my ears or anything and she grins in triumph. I'll be hearing it everywhere soon enough, just like all his other songs. There's no escaping him these days because the universe has a sick sense of humor, I guess.

The all too familiar voice starts to sing and even after all this time, it sends a shiver up my spine and warms my chest. He's only gotten better over the years...*and better looking,* I think when I can't help by shift my gaze to the TV screen. Dark curls reaching his shoulders under his cowboy hat, blue-green eyes, that not-quite-a-beard scruff that looks ruggedly handsome, and a smile that can still make my stomach flip. I cross my arms over my chest and clench my fists, hating him, hating myself, hating whoever picked that stupid shirt that's almost too tight over his stupid arms and stupid chest and—

Then the chorus hits and my arms fall lifelessly to my sides, all thoughts of how good he looks flying right out the window.

"That mother fucker," I say, incredulous.

Beth turns back to me, brow furrowed. "What?"

"That mother fucker!" I say again, slamming my palms on the counter. "I can't believe him..." I'm fuming, my chest is burning, and it's like I'm right back there again. I really shouldn't be surprised, but even after *everything,* I stupidly let myself believe that at least part of it had been real, that there was at least a shred of something truly special between us. Or at the very least, that he wouldn't stoop so fucking low.

"What are you talking about?" Beth asks, turning the volume down and crossing back to the island that separates the kitchen from the living room. "What's going on? You're all red and have big time angry eyes going on."

I grip the counter, trying to figure out how to explain it without sounding like a delusional lunatic.

"He said that to me, once upon a time. I practically helped him write the fucking song," I huff out with a humorless laugh as I replay the chorus in my head. The memories of that night, that perfect fucking night, try to flood my mind but I absolutely refuse, gritting my teeth and forcing them back.

Beth looks more confused than ever and I shake my head, the hurt I'm feeling making me pissed as hell. I shouldn't care. I shouldn't be surprised. It shouldn't fucking matter.

But it does.

"Umm…what?"

I let out a long sigh. "We…dated," I say, though *dating* sounds like such a small word for what we did, for what I felt.

She blinks.

"You…dated," she repeats slowly, still confused. And when I look pointedly at the screen she gapes. "You dated *Bowen Wright*?"

I nod. "When I was nineteen. He turned out to be a huge player and an even bigger asshole…but before I knew he was those things, he was sweet and funny and made me fall completely in love with him. And I thought…" I shake my head. "It doesn't matter, none of it was real. But he told me, among other things, that I could make even a weeping willow smile."

Her eyes bulge with realization, cutting her gaze back to the TV for a second while that very chorus plays again, then back to me and I shake my head in frustration.

"I'm sure he's said it to a thousand girls since then and now the asshole is writing songs about it, making a million dollars, but I was dumb enough to think that it was…just for me," I finish, feeling so incredibly stupid and embarrassed. Beth eyes me, still skeptical. I don't blame her really. If she just casually dropped that she and Jensen Ackles had hooked up at summer camp, I would probably think she was a little crazy too.

"How…what…I thought he was from Texas? I'm so very confused." I hold up a finger, telling her to wait a minute, and I run back to my room. I dig around the closet until I find the old shoe box, only semi-embarrassed that I still even have it. I'm sentimental, ok? Or an idiot. Or both. Yes, a sentimental idiot who apparently enjoys reliving her past trauma. My many therapists have had field days with me, I assure you.

I stride back into the kitchen and tear open the box, tossing the lid on the counter with a loud smack. I rummage around and pull out a handful of old pictures and hand them over to her. She takes them and her brows knit as she studies the photographs. After a few seconds, her eyes fly wide.

"Holy *shit*, you aren't joking!" She sits up straighter and shuffles through the pictures: Bowen and I on a porch swing; the two of us in front of the stage at Johnny's, Bowen's arms wrapped around my waist and looking at me while I laugh; a picture of me asleep in his lap while he writes in a notebook; me drawing a heart on his guitar in Sharpie while he watches with a grin; a group shot of all of us around a campfire.

I wish the memories were all bad. The fact that they're some of the best I have only make it all hurt that much worse.

I keep digging around in the box, pushing aside movie ticket stubs and dried flowers and other odds and ends until I find it. I pull out the old piece of paper and slide it over.

> TO THE GIRL WHO COULD MAKE A WEEPING WILLOW SMILE.
> YOU'RE MY HEAVEN, LANEY THORTON.
> I'LL LOVE YOU FOREVER.
> —BOWE

He'd given it to me just a few nights before it all ended. I can't believe how stupid and naïve I'd been back then, but I guess everyone is that way when they're teenagers and in love for the first time. But even after it went to shit, it still never *felt* like a teenage fleeting crush mistaken for the real thing to me. It always felt real on a level I still can't even explain.

"Holy shit," Beth breathes again, running her fingers over the note before looking up to meet my gaze again. "But if he was an asshole... why do you still have all this?"

I hike a shoulder. "Just because it meant nothing to him doesn't change the fact that it meant *everything* to me." Beth looks like she might cry and I try not to take it as pity.

"What happened?"

I shake my head. "Just typical young love bullshit. Short version is that I fell in love and he was just trying to get in my pants." She looks aghast and like she needs the long version of the story immediately, but I wave her off. "It doesn't matter anymore."

We sit in silence for a few minutes before she finally mutters, "I wish it wasn't such a good song." I huff out a laugh and she grins. Another great thing about Beth is her ability to make me laugh no matter what the situation. When I have a bad day at the hospital, she makes horribly morbid jokes that somehow land exactly where I need them to, or when I have a rough conversation with mom, she's there with an arsenal of stupid gifs and memes.

"Fuck. It is a good one, isn't it?" I sigh. It really is. He's a damned good songwriter, an even better singer. From what I hear, he puts on an amazing concert—and tends to wind up shirtless during them, which no one is complaining about. Despite how much I hate him, I can't deny that he's worked hard and earned everything he's gotten. I can't say that I think he *deserves* it, necessarily, because, ya know, the whole heartbreaker thing, but he *is* talented. He always has been. Even back then, I just knew he would make it. I had this feeling in my gut that he would make it happen, no matter what.

And maybe I'm just too jaded over the whole thing. Maybe he's a great guy now and he was just young and stupid back then. I mean, he was a twenty-two-year-old, *very* good-looking musician—of course he was just enjoying the ride. People make mistakes when they're young and dumb, right? Maybe I should forgive him and just forget about it all like a normal person.

I mean, who still thinks about their first love fifteen years later, right?

I sigh, feeling pathetic, because the answer is me. I fucking do.

"It really is, I'm sorry, Laney Waney." She moves behind me and wraps her arms around me, resting her chin on my shoulder.

"You know I hate when you call me that," I say, leaning my head against hers.

"I know. It's why I do it," she says simply and I can't help but smile. We both laugh a bit and then I sigh.

In a too-cheery tone, I say, "Well, that was a nice little stroll down memory lane. Now I get to go see my dying mother!"

* * *

I NEED to release the death grip I have on my steering wheel before my fingers fall off. I don't really know what to feel about what's coming. I'm not *happy* that she's dying, of course, but I know I'm not feeling the sorrow I should be. I don't know what that says about me, but our relationship has never been easy. We see each other once a year these days, at best, and I can't even remember the last time we had a conversation that didn't devolve into an argument.

Why am I still working at the hospital when private practice is much more lucrative? Why would I choose trauma surgery as my specialty when I could have chosen something more posh like dermatology or plastics? Why am I not seeing anyone? Why am I seeing that guy? Why did I get bangs? Have I stopped working out? Am I really sure that I want to wear that dress to my cousin's wedding? I really should be more involved in the Foundation.

It never ends with her. Though, I guess it's about to. There's a hollowness in my chest when I think of it, but not pain or grief. I'll unpack all of that later with a licensed professional.

"Are you alright?" Beth asks over the Bluetooth in my rental car.

"Define *alright…*"

"The only way through it is through it. And then to go to a bar afterwards."

Despite the cold pit in my stomach, I smile.

"I'll text you later."

"Okie dokie. Uh…good luck? Is that the right sentiment here? I'm bad with this stuff, I'm sorry."

"Good luck is always the right sentiment when dealing with Miranda Thorton, trust me."

We hang up and I try to prepare for this, but I'm not sure how in the hell to do that, so I settle for just not puking or punching anyone. I pull up to the gate and peer up the long, winding drive to my childhood home. I haven't been back here in, God, maybe six, seven years? It looks the exact same as it always has—cream stone façade, wide matching stone steps that taper gradually as they lead up to the towering front doors, ridiculously ornate lion's head door-knockers that I thought went out of style in the 90s—but that's unsurprising, really. Mom isn't big on change or deviations from what she sees as the right way of things.

I let a thousand memories roll over me, good and bad, before taking a deep breath and punching the code into the keypad. The iron gate slowly rolls aside.

"Here we go," I breathe.

I pull around to the detached four-car garage and park just out front. My dad's prized vintage Jag still sits inside, where it always has, and the decades old ache echoes through my chest. Things were so much better before he died. He kept mom balanced, I guess. After he died, she turned into a completely different person. She became cold and detached and all of her focus shifted to making my life miserable.

Ok, that's slightly dramatic. My life wasn't *miserable*, exactly. I know how lucky I am to have grown up in the world I did with the opportunities I was given, but things weren't perfect by any means. Having a big house or fancy car doesn't make having a mom who can't even tell you that she loves you any easier.

I head in through the side door and pass through the kitchen and dining room, memories dancing around me like ghosts. I smile a little sadly at the giant family portrait that hangs over the mantle in the living room, taken just a few months before the accident. I think that might be the last real smile I ever saw on my mother's face.

Jessa, mom's executive assistant, is in a few meetings this afternoon and but said she'd be over afterwards and would bring dinner. Jessa is great, and a saint, honestly, to have put up with mom as long as she has. I suppose that isn't really fair—Miranda Thorton is a much better boss than she is a mother, from what I hear. But either way, Jessa has been a part of mom's life, so by extension, mine, for this side of a decade now, and I'm grateful that she'll be here to spearhead handling everything after…after mom is gone.

"Oh, hello," a voice calls from the stairs. I look up to see a young man with short blonde hair and glasses making his way down. "You must be Delaney."

"Just Laney," I correct.

"Oh, sorry about that. Your mother—"

"Would rather chew glass than use anything but my given name, I know," I say with a smile. He huffs out a laugh and steps from the last stair, leaning his elbow on the ornately carved post.

"I get that. My grandfather refuses to call me Ryan—which is my name, by the way. Sorry," he says, shaking himself. He extends his hand and I shake it, smiling. Judging by the scrubs, I'm assuming he's the hospice nurse mom hired.

"Nice to meet you."

"Likewise. Your mom said you should be arriving today." He glances up the stairs and back to me. There's sympathy in his brown eyes when adds, "It's probably good that you did. It's getting closer now."

"How long?"

"Honestly, could be any day, but a week at most I would think. Then again, your mom is…"

"Stubborn as hell?" I supply helpfully and he grins.

"She is definitely that, so she's been fighting hard, but you know how quickly these things can turn." I nod in understanding. Sometimes a few months can turn into a few hours, and sometimes a day or two can turn into a year. I've seen it go both ways. The human body is screwy that way—it doesn't always behave the way we think it will. But I get the uneasy feeling deep in my gut that she's waiting for me, waiting to have this conversation before she goes.

"She's comfortable?"

"As comfortable as possible," he assures me and runs down what they're giving her and her latest stats. Mom told him I was a doctor, so he gives me far more detail than I'm sure he would a normal (supposed to be grieving) relative.

I let out a long breath and glance up the stairs.

"I guess I better get this done."

"I'll give you some time. There's a button on the side of the bed that'll send an alert to my phone if you need anything." I give him a nod of thanks and start up the stairs, but freeze a few steps up.

"What's your full name? Or the one that your grandfather uses anyway?"

He wrinkles his nose and shudders. "You *really* don't want to know."

I huff out a laugh and climb the rest of the stairs, my heart thundering in my chest. I make what feels like the longest walk in my life to her door. I take a deep breath before pushing it open and step inside.

"Hi, mom."

She's propped up in her bed, and though she's so much frailer and smaller than I've ever seen her, she's still the formidable, no nonsense, Miranda Thorton I've always known. Her once brown hair has liberal streaks of silver in it now, but it's pulled back into a sleek bun, not a strand out of a place. She studies me, her usual judgment missing from her hazel eyes, so like my own.

"How long has your hair been that color?" she asks and can't quite hide the criticism in her tone. *Ok, maybe a little judgment still left after all.*

"Wow. Six seconds, mom. That has to be a new record. Is that why you wanted me to come? So you could just get one last insult in? To make sure I know damn sure that everything about me is a disappointment to you?" I shake my head, suddenly so angry I can taste it in the back of my throat like acid. I'm angry at mom. I'm angry at myself. I'm angry at the world.

I turn to leave but she calls out to stop me.

"Wait. Wait, Delaney. I'm sorry." I grit my teeth at the use of my full name, but she also rarely says the S-word, so I turn to face her again. "Please," she adds and I sigh, walking to the bed and sitting stiffly in the chair beside it, clenching my jaw the entire time. I know I shouldn't lash out but she makes everything so damned hard.

"Delaney—Laney," she corrects quickly when I give her a pointed look, though she looks as if the word tastes like vinegar. I've never understood her refusal to use my preferred nickname. Maybe now is the time to ask, but before I can, she continues on. "I don't have much time left, as I know you're well aware, so I'll cut right to the quick of it. I know that I've been…difficult, that our relationship has never been a good one, or at least not since the accident." She huffs out a quiet laugh at my surprised expression. "I'm afraid I've become quite the cliché. When you know the end of the road is coming soon, it really does force you to look back at your journey. I wish that mine was a more beautiful one to recall."

"Mom, I—" I don't know what to say.

"I know that my life was a good one, all things considered. I never wanted for anything, married the love of my life, had a family, a successful career and did what I hope to be thought of as good things with the fortune we acquired." That part is true at least—mom has always been big on charity work and giving back to the community. The Thorton Foundation has given countless scholarships and raised money for too many good causes to count, has built hospitals and homes for veterans and schools, sponsored field trips and little league teams. And all of that was because of mom. So, credit where credit is due there: she made a lot of lives better. Just maybe not mine.

She takes a deep breath and my chest constricts when I can hear how labored it is. Maybe the end really is closer than we thought.

"I know that you don't particularly like me." I open my mouth to protest, but then shut it again. I won't lie to a woman on her deathbed. "And I don't blame you for that," she adds, giving me a ghost of a real smile, one I haven't seen in so, so long. "After your dad died, I was… broken. I can't explain the love that I had for that man, *still* have for him, even after all this time, other than to say that he was like the sun for me. Without him…everything was just dark. I closed myself off from feeling almost everything else when he was gone because it was the only way I could keep going at all. And that was wrong. I know that it was so, so wrong, but it was the only way I knew to survive. But you deserved better than that, and I'm sorry. I didn't love you the way I should have, the way a mother is supposed to…the way he would have wanted."

I'm alarmed by the tears in her eyes. I've never seen my mother cry, not once. I know she cried when dad died, of course, but she did it alone in her room or when she would sneak off to visit his grave, never, *ever* in front of me.

A cold feeling settles heavy in my chest, making it hard to breathe, and I lean forward and grip her hand. She squeezes it softly back and I can feel the fragile bones beneath her skin. Never a big woman, she must barely weigh ninety pounds now.

"You grew into someone that I am so, so proud of. I know I don't tell you that enough," —*ever*— "but I am. I am incredibly proud of the person and doctor you've become. I like to think that that was partly due to me and the way that I pushed you."

"It was," I admit. I may have resented her for most of it, but she did put that drive inside of me to never settle, to push and push and push myself to achieve my (*her?*) goals. For better or worse, she made me the person I am, the surgeon I am.

She takes another deep breath. "I know it's not fair to want to make amends now, when I'm on death's doorstep, but I'm going to do it anyway."

"It's ok, mom," I say softly. "Things weren't…easy, but it's ok…" I suddenly realize I want her to be at peace. All of the resentment and anger and, yes at times, hatred, I've had for her over the years melts away now that it's all coming to an end. At least for the moment. I know it won't magically disappear just because I'm having this moment of peace, but for now, I can ignore it all. I can put it all aside and have this time with my mom, with a version of her I wish I had known for longer.

She shakes her head, tears shining, but she seems to steel herself.

"I need to tell you something." The look in her eyes makes that coldness in my chest spread through every inch of me, like ice slowly coating every vein. "Something about that boy."

PART ONE

Fifteen years ago

I'LL NEVER GET tired of this. Of singing and performing, of being up on the stage with the lights flashing and the crowd cheering, of the rush I get every time I touch this guitar. I grin over at Jared as he kills the drum solo, as usual, and then share an amused look with my sister, Kelly standing on my left on the stage with her fiddle, before scanning the room. It's a pretty decent crowd, a lot of them regulars who even sing along to some of my original songs now. The steady gigs at Johnny's the past few months have made me feel like we can really do this.

I know everyone fucking thinks that. The world is full of twenty-somethings that think they have what it takes to make it big, to be a huge star on a stage singing in front of eighty thousand people, but I don't know, I just feel it in my bones. This is what I'm meant to do. I snort before grabbing the mic, the chorus coming back around again. *Like every other wannabe country star didn't feel it in their bones too, jackass.*

We finish the song and while the crowd claps and cheers, I take a swig of beer. Jared winks and waves to his newest fling, Annie, sitting at a small table in the corner with a cute brunette. I can't make out much more than that with the lights in my eyes, but I'm sure I'll be introduced later.

"Alright, we got a request for this one—we got any whiskey girls in the house tonight?" A chorus of cheers and whoops erupts and I grin. "Mmm…love me a good whiskey girl," I say, winking at a blonde at the front of the stage.

* * *

I'M HANGING out behind the bar to get some air and have a smoke in between sets when the door opens and a girl walks out onto the deck. I turn and she gives me a small wave, and I realize it's the cute brunette who came with Annie. Now that I can actually see her, I realize that she's more than cute. I straighten and my pulse jumps. She's *beautiful*. Long, loose curls the color of chocolate with streaks of honey blonde winding lazily through the strands, hazel eyes, and—ah fuck me: *dimples*.

"Hey, you're Annie's friend, right?" I say as she makes her way closer and I lean back against the railing, trying for cool nonchalance, but for some reason, I'm actually a little nervous. *What the hell?*

"Yeah, hey. I'm Laney."

"Bowen," I say inclining my head. "Nice to meet you."

She nods and tucks a curl behind her ear. "Y'all were great," she says, nodding back towards the bar.

"Oh, thanks, glad you enjoyed it." She joins me at the railing and leans her forearms on the wood, looking out into the trees in the distance. She's on the short side, probably barely five-three, but somehow her tanned legs seem to go on forever in her tiny cut-off skirt. I clear my throat lightly. "What are you doing out here?"

"It was the quickest escape route." When I arch a brow in question she grins. "Annie and Jared are dry-humping on the couch in the back room and I really didn't need a front-row seat for that, so…" She hikes a shoulder and I laugh loudly. Jared is a fucking horn dog and has zero concerns with privacy, but the fact that this girl just used the term *dry-humping* makes me grin.

One of the waitresses, Taylor, pokes her head out of the door.

"Hey Bowen, you need anything out here?"

I turn to Laney. "You want a drink?"

"Oh, no I'm good, thanks." Her cheeks heat ever so slightly.

"We're good, thanks, Taylor."

"Sounds good. Rick says about fifteen before your second set starts, just FYI." I nod and she heads back inside, the screen door slamming behind her.

"Not a big drinker?" I ask, turning to lean my arms on the railing next to her.

"Well, *officially* no since I'm not actually legally of-age to imbibe…" She wrinkles her nose a bit, and fuck me if it isn't adorable. But also—I need to make sure of something before I let myself keep thinking the things I'm already thinking…

"And how old are you, exactly?" The bar is *supposed* to be eighteen and up, but I'm all too familiar with sneaking into places underaged.

"Nineteen," she says, adding playfully, "totally legal, not to worry." I grin at her, liking how easy it is to talk to her, to joke around. "Just not legal to, ya know, drink in public."

"Good to know," I say and her answering smile makes my pulse race. "So, do you go to Carolina with Annie, then?"

"Oh, no. We've been friends since we were kids, but I don't start college until the fall. Not Carolina, but, yeah. I really should have started last year too, but I graduated late."

"Hey, that's alright. I have a cousin who repeated the second grade four times. It happens."

She laughs and I can't help but smile back like an idiot. I already feel something sparking between us and fuck if that's not just plain stupid. She just said she's leaving in a few months and if things go the way I plan, we'll be moving to Nashville soon too. Starting something now would be like drinking poison on purpose, knowingly putting myself through pain. *But what one hell of a pretty little poison* * *it would be…*

I shake myself. I won't be fucking lame and say shit like love at first sight or anything…but there's an instant connection here that I can't ignore, no matter how much I should.

"Har har…but yeah, I did actually have to repeat seventh-grade. I

---

* *Pretty Little Poison*

was in an accident and missed like half the year." She looks back out at the trees, swallowing hard.

"Oh hell, I'm sorry. I have a tendency to say stupid shit. Feel free to smack me when I do." She turns back to me and her lips curl upwards on one side making one dimple pop.

"Good to know I have permission. But, yeah, I was in the hospital for a while and then had to deal with all this other stuff and…" She stops and shakes her head, brows knitting together. "I don't know why I'm telling you all this, I'm so sorry. I just met you and I'm like word-vomiting my entire life story."

She meets my gaze, eyes dipping ever so briefly to my lips and looking little nervous. I'm wondering if it's because she's feeling this crazy, instant attraction, same as me.

"Nah, keep talkin'. I'm enjoying it." She eyes me to see if I'm serious and whatever she sees there must convince her, because she continues on.

"The accident and recovery and all of that meant that I got to do another year of middle school—every adolescent girl's dream come true."

"Ah yeah, middle school is the worst." She gives me a pointed look, clearly saying *yeah sure, buddy*. "Seriously. I was shorter than you—didn't hit my growth spurt until sophomore year of high school—had killer acne, weighed like 80 pounds soaking wet, played D&D…I was cannon fodder for bullying and got my ass kicked on more than one occasion."

She quirks a brow but decides to believe me I guess.

"Well, you look like you came out of it alright," she says, eyeing me in a way that's half flirty, half dirty, and one hundred percent sexy as hell. I tip the front edge of my hat down.

"Well, thank ya, ma'am." She giggles. "So, where are you going then? To school I mean?"

"Oh, uh…Princeton, actually…" She says it shyly and my eyes go wide.

"Wow, I'm talking to a certified genius out here." She rolls her eyes. "That's amazing. No, seriously, that's awesome and impressive as hell. I bet your parents are crazy proud."

"My dad would have been, I know," she says a little sadly, and I realize that he must be gone, "but my mom…well, I don't think proud is the right word. More like just checking the next box off the list. She's had my entire life all mapped out since…well since just after the accident, I guess."

"Ahh, one of those."

"The epitome of *One of Those*," she says with a laugh, and I'm glad that she can at least joke about what appears to be a tense relationship. She turns to look at me, narrowing her eyes. "You are weirdly easy to talk to."

"Back at ya, Ivy League." She smiles at that, those dang dimples peeking out, and I know I'm grinning like a fucking moron. I pull out my cigarettes and lighter, and she wrinkles her nose.

"Not a fan of smokers?"

"Well, I don't know if you've heard this or not, but it's actually *bad* for you." I drop my jaw in mock surprise and she plays along, acting like her mind is blown. "I know, right? It's crazy! Who woulda thought putting toxic chemicals into your body is actually not a great idea?" We both laugh and then she adds, "Plus, kinda makes you taste like an ashtray."

I eye her to make sure I'm reading what I *think* I'm reading in those words, in the feeling bubbling up in my chest…and oh yeah, it's there. I can't stop myself from licking my bottom lip as I imagine kissing hers, and that pulse-racing anticipation settles in the air around us. Which is insane. Musicians get a bad rap, but I don't actually make a habit out of hooking up with random girls that I've known for exactly two-point-five seconds in between sets.

"And you don't like kissing ashtrays I take it?…" I ask slowly as I turn towards her.

"Not so much," she says, eyes darting to my lips again as she turns my way and takes a step closer.

"But if someone were to *not* taste like an ashtray…"

She smiles and I don't think I've ever wanted to kiss someone as badly as I want to kiss Laney right now.

"I might be persuaded, then."

"Well, in that case, I'm officially a non-smoker," I say, pretending to throw the pack out into the woods. "I'm not really going to throw them out there because that would be littering which is also bad." She laughs, tucking that curl behind her ear again. "But I'm quitting. Cross my heart." I shove the cigarettes back in my pocket and draw an X over my chest with my finger, and she tries to fight a smile, biting her lip in a way that's cute and sexy and God, what the hell is it about this girl?

The screen door slams against the side of the building and Jared comes barreling out, lurching a bit. Laney laughs quietly and takes a half a step away from me. I hadn't even realized how close we'd gotten. I kind of want to punch my best friend's fucking lights out right now for interrupting. Laney hikes a shoulder and I huff out a laugh as Jared rushes towards us. I like that she isn't freaked out or shy about our little interlude—not that anything really happened, but plenty of people would be awkward or embarrassed after it.

"Yooooo, Bowe, time to get back there, man! There's a blonde who's asking about you—Oh, hey, Laney," Jared says with a drunken grin her way.

"Hey, Jared," she says indulgently, and I realize that they must know each other, or at least have met before. I plan to get more info out of the drunken idiot about this girl later, then.

"You staying for the second set?" I ask Laney, trying not to sound too damn hopeful.

"Yeah, I think so."

"Y'all are definitely staying," Jared says. "Annie's already back out there looking for you."

Kelly comes out then, rolling her eyes and looking annoyed.

"Alright boys, back on stage. And you," she says pointing a finger at Jared. "No more shots. I mean it."

Jared stands straighter and gives her a mock salute.

"Sir, yessss, sir." He grins and she tries to hide her exasperated smile as he heads back inside.

"You too, B. And I mean it, don't let him take another shot. He's gonna fall right off his stool if he keeps it up—or puke on the stage and no one wants to deal with that again."

"I'm going, I'm going," I say, pushing away from the railing.

"Laney, this is my sister, Kelly, by the way. Plays the fiddle and keeps us all in line, obviously."

"Hi," Laney says with a smile. "You're amazing by the way—at both." Kelly laughs and runs her hand through her short blonde hair.

"Thanks. The first one is fun, the second is a full-time job, honestly, but I love the idiots so, what can ya do? Alright, come on, hot shot, get your ass back on the stage."

I tip my hat to her. "Yes, ma'am." I turn back to Laney. "I'll see you after…?"

She nods and I smile. The three of us walk back inside and I've got a weird, nervous energy sizzling in my veins this time around at the idea of Laney watching, of singing directly to her…because fuck if I won't be.

Chapter Three

LANEY

I'M AN IDIOT. I can't really be into some wannabe country music star I met five seconds ago in a bar.

But here I am, being *completely* into some wannabe country music star I met five seconds ago in a bar.

Except I don't think he's just some wannabe. I think he might be the real deal. He's got that stage presence that has everyone in the room watching his every move, has every girl swooning and hoping that the little wink or swagger is for her, and her alone. Don't get me started on the shivers his voice sends through my spine. It's got that touch of rasp that's way too sexy and man does he know how to use it. And of course, he can actually write too. Their original songs—which I'm shocked to hear the crowd singing along with—are actually really good. They could totally be on country radio in a heartbeat.

I get the feeling that I'm watching a star in the making as he struts across the stage, smiling and drinking and flirting, and damn it if I'm not out here hoping every little thing he does is just for me too, just like the rest of them. *Idiot, idiot, idiot.*

"Soooo you were outside with Bowen, huh?" Annie leans in and yells in my ear while The Outlaws do their *Fishin' in the Dark* cover.

I can't take my eyes off of Bowen, but yell back, "Yeah, we were just talking. He's...something," I tear my gaze away from him long enough to meet Annie's. She gives me a knowing look, and I roll my eyes. "Shut up."

They finish up their set and after they get done chatting with what I assume are the regulars, the boys mosey on over while Kelly heads up to the bar.

"Whatdya think, baby?" Jared asks, slurring a bit. He throws an arm around Annie and kisses her a little sloppily. I try to hide my smile when Bowen and I catch each other's eyes. His are a really pretty blue-green color that I haven't seen before. They remind me of the sea glass that we collected on a beach trip when I was maybe ten or eleven that's still in a jar on my desk.

"Awesome, as always," Annie says when Jared finally pulls away. "Bowen, you killed it!"

"Thanks. It was a fun show." He cuts his eyes back to me and my stomach does that annoying little flutter thing.

"Laney, you gotta come out to the lake tomorrow," Annie says, looking between the two of us, and I can tell she's scheming.

"Oh yeah, you should! Bowe and I rent a little cabin out there from my uncle and we're gonna cook out and shit."

"So, you're gonna shit after you cook out?" I ask innocently and Bowen snorts with laughter.

"Ha ha ha. Always the smartass," Jared says with a smile.

"Who's a smartass?" Kelly asks stepping up to the table and handing a beer to Bowen and a bottle of water to Jared. He shoots her a *what gives?* look, but when she gives him one back that clearly says she's not in the mood, he gives in and takes a big swig.

"Me, apparently," I say.

"We were just inviting Laney to the lake tomorrow," Jared says.

"Oh you should definitely come! We do it pretty much every weekend, so some new blood would be a nice change of pace." Kelly smiles at me and I can't help but return it. She seems really cool, like the kind of girl Annie and I would have been friends with at school.

"Sure, sounds like fun." I don't have anything going on tomorrow after a couple of tutoring sessions in the morning, and the thought of spending the day with Bowen is far too enticing to pass up. To be quite honest, I would have cancelled any plans I had anyway just to be able to go.

"Yay! Ok, we gotta head out," Annie says with a pout. "I'll see you tomorrow." She gives Jared a kiss and we all try to ignore them.

"It was really nice meeting y'all," I say to Kelly and Bowen. Jared finally comes up for air and I nod to him in goodbye. He grins and gives me a little wave. We ran in a few overlapping circles of friends before he went off to school a couple of years ago, so I wouldn't call us friends, exactly, but a step up from acquaintances. He always seemed like a pretty decent guy and was a good beer pong partner at parties. Annie seems to like him well enough and she's got a pretty low bull-shit tolerance, so he's alright in my book.

"You too," Kelly says.

Bowen nods. "So, I'll, uh, see you tomorrow?"

"Yeah, Romeo, don't worry, she said she's coming, geeze," Jared says, rolling his eyes. My cheeks heat a little bit but everyone laughs. Bowen looks torn between amusement and wanting to punch Jared in the jaw.

"See ya tomorrow," I say, but I don't want to walk away. I want to sit here with Bowen until they kick us out and I know how stupid that is. I literally don't know a thing about him apart from his name and that he can play the shit out that guitar, sing the hell out of those songs, and wear the absolute fuck outta that hat…

"Bye," he says, and I would swear there's reluctance in his eyes. Maybe he wants to sit here all night with me too…

"Bye!" Annie calls as she drags me away.

I smile like an idiot the entire way home.

* * *

MOM IS ALREADY GONE by the time I wake up the next day. It isn't uncommon, but I'm extra thankful today because I really just don't feel like dealing with her disapproving look from being out late at a bar with Annie. She doesn't dislike Annie, exactly, but she wasn't sad when Annie left for college last year so I could, and I quote, "stop wasting time on frivolous things and focus on my future."

Because having fun and friends and enjoying life is totally frivolous in the eyes of Miranda Thorton.

After a quick workout, coffee run, and a couple of tutoring sessions, I rifle through my drawers, trying to decide which swimsuit to wear. Ok, so *maybe* I'm actually trying to decide which swimsuit might catch a certain lead singer and guitarist's eye. I can't stop thinking about Bowen, and the anticipation of seeing him today has ridiculous butterflies going crazy in my stomach.

I settle on a yellow bikini that my mom hates, and grin at the thought of Bowen seeing it. Mom might not love it, but every guy I know sure does. I pull on some cutoffs and a tank top over my swimsuit, throw a towel, sunscreen, and bottle of water into a bag, and head downstairs. I scrawl a note telling mom that I'm out doing frivolous things and not to wait up, and smile as I stride out to the garage. I give dad's old Jag a loving pat as I pass by, like I always do.

"Love you," I whisper. It's my weird little tradition every time I leave the garage and pretty much the only thing I'll miss when I leave for school in a few months. I climb in my SUV, open up the sunroof and all the windows, and head towards the lake blaring my radio as loud as possible. The lake is only about half an hour from our place, so I don't have long to be nervous about spending the day with Bowen. I don't typically get nervous about much of anything, and especially not about guys…but there's something about him that sends my nerves jingling in the best possible way. I don't know that I've ever instantly clicked with someone like this. I'm not sure what it means and am trying really hard not to read anything into it or sound like a complete, raging moron by thinking words like *love at first sight* and *meant to be*, but…well, I can't stop my imagination from running off the rails, honestly.

I tell myself to chill out as I drive through the tree-lined streets that wind around the far side of the lake until I find the address Annie gave me, and head down the gravel driveway. The cabin is super cute, with a big wrap around porch and a tin roof. Man, I would love to lounge around on that porch during a thunderstorm, just listening to the rain fall. The thought makes me long for a few days at the farm. It's about two hours east and has been in our family for generations. It was one of dad's favorite places and quickly became mine too as I'd grown up. Mom has refused to go there since dad died—whether because she just can't stand to be somewhere that he loved so much without him or because she blames the farm in a way, I'm not sure—so I haven't gotten to spend as much time as I would have liked there over the past few years. I go alone sometimes though, when I just need a break from mom and her overpowering and constant presence. I usually use the guise of needing a quiet place to study and she lets it slide without much of a fight, but I know she doesn't like when I spend time there either.

But it has a big old farmhouse with a tin roof, just like the cabin in front of me, and I could sit outside on the porch swing for hours listening to the rain. I think maybe one day I'd like to live there. Dad left it to me, after all, knowing how special it was to me, so it's mine to do with what I want. For now, my Aunt Shelby acts as groundskeeper to keep things maintained and in good shape, but one day, I can imagine myself there with a family of my own, kids running around in their bare feet, climbing the trees, picking honeysuckle, swimming in the pond—all the things I'd done with dad more times than I could count. Even mom was happy there once upon a time, and it's nice to cling to those memories.

I pull myself from thoughts of the farm and happier days, and grab my stuff from the passenger seat. I get out of the car just as Annie comes running around the corner of the house, waving.

"You made it!" She hugs me and loops her arm through mine, leading me back the way she just came. "Bowen has asked me at least six times since I got here if you were still coming," she mutters with a grin. "I think you worked some magic on the boy, Lanes. Jared said that he hasn't been serious about anyone in…well, ever, at least not since they've known each other."

I tell the stupid butterflies in my stomach to chill the fuck out and roll my eyes, trying to play it cool. "Not like he's serious about me, Annie. We literally just met like twelve hours ago."

"And you like him too, I know it," she says, ignoring me completely. I laugh as we round the side of the house to the backyard.

"Wow," I say, scanning the view. The backyard slopes down gently to a beachy area at the water's edge beside a long dock, thick trees lining the yard on either side to give it privacy from the neighbors. Jared's uncle has quite the spot, that's for sure.

"Hey, Laney," Bowen says from behind me, that Texas twang making me shiver. I turn and make a ridiculously embarrassing choking sound that makes Annie silently crack up beside me. Bowen grins and I have a feeling he heard it too. *Well, shit.* I'm already caught, so I figure I might as well take the opportunity to take him all in as he strides off the back deck. He's shirtless, his broad chest and taut stomach on full display and *fuck me* he even has those stupid dents beside his hips that I thought were photoshopped onto Abercrombie models. He's toned and tanned...and I really need to stop staring.

"Hey," I say a little breathless when he makes it down the stairs and sidles up to us. He swapped out the cowboy hat for a Longhorns ballcap and damn if he doesn't look just as good in it. *And lord help me if he turns it around backwards...*

We head down towards the water where Jared, Kelly, and a handful of other people I don't know are hanging around, some in the water up to their knees, others in lawn chairs in the sand.

"Hey!" Kelly calls as we get closer, coming out of the water to meet us. Pointing to the people in turn, she introduces everyone. "This is Miles, Jessie, Smith—well, his name is actually also Jared, but we already have one of those, so he's Smith—Seth, and Tommy. Everyone, this is Laney."

I wave to everyone, thinking that I might have met Miles and Tommy before or at least have seen them somewhere around town, but I'm not completely positive. I take a seat on a towel next to Annie, setting my bag on the sand. Bowen heads over to a cooler and lifts his brows in question, pointing. I nod and he grabs a couple of beers and heads our direction.

He holds out a beer to me but snatches it away again before flopping down in the sand in front of us.

"Can I see some I.D., young lady?" I give him a dry look and he chuckles, handing the beer over. I pop the top and take a long sip.

"So, Laney, are you from here?" One of the guys—Seth, I think, though he looks really similar to Smith, so I may have them mixed up —asks, and Jared snorts.

"From here? Dude her family practically *owns* Riverbend," Jared says and I wince, wishing he had kept that under wraps. A lot of people act different once they know who I am. Or, who my family is, rather. Bowen quirks a brow but doesn't comment.

"You're not…oh shit are you Laney *Thorton*?" Jessie asks. I've been in the paper plenty beside my mom at Thorton Foundation events and ribbon cutting ceremonies, and everyone in the tri-county area heard about my accident all those years ago, so it isn't completely shocking that she knows my name if she's from around here.

"She is! I knew you looked familiar. We went to Bradford," Miles says and the lightbulb goes off. Bradford is another private school one town over and was our big rival as far as sports and everything went. Now I remember seeing Miles at basketball games—he was really good. I think he even got a scholarship somewhere—and I'm pretty sure I wiped the floor with Tommy in debate two years ago.

"Guilty," I confirm, taking another drink.

"Yes, yes, her family is small town royalty and she's mega loaded. Moving on," Annie says, bumping my shoulder with a wink and I huff out a laugh. God, I've missed her. She was one of the main reasons I made it through the accident and losing dad at all. She came to visit me in the hospital almost every day after school, even when I was still unconscious, and she made the first year back at school bearable.

We play a few more rounds of the *Get To Know The New Girl Game* but it's not too bad, actually. Everyone seems really nice and chill, and soon everyone is just having normal conversation not focused on me. Annie moves to sit in Jared's lap and Bowen takes her spot beside me. I can't say I'm mad about it. We're close enough that his arm brushes mine and every cell in my body reacts. I might *accidentally* rub my thigh against his a few times here and there too and with the way he tenses and glances my way, I'd say I'm not the only one feeling the sparks.

"Hey, Bowe, lemme bum a smoke," Tommy says.

"Oh, I don't have any—I quit." I whip my head towards him and I can tell he's fighting a smile.

"What? Since when?" Tommy asks, sounding shocked maybe a little disgruntled.

"Since last night," Bowen says simply, holding my gaze as his lips curl up into a crooked grin. My stomach doesn't just flutter at that, it does a fucking back flip. *He can't be serious…can he?* He finally cuts his eyes back to Tommy and adds, "Apparently they're bad for you. Who knew?" I can't stop myself from grinning at him and I know damn well my cheeks are flushed. *I am in so much trouble.*

"Ok, so how did you three meet then?" I ask, trying to change the subject. "How did the Outlaws become a thing?"

"Me and that asshole were roommates our freshman year at College of Charleston," Jared says, nodding towards Bowen. I turn to Bowen, arching a brow and he ducks his head.

"We partied too much and didn't study nearly enough, and realized that neither of us really wanted to do the college thing after all and just wanted to play music instead. So, we moved back here when Jared's uncle said he could get us jobs and then my bratty big sister decided to follow me around like always and—ow!" he cries when an empty beer can smacks him in the leg.

"What he means by that is that he called and *begged* me to move out here with him and start a band with his idiot roommate, and I graciously said yes," Kelly says, scowling good-naturedly at her brother. "College wasn't for me either," she adds.

"The world may never know the truth," Bowen says and everyone laughs, "But, yeah, that's how we all ended up here and how the band got started."

"Alright, enough chatting, it's too hot out here," Annie says, swatting Jared's hand away from her ass so she can get out of his lap. She strips off her sundress and Jared cat-calls, earning him a flirty wink before she turns to me. "Come on, Lanes, last one off the dock is a rotten egg!"

"Are you five?" I call after her as she, Jared, and the others all make a break for the dock, hooting and hollering, and I can't help but laugh. Bowen hops up and holds out a hand to help me up.

"Wouldn't wanna be a rotten egg, would ya, darlin'?" That *darlin'* rolling off his tongue with his accent makes goosebumps erupt across my skin and heat flood my stomach. I try to play it cool but I think he knows exactly what he just did to me.

I let him haul me up, trying to ignore the jolt that goes through my entire body when our hands touch. I know how much I sound like one of those awful Hallmark movies but I can't help it. Apparently, there's some truth to all those cheesy clichés—who the hell knew? Bowen's eyes spark with something dangerous and my pulse races. He smiles and releases my hand, though I would swear it takes him a great deal of effort to do it.

A shot of anticipation snakes up my spine, a mix of nerves at Bowen seeing me in a swimsuit for the first time, and that wicked confidence that I always get knowing that I look pretty damn good in a bikini—I workout four days a week and am proud of how my body looks. There's always that moment of apprehension because of the scars on my back, but I force it away. They are what they are. I can't change them and they remind me of everything I've been through. They're a part of me and if someone has a problem with them, then fuck them.

I shimmy out of my cutoffs and don't miss the way Bowen's eyes seem locked on my every movement. I reach down and grip the hem of my tank, catching his gaze and giving him a flirty quirk of my brow before I pull it upwards and toss it to the ground beside my shorts.

"Mercy," he rasps, running a hand over his mouth. I huff out a laugh, but shiver as his eyes rove over me. It isn't a skeevy kind of look like you get from random guys at the beach, but a look that says he's admiring every inch of me, almost worshipping me with his eyes. It's a damn sexy look.

"Laney Thorton, I think you're going to be the death of me…"

I don't know why I'm so breathless when I say, "back at ya, Bowen Wright."

Chapter Four

BOWEN

JESUS.

Laney in that tiny excuse for a bikini has me in a chokehold. The yellow looks brilliant against her tanned skin and makes her eyes sparkle more green than brown today. I can't stop my eyes from skating over her body, admiring every inch: two small triangles cover her breasts, a flat belly with a ring hanging from her navel makes my pulse race, and could the bottoms hang any fucking lower? *Dear God.* Thin strings connect the front and back, tying on her hips and making my mouth water.

She gives me a flirty look that tells me she knows exactly how good she looks and it makes me grin wider.

"Come on, you," she says, reaching up to pull the bill of my hat down over my eyes before she takes off running for the dock. I take a second to carefully adjust a few things before running after her. I catch sight of some wicked looking scars along her spine, but the view of her ass in that tiny bottom makes all thoughts of the scars disappear in an instant. I leap off the dock and make her squeal and giggle when my splash crashes into her.

The rest of the day passes with lots of swimming, laughing, lounging, eating and drinking, and it's practically fucking perfect. After dinner, Kelly suggests a walk around the lake, but I grab Laney's hand before she walks off with the group.

"Wanna hang back with me instead?"

She smiles and nods, and I grab an old quilt off the porch. We walk down the dock and I spread the blanket out over the wood, still warm from the sun. We sit on the very end, legs swinging back and forth as the sun starts its slow trip beneath the horizon. Streaks of brilliant orange and pink color the sky, and for a second I wish I could paint like my dad so I could capture the perfection of this moment, but the art gene skipped me completely. I can barely draw a stick figure.

"So, this is a pretty sweet set up," Laney says, nodding back towards the house.

"Yeah, it really is. Jared's uncle is pretty cool about letting us party as long as we don't do stupid shit like burn the place down or get arrested for streaking—that only happened twice, don't worry," I say with a wink and she grins. "We both work at his uncle's construction business, so it would be extra dumb of us to piss him off when he's got our jobs and the roof over our heads in his hands."

"Until you make it to the big time, right?" she asks, taking a sip of water.

"That's the plan," I say, leaning back on my hands. "We've been saving up like crazy to make the move to Nashville. Try to give this thing a real shot."

"That's amazing. I can't imagine doing something so…scary."

"What do you want to do?" I ask. "I mean, other than run off to Princeton like a smarty pants." She rolls her eyes. "Not something scary?"

"I'm going to be a doctor," she says, almost automatically. "I mean, that's the plan anyway. Always has been." I look at her like she's insane.

"And you don't think *that's* scary??" She hikes her shoulder as if it's no big deal. "You are one brave son of a bitch, that's for sure." She huffs out a laugh, but I can tell she enjoys the compliment. I get the feeling she doesn't get them often, at least not ones that really matter. She tucks a lock of hair behind her ear. The strands have dried into loose waves that I want so badly to run my fingers through that it makes me want to kick my own ass for being such a sap.

She peeks back up at me and our gazes lock, a feeling of complete connection snapping into place between us. I feel like this is where I'm supposed to be, like Laney is…fuck, like she's the one. It's a batshit crazy feeling, I know it, but that doesn't make it go away or seem any less real.

She clears her throat before asking, "So, um, what do your parents think? About the two of you wanting to run off and be rockstars?"

"They're so supportive it's nauseating," I say with a grin and she laughs lightly. My stomach clenches when she skates her pinky gently over my fingers where our hands rest beside each other on the blanket. I swallow hard, wondering what the fuck is wrong with me that such a simple touch can set me on fire. "But no, really, they're so supportive, it's insane. I mean, I can't imagine not one, but both of my kids deciding that they're gonna start a band and run off to Nashville. But Kels and I have both had the bug since we were toddlers. Mom's a music teacher and runs the church choir, and dad plays guitar, piano, and fiddle, so I guess it isn't too surprising that we grew up with music in our blood."

"What's your dad do job-wise?"

"High school science teacher and football coach. So…when did your dad pass?" She blinks in surprise and I clarify softly, "At the bar, you said your dad *would have* been proud of you…"

"Ah, caught that did ya?"

"We don't have to talk about it," I assure her, but she gives me a soft smile.

"No, it's ok, I…want to, actually," she says, almost as if she's surprised by that fact. "I don't get to very often. My mom…well, it's not a topic that's ever on the table." She takes a quick breath like she's preparing herself. "That accident I told you about? Well, I wasn't the only one in the car."

My heart clenches for her. I can't even begin to imagine losing my dad. He's one of my best friends in the world. He's my rock and my teacher and my moral compass for the man I want to be. A world without him in it? I get sick just at the mere thought of it.

"Ah fuck. I'm so sorry, Laney."

"It's ok. I mean, it sucks, but there's nothing I can do about it. I miss him so much, miss the way my mom used to be before he died. After, she just became like a robot. I know she blames me in a way, even resents me maybe? I survived but he didn't? I don't know, I mean she's never come out and said that or anything, but we were only in the car because *I'd* wanted to go out to the farm that weekend, so whether she blames me for surviving or for the accident in general, I dunno. But things with her have been hell ever since it happened. She's cold and I don't even know the last time she hugged me or told me she loved me. Nothing I do is good enough, no decision is the right one. No matter what it is, I could have done better." She sighs and I cover her hand with mine on the blanket. Her eyes slide closed for a second in what I think is contentment.

"At first, I thought it was just typical depression or a way of coping that comes after something like that, ya know? So I walked on egg shells, trying to do every little thing perfectly, obeying every command, just hoping if I did it all right, it would bring her back again. But after a while, I learned that the mom I used to know was gone forever. I stopped being quite so pliable and compliant, and now it's almost a game—how far can I push her, how annoyed can I make her before she loses it." She gives me a half smile.

"I can't lie and say I know what that's like, but I can imagine that it's…rough. I'm really sorry. I know I've only known you for like five seconds, but…well, you seem like someone who deserves much better than that."

She turns towards me again and just like that, I'm gone. It's stupid and reckless and makes no fucking sense at all, but there's no stopping it. The saying *when you know, you know* exists for a reason right? Something passes between us, something sparking in the air around us like electricity, and I know she feels it too.

"Did you really quit smoking?" she asks, breathless, eyes darting to my lips.

"Haven't had one since before the show last night. Scout's honor." She grins and before I can stop myself, I'm leaning in, one hand sliding across her jaw before tangling in her hair.

"You're gonna break my heart, aren't you Bowen Wright?" she whispers with a smile.

"Never," I promise softly just before her lips meet mine. Fire explodes in my veins and a soft tremor ricochets through my entire body. Her lips are soft and sweet, tasting like the strawberry pie we had for dessert, and when they open for me, I groan softly as her tongue strokes mine. She rests her hand on my side and I wish I hadn't put on a shirt. I want to feel her hands on my skin, want to spend the rest of forever touching and tasting and wrapped up in this woman.

All too soon, cat-calls sound from the other end of the dock and we pull apart, both laughing lightly as the others come strolling towards us.

"Bowe and Laney, sittin' in a tree, k-i-s-s-i-n—ow!" Jared cuts off when Kells smacks him in the back of the head, and I give Laney one more soft kiss before leaping up.

It's time for Jared to take a swim.

* * *

"DUDE," Jared groans as he stumbles into the living room. "I need coffee. And food. Both in copious amounts."

I laugh as I finish tying my shoes.

"Don't try to use big words when you're hungover, buddy."

He scrubs his hands down his face and then blinks several times, eyeing me.

"You aren't seriously going to the gym right now, are you?"

"Yep, and you're coming with me. Get dressed."

"I hate you," he gripes, flopping down on the couch and putting the pillow over his face.

"It'll make you feel better. Sweat it all out. Plus, I'll buy you breakfast after," I promise, coaxing him to remove the pillow and grudgingly pull himself up again.

"I still hate you." I blow him a kiss and he flips me off as he shuffles back to his room to get dressed.

"You love me!" I call, pulling my hat on and checking my phone. I want to text Laney, but decide it's too early and I don't want to come off as desperate. I've pretty much accepted that I'm already in trouble with this girl, but that doesn't mean that I'm not going to try to play it at least a *little* cool.

Jared pulls his hood over his head and naps on the way to the gym and I barely resist the urge to brake check him multiple times. He does start to perk up a bit once we get started though, just like I knew he would.

"So, you and Laney..." he says as I spot him on bench.

"What about us? Come on, four more."

He grits his teeth and pushes himself through a few more reps. When he's done, he sits up and wipes sweat from his face.

"I mean, you seem pretty infatuated, and I don't know when the last time I saw you infatuated was. First semester maybe? With Jill Collins?"

"I like her." I shrug, trying to play it off and not bothering to correct him that he was the one into Jill, not me. "No big deal."

"Bullshit. It's a big deal and you know it."

Sometimes I wish he didn't know me so well.

"Ok fine, it's a big deal and I'm in deep shit, but it's insane. I *just* fucking met her, dude. And she's about to go off to school—fucking *Princeton*—and we're moving to Nashville and I don't know how the hell that's supposed to work."

I slam a weight back onto the rack with a little too much force. Saying everything out loud makes it real. Real, and painfully obvious that there are big obstacles in our future. *If* there's even a future to worry about. It seems batshit crazy to even be thinking of all that, so I try to rein it back in.

"Plus, I'm getting way ahead of myself. We just met, we aren't even actually dating or whatever, and I have no idea what she's thinking."

"Well, I know she likes you. For one, it's kind of obvious. And for two, Annie told me that she does. Like *a lot*." I wave him off, not wanting to talk about it anymore. We head out to the truck and I wonder if this is seriously insane...

Or if maybe, just maybe, we can just embrace the insanity, say fuck it, and take the leap together. I smile as we head to get breakfast burritos, thinking that this might just be the best idea I've ever had.

Chapter Five

LANEY

I WAKE the next morning with the feel of Bowen still on my lips. The kiss had been *just* a kiss but the promise beneath it was enough to make me want to combust. If we hadn't been interrupted, I would have taken it so much farther right there on the dock in front of God and the fish and everyone. I'm not a prude, but I'm not usually one to hook up with someone so fast after meeting them either. I also don't really do the boyfriend thing usually either, actually, more just casual dating with some fun thrown in before I get restless and break things off. But with Bowen, I want more than just stupid fun and casual dating.

I want...

"Fucking idiot," I mutter to myself, throwing my arms over my head. What I want is ridiculous and stupid. I literally just met him two days ago, and I'm over here already thinking that I...what? *Love* him? That's impossible! Except...I don't think it is. As crazy as it sounds, I know what I'm feeling. I'm sure every teenage girl has had this exact same conversation with herself at some point and ninety-nine percent of the time, it turns out she was just being a naïve idiot, but I'm going to go ahead and say I'm the one percent who's fucking *right*.

I'm already falling in love with Bowen Wright. There's something between us that I can't deny and that I know means something important, and I honestly don't care if it's crazy. Dad always said he fell in love with mom the minute he saw her walk into the Ice Cream King when he was seventeen. No contact. No conversation. Just one look and that was it. So, it happens, I know it does.

Bowe—which is what his friends and family call him and I'm apparently counted in that number now—and I talked for *hours* yesterday, the conversation always easy and comfortable. We'd laughed almost non-stop, jinxed each other too many times each quoting the same stupid movies at the same time, and I felt like I'd known him for years instead of just hours. I've definitely never felt so physically attracted or in tune with someone before, that's for damn sure.

My phone buzzes and I open it to find a text from him.

Bowe: Dinner tonight?

I can't stop the stupid smile from spreading across my face and I roll over on my stomach to text him back.

Me: ...Who is this?

Bowe: The ruggedly handsome country singer you were making out with last night on the dock...

I huff out a laugh.

Me: I wouldn't call that making out, per se...

Bowe: Hmm, I think you'll have to show me exactly what your definition of making out is then. ASAP please.

I bite my lip, my stomach clenching at the thought of kissing him again, of doing a hell of a lot more than that...

Me: Dinner sounds great

Bowe: Pick you up at 6:30?

I wrinkle my nose, not really wanting mom to meet him yet. People always say that dads of teenage girls are terrifying, but my mom can put them all to shame.

Me: I can just meet you.

Bowe: Let me pick you up, Laney. Your mom doesn't scare me.

I shake my head, loving that he can so clearly read my mind already.

Me: Ok, it's your funeral.

Bowe: Will you throw yourself on my casket, weeping dramatically? Preferably wearing something very short and possibly see-thru...

Bowe: I gotta get to work helping a neighbor install a fence. Feel free to imagine me all hot and sweaty and being very, very manly all day.

Me: Make sure you shower before dinner, Mr. Manly Man. Talk to you later.

I want to squeal and kick my feet. I settle for just grinning like an idiot as I head down to the kitchen to find some breakfast.

"And what kept you out so late, Delaney?" mom asks from the other side of the fridge door. I roll my eyes but school my features before straightening and closing the door, orange juice in hand.

"Oh, I found a flyer for a midnight orgy that looked super fun. Didn't I leave a note?" I tap my chin and she presses her lips into a thin line.

"So amusing," she says dryly. She's very used to our little song and dance by now and has resigned herself to the fact that I'm not the obedient little doll anymore. I still do what I'm supposed to—get perfect grades, do all the extracurriculars that look fantastic on college applications, show my face and smile pretty for the cameras at all of the Foundation functions—but I also live my life and let her know my feelings on things without holding back. So long as I look perfect on the outside and check all her boxes, she tolerates the rest.

"I went to the lake with Annie and her new boyfriend, and some of their friends I met at his show I went to the other night."

"Show?"

"He's a musician."

"Oh lovely," she quips with a roll of her eyes. "Have you looked through that mentorship information I left for you."

"Mom, I don't need to do anything else this summer. I've already been accepted, another thing to add to my mile-long list of extracurricular activities and achievements isn't going to make a difference at this point."

"It can never hurt to have more. It will put you above your peers, Delaney." I grind my teeth at her refusal to call me by my preferred name. I swear she does it just to irritate me. I let out a long, slow breath, not wanting to let her ruin my good mood and decide to call a truce on this one. It actually might be fun to do a mentorship with some of the Honor Society newbies, and it'll give me something to pass the time aside from laying by the pool and, hopefully, spending as much time as humanly possible with Bowen.

"I'll look at it after my workout, alright?"

She nods and turns and strides out of the kitchen without another word. No *see you later*, no *love you, kiddo!* Our relationship is so far from normal it's scary sometimes. I wonder what it would be like if dad hadn't died, if mom never broke so completely that there was no hope of fixing her again. Would we actually enjoy each other's company? Would we have movie nights or mani-pedi dates like Annie and her mom?

Would I tell her that I might be falling in love with a boy I just met?

A pang echoes through my chest, a longing for that kind of relationship hitting me like a wrecking ball. I miss my mom, the way she used to be. I miss the mom I *should* have, the mom I *deserve*. I deserve to have someone love me and be proud of me, someone who might actually miss me when I'm gone away at school.

I angrily wipe the tears away, shaking myself and finishing my juice. I get changed and head to the gym for kickboxing class, trying and failing to keep my mind off of Bowen Wright.

* * *

"SO YOU'RE GOING on a *real* date?" Annie asks as we sip our iced coffees.

"Apparently, though I have no idea where, just that we're having dinner."

"And you're even letting him pick you up? Dear God, you're in love with him already aren't you?" I throw my straw paper at her and she bats it away. "It's ok if you are. Sometimes it's fun to be reckless and stupid and fall in love so hard and fast that it feels like you're flying."

"Is that how you feel with Jared?" I ask.

"Oh, definitely not," she says, making me laugh. "He's just fun. I mean, he's a good guy and I definitely like him, but no long-term sparks there. But that's how I felt about Max. I met him at the very first party I went to last year at school and man, it was like *that*." She snaps her fingers loudly. "Instant, crazy, really fucking stupid love."

"What happened then?"

She sighs and gives me a sad smile. "Sometimes, that kind of love lasts. Sometimes, it doesn't. It isn't anyone's fault, it's just how it goes." She shrugs.

"Is it worth it?" I ask quietly, studying my drink like it holds all the answers in the universe. She reaches over and grasps my wrist, making me look up to meet her eyes.

"I would fall in love with him all over again in a heartbeat, even knowing that it would end. It's *so* worth it." I let out a long, almost shuddering breath.

"You've gotten really wise in your old age, ya know," I say with a grin, breaking the serious moment. She presses her lips into a thin line, looking entirely unamused.

"I am literally two months older than you."

"Yeah, but you're a whole year ahead in school, so that makes you exponentially older. It's science."

We laugh and then my phone buzzes. I open the message and

inhale sharply when I see the selfie that Bowen sent. He's holding the phone up above him so I have a good view of his panty-eviscerating smile but also his very shirtless body. He's covered in sweat and dirt and *dear God*, why is that so sexy?

"What?" Annie asks and I turn the phone so she can see. "Holy. Shit," she whispers. "That's...he's..." She sputters trying to find the words and I can't help but laugh. "You are a very, very lucky girl, Lanes. That's all I'm sayin'."

Me: Straight to jail 😇

Bowen: What? I was just trying to show you the progress on the fence! 😊

Me: You lie like a rug.

Bowen: 😏

I shake my head and put my phone away, and Annie and I settle back into less serious conversations about some concerts we want to go to before we both leave at the end of summer, and her sharing way too many details about her and Jared's sex life. I'm far from a virgin, but *damn*. And ok, I might make a few mental notes for...reasons...

As we're walking out to our cars, she eyes me.

"I have it on good authority that he's feeling the same way you are, in case you were wondering..." My brows fly up. Do I dare believe it? I mean, I got the feeling that it was a two-way connection, that he was just as hung up as I am, but to hear it out loud makes my pulse race a bit. "Just, ya know, food for thought," she adds with a wink, before getting in her Jeep and waving as she pulls out of the parking lot.

Sometimes, that kind of love lasts. Sometimes, it doesn't.

Maybe ours will be the kind that lasts forever.

BOWEN

I PUSH the button at the gate of the Thorton mansion. I'm not sure if there is an actual official size requirement for a house to be considered a mansion, but this place is pretty fucking big whether it's officially one or not, especially for just two people. I expect someone to come on the intercom and ask what my intentions are or for a secret password or something, but there's only a quick buzzing sound and then the iron gate rolls out of the way. I pull my truck around the circular drive, eyeing the place. It's…stately, I guess is a good word for it. It looks like somewhere a Senator would live.

I'd be lying if I said I wasn't actually a little nervous to meet Laney's mom, even though this is just an innocent first date. She can't possibly know that I'm already falling for her daughter.

As fucking stupid as that is, it's true. Talking with Laney last night had been like coming up for air after being under water for too long. It was a relief, like I could finally breathe easy. I can't explain it, but I woke up early this morning and wrote two new songs about it before we hit the gym, so there's that.

I take a deep breath and hop out of the truck, striding to the imposing front doors and ringing the bell. I barely resist the urge to run my hands down my shirt and the front of my jeans, worried about looking presentable. Laney opens it, smiling.

"Wow, you look amazing," I tell her. She's in a short, white sundress with thin straps that tie on the tops of her shoulders. It hugs her curves in a way that makes me wanna rip it right off. I try to keep my thoughts in check as my gaze travels down, over her chest and waist, down her legs and—no shoes? I arch a brow, meeting her eyes again, and she laughs, holding up a pair of flip flops and a pair of boots—Lucchesses, looks like—in one hand, and a pair of strappy heels in the other.

"I wasn't sure where we were going," she says by way of explanation.

"Go with the flip flops or boots for tonight...but I'll need to see you in those heels at some point..." I add, quietly. She wiggles her eyebrows and bites her lip in that playfully sexy way she has and I barely stifle a groan. I force my thoughts to behave. I don't want to meet her mom with a raging fucking boner.

"Who's at the door, Delaney?" a voice asks from inside and Laney tenses. *Speak of the devil...*

"Delaney?" I mouth and she rolls her eyes before sighing and stepping back. She opens the door wider so her mom can join her in the doorway.

"Hello, Mrs. Thorton. I'm Bowen Wright." I reach out my hand. She eyes me in a way that leaves me feeling like an insect under a microscope, but I try not to fidget. I've known people like Miranda Thorton in the past. I'm not really intimated or cowed by people with money or status, but I *do* want her to like me since I'm already in it deep with her daughter.

"The singer," she finally says, somehow making the word sound like an insult without actually being rude about it—that's quite a talent —and shakes my still outstretched hand. Laney had described her as cold last night, but I think this lady sank the fucking Titanic.

"Yes, ma'am."

"And how old are you?"

"*Mom*," Laney breathes in frustration and my lips curl.

"Twenty-two, ma'am."

"Hmm," is her only response. It seems almost like she hoped I was older, like there weren't only three years separating me and her daughter so she could forbid this relationship outright. But three years is really nothing and Laney is over eighteen so, really, there's not much she can say and she knows it. Laney looks between us, tosses her heels and boots somewhere off to the side, and drops her flip flops to the tile floor with a loud smack. She shoves her feet in them and smiles.

"Ok, mom. He's twenty-two, not a serial killer as far as I know, from Texas, has a steady job, lives in an actual house with a roof and everything, and has a fully functional vehicle." She throws her arm out towards my truck. I wonder what the story is behind this one—assuming a bad date with someone who *didn't* have a fully functional vehicle? And what was the roof comment? Did she date someone who lived in a tent or something?—and quirk a brow, trying to hide my smile. "So, there you go. We can cover blood type, credit score, and investment portfolio next time. We're leaving now."

"Nice to meet you," I say as Laney steps out onto the wide stone porch beside me and takes my hand, tugging me towards the truck. I nod at her mom, giving her my most charming smile, and turn to follow Laney.

"Oh, and don't wait up—I looked at the date on the flyer wrong. The midnight orgy is *tonight*!" she calls over her shoulder. My eyes bulge and I look back in time to see Mrs. Thorton rolling her eyes, lips pressed into a thin, unamused line, and slamming the door shut. Laney laughs loudly and hops in the truck when I open the door for her.

"Do I even want to know?"

"Nah, probably not. So, where we going, Mr. Manly Man?"

"Buckle up, Ivy League. You're in for a treat tonight."

* * *

"HOW DID you even find this place?" she asks, taking another bite of pizza. "I've lived in Riverbend my whole life and I've never heard of it."

"Kelly dated the owner's son for a while. It's the best kept secret in Marshall." It's a few towns over from Riverbend, and just a little hole-in-the-wall place, but Ransom's Pies has the absolute best pizza in the tri-state area and a great outdoor seating area that looks over a scenic little creek.

"It's amazing," she says. "I'm absolutely stuffed but I want to keep eating."

"I love a girl who loves her pizza," I say with a grin.

"I think I could eat pizza every day of my life and never get tired of it. What's that saying? Pizza is like sex: when it's good, it's really good, and when it's bad, it's still pretty good?" I laugh lightly and then she purses her lips. "A dude definitely came up with that though, because bad sex is definitely *not* still pretty good. At least not for girls."

"Ok, I'll give you that—for guys that's probably truer than for girls, but not *all* sex is good. I've had some pretty bad experiences too." She takes a drink of her sweet tea, her eyes sparkling.

"Alright, I'll tell you mine and you tell me yours, best worst sex story wins." It seems like a challenge and my lips curl. I cross my arms over my chest, knowing I'm going to win this little game. I've got a fucking doozy, but I gesture for her to go ahead.

"Ladies first."

"Alright. My junior prom date chose *mid-sex* as the perfect time to tell me that he was gay and that he'd been imagining the starting defensive end the entire time just to get it up."

I wince. "Oof, ok, yeah, that's not great," I admit.

"They've actually been dating for the last year, so I guess it worked out alright, but, yeah, it was quite a blow to my seventeen-year-old-ego because at the time my mind decided that I was somehow so bad that I'd *turned* him gay right then and there." I can't help but bark out a laugh and she wrinkles her nose. "I know, I know, it's stupid and makes no sense, but in the moment, that's literally all I could think. Oh! And that was also me losing my V-card. So. Yeah. I'll go ahead and take my win now."

"That's a contender, I'll give you that, but hold on to your horses, darlin' because I've got something even better for ya."

She quirks a dark brow in interest.

"Well, bring it on then."

I lean forward and rest my elbows on the table, giving her a little smirk.

"A girl broke my nose in the middle of it." Her mouth pops open.

"Oh my God, like…*in the middle* of it?" she asks pointedly and I nod. "What!?"

"Yeahhh. Ok, so, things are going good, right, but then she keeps saying she wants to try some crazy thing her cousin told her about. I have no idea what she's talking about and honestly, I'm not really paying attention, I'm just trying to concentrate on, ya know, lasting. So, anyway, she's trying to maneuver into some insane position—we were in a car, by the way, because I was sixteen and I had no place to take her other than parking the car out in in the woods. Super classy, I know." I shake my head and she laughs.

"But anyway, she's trying to switch positions into God only knows what and the next thing I know, her foot is flying at my face like a fucking cannonball. She catches me square across the jaw, and then when I yell out, she turns around too fast to see what happened and *bam!* A forehead right to my nose. It cracks, blood starts pouring everywhere, she tries to scramble off me and ends up kneeing me right in the goods, which, let me tell you, hurts even worse when you're, uh, standing at attention, and when I crumple over to cover the jewels, she hits me in the nose *again*!"

Laney is practically crying she's laughing so hard, clutching at her sides.

"Oh my God, I can't breathe."

"It gets better. Next thing we know, there's a knock at the window."

"*Oh no.*"

"Ohhhh yes. It's the Park Ranger coming to tell the horny teenagers to keep it moving only to find two half-naked idiots covered in blood, one of them crying *very* manly tears of pain. He was extremely helpful though, once he figured out that I hadn't just tried to murder her—or her me, I guess—going so far as to call an ambulance for me, and did a pretty good job of hiding his laughter. Mostly."

"Stop," she pants between gasping breaths and laughter. "I can't."

"Annnnd the piece de resistance: the EMT was my fucking *little league baseball coach*."

I start laughing at the memories and the two of us are nearly hysterical before long, and God, it feels good. How can I feel so at ease with this girl, so connected and happy?

"Ok, ok, you win. That has to be the worst sex story I've ever heard."

"What's my prize?" I ask, wiping tears from my eyes.

"Hmm, ice cream?"

"I thought you were stuffed?"

"Oh, I'm never too stuffed for ice cream," she says seriously.

"Ice cream it is then." I signal to our waitress for the check.

We grab a couple of cones from a place down the road and eat them sitting on the tailgate of my truck. Halfway through, she eyes me. Or, more accurately, my ice cream.

"I should have gotten cookies-and-cream," she says with a frown.

"Wanna switch? I love me a good chocolate-chip-cookie-dough."

She grins widely and we swap cones.

"So, your mom is, uh…"

"A frigid, uptight bitch?" she supplies, licking the cone in a way that makes all thoughts of her mom and everything else in the world fly right out of my head. I shake myself, forcing my thoughts to heel, but it's far from easy.

"You said it, not me," I say with a laugh.

"She's…a lot. I've learned to roll with it over the last few years, pushing back just enough to make her know that I have my own thoughts and feelings on things. But…" She lets out a long sigh, looking thoughtful. "I honestly can't even tell you the last time she told me she loved me."

That makes my heart hurt. My mom and dad both text me and Kells at least twice a day just to say hi and remind us that they love us and are proud of us, or to make sure we're doing alright. I can't imagine not having that in my life.

"I'm really sorry, Laney."

She shrugs. "It's alright. I mean, it *isn't*, but I'm as alright with it as I can be for now. I'm sure I'll unpack it all later in years upon years of therapy." We both laugh at that. "So, when's the next gig? Is that what we call 'em? Gigs?"

"You gonna come?" I ask with a grin.

"Oh for sure. I'm officially an Outlaws Groupie. That fiddle player is pretty hot…"

"I don't know if I should be offended…or intrigued…or, ew no, wait, I'm disgusted. That's my sister!" I shudder violently, making sounds like I'm throwing up. She snorts and bumps my shoulder with hers.

"We play at Johnny's pretty much every Friday, and we've got some other bar shows lined up over the next couple of months, a county fair, and a music festival."

"Oh wow, you're pretty much a big star already. Think you'll still remember little ole me when you're a big famous country singer?" she teases.

"I think that I'll remember you forever, Laney Thorton," I tell her honestly and she flushes slightly, eyes dipping to my lips. Suddenly, the air around us shifts and all thoughts of anything else disappear.

"You 'bout done with that ice cream?" she whispers. The look in her eyes says she's hungry for something else entirely. I hold my hand out for her cone and hop off the tailgate, tossing both in the trash can a few feet away. I stride back over and she widens her knees, giving me a place to settle between her thighs. She wraps her arms around my neck and I settle my hands on her hips before leaning down and brushing my lips to hers.

"You taste good," I whisper and I can feel her grin against my lips.

"Like cookies and cream?" she asks, biting at my bottom lip before sucking gently. I groan, fingers flexing on her waist as I pull her forward on the tailgate, wedging my hips harder against her.

"Like heaven," I correct and I don't even give a shit how cheesy it sounds. She runs her hands down my chest and over my stomach, knotting in the material of my shirt to pull me closer. "You're about to make me wanna do very ungentlemanly things to you in this parking lot, Laney Thorton."

"Is that a promise?" she asks and I make an obscene noise that makes her giggle in my arms.

"Get a room!" someone yells from our left and I almost growl in annoyance. I sigh and begrudgingly pull my lips from Laney's, flipping Kelly off in the process.

"Go away or I swear I'll send you back to Texas in a cardboard box," I call to Kelly, not even bothering to turn to look at her.

Laney laughs but to my surprise and delight, she doesn't push me away or move to disentangle herself from me. She actually hooks her foot around the back of my leg, holding me in place. I grin, kissing her once more before finally turning to scowl at my sister.

"I'd make sure he poked holes and threw some fruit snacks in there first, don't worry!" Laney calls and Kelly throws her head back and laughs as she walks over with her milkshake.

"What are you doing out here?" I ask.

"Hanging out with Patrick tonight. Good to see you again, Laney," she adds and Laney smiles easily at her.

"We just went to his dad's place for dinner. I didn't know y'all were talking again."

She quirks a brow. "Well, technically speaking, we aren't really doing much *talking*…" I throw my hands up, clamping them over my ears.

"Enough, enough, I don't want to know!" The girls share a look, grinning. I drop my hands, settling them on Laney's hips again and lift her from the truck, tossing her over my shoulder. She yelps and giggles. "We're outta here. Go do…whatever it is you're doing with Patrick and do not ever tell me any further details, k, thanks."

"I wouldn't mind details!" Laney calls as I carry her around to the passenger side of the truck, and I can hear Kelly's answering laugh. I settle her into the seat, leaning in close when I set her down.

"You are trouble, do you know that?"

"Oh you have no idea, Bowen Wright."

I groan as I lean in and kiss her again, nipping at her bottom lip and making her shudder in my arms.

"Take me to your place," she whispers against my lips and I pull away, cradling her face between my palms. The look in her eyes makes my stomach clench.

"Yes, ma'am."

Chapter Seven

"AND…JARED ISN'T…HOME?" I ask between kisses as we manage to make our way up the porch steps tangled up together.

"Nope, movies with Annie," Bowe answers as he kisses across my jaw and down my neck, making my toes curl and my pulse race. His back hits the front door and I press my body to his, wrapping my hands around his neck and sliding them up into his hair. His hands slide down my sides, over my hips and around my ass.

"Good," I pant.

He uses his grip to lift me up, twisting as he does so that my back is against the door. I wrap my legs around his waist, moaning quietly into our kiss as he shifts forward, pinning me to the cool wood and *dear God* the feel of him against me is enough to make me lose my mind. I wrap my arms around his neck, holding on like my life depends on it. He somehow manages to get the door open with one hand and we tumble inside. He walks us back to the couch and falls into it, settling me over his lap, knees on either side of his hips.

I kiss him again, fire spreading through every inch of me. I slowly move across his jaw, down his neck, tugging his shirt aside so I have better access. He grips my waist tighter when I lick the spot where his shoulder meets his throat.

"Hmm, like that spot, do we?" I whisper before kissing the same spot again. He makes a sound that's half growl, half groan, and why the hell is that so sexy?

"You're sin incarnate, Laney," he rasps, ever so subtly rocking my hips over his lap and making me gasp loudly. From the feel of things, Bowe is packing some serious heat, and I gulp a little at the thought. I move to kiss him again, languidly thrusting my tongue against his.

"Ever had a sin this sweet?*" I ask, grinning against his mouth.

"Never," he admits. "Not even close." I spread my knees and settle more firmly atop him, and he hisses in a breath before pulling back. "Wait, wait. One second. I need to say…something," he groans when I lean in and run his ear lobe through my teeth, but then he uses his grip on my hips to push me gently away. I pout and he leans in and gives me a quick kiss. "Let me get this out now or I never will."

"What is it? What's wrong?" I ask, brows knitting together.

"I just want to make sure you're…good. This is super fast and I don't want you to think I'm like, expecting shit or anything like that. We don't have to do anything, you know that right?" My chest twists at that, the fact that he's even thinking about that cementing the fact that he's a decent guy. I slide my hand to his cheek, gently stroking as I meet his gaze, liking the way his stubble feels against my palm.

"You are very sweet, and I appreciate you saying that more than you can possibly understand." I think about it for a second, chewing on my bottom lip. "I think, yeah, maybe we should wait until we've known each other at least a week or two before…*ya know*…" I say meaningfully, and he laughs lightly. "But that doesn't mean there aren't lots of *other* things I want to do in the meantime…" I lean in and kiss him, sucking on his bottom lip. "And I really, *really*, want to do them…"

That seems to be all he needs to hear, and it's like a dam breaking. Suddenly hands and lips and tongues are all over the place, clothes are gone, and lights are exploding behind my eyes as I reach heights I've never reached before…more times than I've ever reached them. Bowen Wright knows what the hell he's doing, that is for damn sure, and with

---

* *Sin So Sweet*

the way he reacts to my touches…well, I'd say I'm no slouch either. I can only imagine what sex with him will be like. Epic, most likely.

I'm honestly surprised that we managed to stop ourselves. I'd been all too happy to throw my declaration about waiting right out the window, but he'd actually been the one to make sure we stopped, trying his best to obey my wishes.

In the moment, I was pissed I'd made such stupid freaking wishes. Who cares that I've only known him a few days? I already know I'm completely and totally gone for him…but now, lying tangled up together in his bed, I'm glad he somehow had the level head. I don't want to sound like a stupid cliché or an after school special, but when we do go there, I want it to mean more than just two horny idiots who couldn't control themselves. I've never felt this way before. Everything with Bowe is so different, so maybe sex should be different too. I've never thought too much about waiting or not waiting with anyone else, I just did what I felt like doing in the moment. But now…as cheesy as it sounds, I want it to be special. So, yeah, waiting is the right call.

Plus, all the anticipation can only make it that much better, right?

I rest my head on his bare chest, and the sound of his heart slowly settling into a normal rhythm is enough to make my eyes heavy and my heart happy. *Thump thump. Thump thump. Thump thump.* Suddenly, it's the single most important sound in my world. It eases the constant tension in my chest in ways I never thought possible. He slowly runs his fingers through my hair and I sigh in utter contentment.

"Do you wanna stay?" he murmurs.

"Forever," I say sleepily and feel his shuddering exhale more than hear it.

"That is just fine with me, Laney. Just fine, indeed."

I drift off to sleep with Bowen's arms around me, his heartbeat lulling me into oblivion, and it's just about the most perfect night I've had in my life.

* * *

THE NEXT FEW weeks fly by in a blur of pure happiness. I spend as much time as humanly possible with Bowe, becoming a regular at all of their sets at Johnny's. By some miracle, we're still waiting to have sex, but man if everything else that we fill our time with isn't enough to make my cheeks blush and my toes curl just thinking about it. We hang out at the lake, go to movies, he attempts to teach me to play guitar and it's agony for everyone within earshot, and I try not to think about the future too often.

I know that won't work for much longer, though. I'm supposed to leave for school in a little over a month and The Outlaws are heading to Nashville soon after that if all goes according to plan. But the thought of being away from Bowen feels like a knife to the chest. I know long distance relationships can work...but I don't want that. I want to be with him, I want to spend our nights together, I want to be able to watch him play and lie in his lap while he writes songs. I want him to tease me while I study or distract me when I get stressed out. He's very, very good at distractions.

So...what if I changed things up? What if I said fuck the checklist and did things my way for once in my life? My gears start turning with ideas and options and though I'm not quite ready to share them with anyone yet, I see the path before me so clearly in my mind. I smile at the thought and Annie knocks my shoulder with hers.

"What are you thinking about over there that's got you grinning like you just solved world hunger?"

"Just...things."

"Things. And stuff, I'm sure."

"Yep, exactly." I grin and she rolls her eyes. We're watching the boys toss a football around and it's quite the show, indeed. Bowe's in low-hanging shorts and a backwards hat, his bare chest slicked with sweat and spotted with dirt and grass, and I don't know how it isn't illegal to look so damned good. He catches my eye and winks, and I bite my lip to hide my smile.

"Y'all are absolutely disgusting, you know that right?" Annie asks.

"I'm aware," I say, sticking out my tongue at her but then I sigh. "I can't believe you're leaving us early."

"I know, I wish I could stay until the end of summer, but I've been on the waitlist for that apartment for six-months. If I don't move in now, I'll lose it. It's in this really cool old house that was built in like 1900 or something that they converted into individual apartments."

"So, it's definitely haunted."

"Oh absolutely. That's part of the draw," she says with a grin. "Ghosts and my own private balcony, and the landlady said I can paint the walls if I want—most apartments don't let you do that. She's kind of an old hippie and I kind of love her."

"Well, consult with Casper before you pick a paint color—wouldn't want to make him upset."

She laughs and then slaps me on the thigh.

"You've got to come visit me. Maybe for Spring Break? I would say I'd come visit you, but Jersey sounds too cold for my southern blood." She shudders dramatically.

"It sounds too cold for mine, too, but I've got a parka." She grins. "And I'll come visit, I promise..." I literally just said I wasn't ready to share my plans with anyone but...well, I suddenly need someone else to tell me it's absolute insanity. I toy with the end of my braid and try to sound super casual when I ask, "Hypothetically speaking...would you visit me somewhere like...Nashville?..."

Her eyes go wide. "Seriously!?"

"Don't get too excited," I say quietly, shushing her and cutting my eyes to the guys to make sure they hadn't heard anything. "It's all just very, *very* hypothetical but...I don't know, why not? I could go to Vandy and still be a doctor."

"Holy shit," she breathes. "You really are serious about him, huh?"

I bite my lip and nod.

"Really, really."

"You know your mom is going to have a coronary."

"I honestly don't care. I'm still following her stupid checklist, just in my own way. I'm still going to college, still going to med school after that, still going to not do anything up to her standards no matter what state I'm in..." Annie snorts, but gives me an *I'm sorry your mom sucks* look.

"Do you think she'll cut you off?"

"Maybe. But if she does, oh well. I've got my trust fund from dad that I can tap into already now that I'm nineteen, and a decent amount saved up from all my tutoring, and I'll get a job or student loans like everyone else if I have to. If it means a future with Bowe..." I shrug, my gaze shifting to him and Jared play fighting now while Smith and Miles look on, laughing, the football completely forgotten.

"Well, I for one fully support it if it's what *you* want, not just what you're doing for some guy. I know, I know," she says holding up a hand, "I know he isn't just *some guy*, but you know what I mean. If *you* want to take control of your own life and future and if *you* want to pick a different school that happens to be near the man that *you* want to spend the foreseeable future with, then hell yeah, baby girl, let's fucking do it." I smile and she gives me a serious look. "You deserve happiness after everything you've been through, Lanes. And if going to Nashville to be with Bowen is what gives you that happiness, then nothing else matters."

I blink away tears, not even sure where the giant swell of emotion in my chest came from. But, she's right. I'm a Thorton, so on the surface, my life's been a cake walk, but really, it's been fucking hard. I lost my dad *and* my mom in one fail swoop, really. I've been so alone in that big house with the ghost of both of my parents, the overwhelming disappointment constantly surrounding me every time my mom looks my way.

But when I'm with Bowe, I feel treasured and loved and like I'm the most important thing in his life. I feel like I actually matter.

He's what I want. One thousand percent, without a single doubt, my future is with Bowe. It's so fast and I know everyone will think we're crazy, but I just don't care. All I care about is finally feeling completely *sure* about something for the first time in my life. It brings me a kind of peace that I didn't even know I was missing until now.

"Don't say anything to anyone yet, not until I figure everything out."

"My lips are sealed, no worries." Annie bumps my shoulder again and I feel better about everything.

Yes, it's fast. Yes, we're young. Yes, it's insane.

But none of that matters. All that matters is that he's mine, and I'm his, and together, we can get through anything.

Chapter Eight

LANEY

"YOU'RE SPENDING TOO much time with that boy," mom says over dinner a few weeks later. She says it casually as she demurely cuts into her grilled asparagus, but her voice is hard and laced with disapproval. *Must be Tuesday.*

"Mom, can we just not? Please?" I'm not in the mood to deal with another episode of *How Laney is Fucking Up Now* tonight. I had an amazing day at a small music festival a couple of hours up the coast and really don't want her to ruin it. The Outlaws hadn't been on the main stage, but not far into their set they were drawing a huge crowd, pulling plenty of festival-goers from the bigger areas. I'd been given a special pass to watch from a roped off area just to the right of the stage and though of course Bowe put on his typical swagger and sexy little flirtations for the crowd, he would catch my eye every chance he got.

"You know I don't care, right?" I'd asked him afterwards.

"Don't care about what?"

"You schmoozing the crowd, giving them a good show. Flirting," I clarified. "Like, I'm not jealous or whatever." I scrunched my nose, hating how it was coming out and he knew exactly what I was thinking because he grinned, watching me flounder. "I just meant you can do you up there, I'm not going to think anything of it or be worried or anything like that."

He'd thrown his arm around my shoulder and pulled me into his side, kissing the top of my head.

"You're adorable when you're jealous."

"I'm *not* jealous," I said, rolling my eyes and smacking him in the stomach before wrapping my arm around him.

"It's ok to be. I'm very, very sexy, you know."

"Someone please punch the cocky out of him," Kelly said, turning her eyes skyward as if she were praying—for patience or for divine intervention to take care of said punching, I wasn't sure—and leaning into Patrick's side. They'd sort of kind of started dating again, but Kelly was always quick to say it wasn't anything official. Bowe had tossed his head back and laughed and he looked so completely happy and at ease that it made my chest feel tight. He was always like that after a show, almost high from the joy of it, and I wanted him to have that joy for the rest of his life. *He has to make it, he just has to.*

"You're leaving soon for school. There's no reason to be getting this...involved with him," mom pushes on, drawing me from the memory.

"Haven't you ever heard of long-distance relationships?" I snap, frustration boiling over. She scoffs at that. Actually fucking *scoffs.*

"Please, Delaney. You know that this is nothing more than a summer fling, at best."

"At best?"

"Musicians have a reputation for a reason," she says coldly, making her meaning perfectly clear: he's just looking for a good lay and will take it from anywhere he can get it. "You're a smart girl. Act like it for once."

I stare at her, mouth agape. Both fury and hurt rise up in my chest and I don't know which one is causing my eyes to sting with tears. But I force them back. I stopped letting mom see me cry years ago, so I clench my teeth and stand, throwing my napkin on the table.

"I'm going to bed."

"It's only seven o'clock."

"I'm exhausted," I tell her honestly. Exhausted of this entire fucking relationship. Exhausted of feeling this way every time she opens her mouth. Exhausted of never having the right answer or doing the right thing or being good enough. A normal mom might have some reservations in this situation, sure, but she would still be supportive and happy for her daughter who is so obviously in love. A normal mom wouldn't be seemingly rooting for it to fail.

I leave the table before she can say anything else. Part of me wants to find Bowe immediately and just lose myself in him, let his arms make all of the hurt and anger disappear. But, as much as it pisses me off, a part of my mind whispers that maybe mom is right. Maybe this is just a stupid fling for him or he's just wanting to get some or just passing time before he goes on to bigger and better things. I don't think Kelly or Annie would let him get away with running around with other girls at the same time as me, but…now I'm spiraling and I just want to go to bed.

So, even though it's only seven o'clock, I go upstairs, send a quick text to Bowe telling him I'm not feeling great and that I'm going to sleep early, and curl up in my bed.

Only then do I let the tears fall.

* * *

I SHAKE off the conversation with mom by the next morning, kicking myself for even letting her get in my head and making me doubt Bowe and our relationship. It's like she forgot that love and happiness could exist after dad died, or maybe it's like if she can't have them, no one can. I don't know, but either way—fuck that. I'm not going to let someone so bitter and cold try to lessen what I know I have with Bowe.

I haven't made any official decisions yet, but I smile widely as I look at the email from Ed Mundie, Dean of Admissions at Vanderbilt. My uncle Josh got us in touch—apparently they're old friends and I take that as a sign telling me this is the right direction—and though I've missed the deadline for the fall semester, he's pulling some strings for an old friend's niece with a truly exceptional resume—his words, not mine. Uncle Josh is mom's older brother, but he would never rat me out, so I'm not worried about him spilling the beans before the time is right.

I type out a quick reply, thanking him profusely, and letting him know that I'll be back in touch with my final decision soon. I can't contain my excitement and send Annie a text. She left a few days ago to go back to school and move into her definitely haunted apartment, and I miss her already.

> Me: 🙂 Vandy is a go if I want it.

Annie: AHHHHHHHHHHH!!!!!

> Me: still top secret, but…yeah! I just got the email!

Annie: That's so amazing! When do you have to decide?

I bite my lip.

> Me: Soon. Within the next week or so.

Annie: Eeek!

> Me: Does Casper like you so far? 👻

Annie: No Poltergeist-esque situations yet, so I think we're copasetic.

> Me: Glad to hear it! Ok wish me luck – going to ask Bowe to enter the vipers' nest.

Annie: god speed 🤞 And keep me posted on Vandy!

I laugh and toss my phone aside, wondering how the hell I'm going to approach this.

Chapter Nine

BOWEN

THINGS ARE FUCKING PERFECT. Or damn near, anyway. Quitting smoking was admittedly a little harder than I initially thought it would be, but I've gone cold turkey, not having a single cigarette since the night I met Laney, and don't regret a second of it if it means getting to kiss her anytime I want. The gum helped a lot in those first few weeks, and the cravings are almost completely gone now, so if that's the only even remotely negative in this situation, I'll take it.

Somehow I fall more in love with her every day. I've stopped giving a fuck that it's fast and crazy. It doesn't matter. All that matters is how we feel and I know that I love her more than anything else on this earth. When I'm with her, my soul feels settled in a way that I've never had before. When things get stressful or I get frustrated with the music or work or just life in general, one touch from her calms me and makes me know everything will be alright.

"So, I have a big, big favor to ask," she says as she settles on my lap, her knees on either side of my hips. I automatically reach out and rest my hands on her waist, pulling her towards me for a kiss as she drapes her arms over my shoulders. Every kiss is like fire, burning away my self-control bit by bit. She wants to wait to have sex and that's totally fine with me, but damn if it isn't getting harder and harder to stop ourselves. But I will. I'll wait forever for her if I have to.

"I don't think it's very fair to ask favors when we're in this position. You know you could ask me for just about anything with you in my lap and I'd say yes, woman," I say against her lips, sliding my hands up her back beneath her tank top. She shivers as my fingers skate up her spine, gliding gently over her scars, and I smile, loving how responsive she is to my every touch.

"I'm counting on that."

I pull back, quirking a brow in question. "Uh oh…"

"It won't be that bad, I promise…"

"Spit it out, Ivy League," I say, eyes narrowed.

"Ok, ok, fine. Will you go to this fundraising gala with me for the Thorton Foundation?"

"That's it?" I ask, surprised. I don't know what I was expecting, but it definitely wasn't something as easy as going to a fancy party.

"That's it?" she repeats, incredulous. "You know who runs the Thorton Foundation, right? Who will be in attendance and scrutinizing your every move and probably judging the shit out of you for them?"

I wave her away. "How many times do I have to tell you that your mom doesn't scare me, Lanes? Yeah, I'll go with you. You could use some arm candy." I grin and she laughs, but then searches my eyes, as if checking to make sure I'm for real.

"You're sure?"

I roll my eyes. "Yes, I'm sure. Just tell me when and where, darlin'. I'm there."

She leans in and kisses me deeply, running her hands over my chest before pulling back and yanking her tank off and tossing it on the floor. I groan, hands moving to grasp her waist again, her bare skin setting mine on fire everywhere we touch.

"Well, that just earned you a treat, Bowen Wright," she whispers, that sexy little flirty look in her eyes as she slides down my lap and lands on her knees in front of the couch.

"In that case, I'll go to every Foundation event until the end of time," I rasp, swallowing hard. She huffs out a laugh as she unbuckles my belt and unzips my pants, and then all my thoughts become a jumbled mess of desire and *oh God* and *just like that* and *fuck do I love this girl.*

* * *

"HOLY HELL, BOWE," Laney gasps from the top of the stairs. I'm waiting for her in the middle of the grand foyer in my borrowed tux. I turn towards her voice and lose my breath.

She slowly descends the stairs and I swear to God it's like something out of a fairytale or one of those romance movies Kelly loves but pretends she doesn't. Everything seems to disappear around us and time itself seems to slow. Her hair is pinned up in a loose knot, a few loose curls falling elegantly around her temples. She's in a long black silk gown. It's shimmery and flows over her body like water, hugging her curves and showing off her tanned legs with a slit clean up to her mid-thigh, and strappy sky-high heels that I have a sudden, desperate urge to see her in with *nothing* else. I clear my throat lightly and shift my stance subtly.

"Mercy," I breathe. "You look beautiful, Laney. My God…"

"Oh this old thing?" she says, waving me away with a flirty smile. I meet her at the bottom of the stairs and give her a quick kiss, not wanting to ruin her make up or have her mom walk in on us making out.

"You look like a movie star." She eyes me and pulls playfully at my lapels before smoothing them back down. "Or a country music star walking the red carpet at the CMAs, actually," she corrects and I grin. One day, I hope that's true. And I hope she's right there beside me.

"You ready to go?"

"Yep, let me just grab my clutch and then we're good to—"

"Ahem." Miranda Thorton strides into the room, looking almost regal in her deep navy gown. She looks me over with her customary indifference and complete judgment all at the same time, and I really wonder how she learned to do that. *Do they teach a class on it at the Country Club?*

"Nice to see you again, Mrs. Thorton," I say politely, inclining my head. "You look lovely this evening." She gives me a small nod of hello and acceptance of my compliment, walking between me and Laney.

"You look…presentable," she allows, and from her I'll take that as high praise. Even Laney raises her brows and mouths *wow* over her mom's shoulder. Miranda turns to look at Laney. "I thought we discussed you wearing the red Dior, Delaney?"

Though she hides it well, I can see the flare of hurt flash in Laney's eyes, her mother's criticism hitting like the lash of a whip. Protectiveness for her rears up inside me, hot and swift. I know I need to keep my cool but someone needs to make this woman see what she's doing to her daughter, to make her realize the amazing person she's tearing down bit by bit. As much as I don't want Laney to leave, I think the sooner she gets away from this woman and out of this house, the better.

"I think the black looks perfect," I say, voice polite but with a hard edge to it that Miranda doesn't miss. She turns back to me, narrowing her eyes slightly. I meet her stare and hold it. She can say or think whatever she wants about me, I don't give a shit, but I won't let anyone hurt Laney. Something that looks almost like respect flashes in her hazel eyes, and I realize then how similar they are to Laney's. The two of them don't resemble each other much beyond similar builds, but the eyes are nearly identical.

"Yes, the black will do," she concedes as she turns back to her daughter. "Well, hurry up, we can't be late to our own function." She strides out of the room leaving us alone in her wake.

Laney throws her arms around me, kissing me long and deep. I settle my hands on the small of her back, pulling her tight against me as I gently kiss her back.

Eventually we pull apart and her eyes are shining, but she smiles brightly.

"Let's go."

* * *

THE GALA ISN'T TOO bad at all. We dance, we laugh, we eat really amazing food, and apparently raise a lot of money for a new something or another for the children's hospital—I wasn't quite sure if it was an MRI machine, or an entire new wing that housed an MRI machine—but all in all, it's a great night in my book.

Laney's mom eyes us like a hawk throughout the evening, but never outwardly objects to anything we're doing or to my existence, in general, so I'll take it. She seems to know that I'm not going to back down just because she might give me the evil eye or obviously thinks I'm not good enough for her daughter.

On that point, we're in agreement. Laney deserves the entire fucking world, and I'll never think that I'm good enough to give her that. I'll try my hardest and will spend every day being better than I was the day before, to be a man that she can be proud to stand beside, but she will always deserve more.

We're dancing now, something slow and sultry playing in the background. I hold Laney probably a little too close as we slowly turn around the dance floor, but I can't quite make myself care too much. She toys with the edges of my hair at my nape, making me shiver, and I trace my fingers lightly down her back. She tilts her head to look up at me, a soft smile on her lips. The light from the oversized chandeliers hanging above us make the gold flecks in her eyes sparkle, and I've never seen anyone look so damn beautiful. That feeling of perfect connection settles over me, the one that tells me this thing with Laney is the real deal, that we're meant to be together.

When you know, you know.

I open my mouth to blurt out those three little words, but someone comes over the speakers then, giving the five-minute warning for the end of the silent auction. A handful of people rush over to place last minute bids and the moment passes. I'll tell her soon enough. There's no way I'll be able to stop myself for much longer. I don't think she'll be freaked out by it or anything, but I'm still a little nervous, truth be told. I've only said I love you to one other girl before, and I'm not really sure that I meant it. I cared about her, of course, but I was sixteen and mostly just said it because she said it first. We broke up a few weeks later, so even if it was a sort of love, it was nothing like what I feel for Laney, so I'm in completely new territory here.

We finally leave the gala around eleven, not even bothering to say a proper goodbye to Mrs. Thorton. Laney gives her a wave from across the room and then grabs my hand, tugging me along after her. Once in the car, Laney suggests grabbing some late-night ice cream, despite sampling at least one of each of the insanely delicious dessert options at the catering tables. I might have had three of the banana pudding shooters. Who even knew that was a thing? Not me, but damn if they aren't my new favorite thing on the planet.

"I don't think anything is going to be open, Lanes. It's almost midnight."

"I know a spot, don't worry," she says with a grin. "Franklin's stays open until three a.m. in the summer." I laugh and reach over from the passenger seat to put my hand on her thigh. I'd only had a couple of drinks and was probably fine to drive, but Laney hadn't had anything so we both agreed it was probably better for her to jump behind the wheel. Plus, it's really hot when she drives my truck, so I'm happy to just sit back and enjoy the ride.

She turns her head for just a second to give me a wide, flirty smile and then something slams into the windshield, shattering the glass.

Laney's blood-curdling scream rips straight through my heart.

Chapter Ten

LANEY

EVERYTHING HAPPENS in the blink of an eye and somehow in slow motion at the same time. I turn to smile at Bowen, feeling happier than I've ever felt after what ended up being the perfect night, and then the truck is jerking from a jarring impact and I'm being showered with broken glass and I'm screaming and Bowen is yelling my name I think, but it's muffled, and I'm trying to remember how to function and I can't breathe and—

I slam on the brakes more out of reflex than actual thought.

It's all too familiar.

I'm suddenly thirteen again, and dad and I are hanging upside down in the wrecked car after the drunk driver hit us nearly head on. I'm right back in that nightmare, screaming and crying and hurting so badly that I don't know how I'll ever stop and dad is telling me that it's ok, that everything will be alright.

I can't breathe. I can't move. I can't do this again. *I can't, I can't, I can't—*

"Laney. Laney, baby, look at me. Laney!"

Somehow the voice cuts through the memories trapping me and the ringing in my ears.

Bowen.

I cling to his voice like a life raft in the middle of a hurricane and slowly, oh so slowly, he pulls me back. I blink and turn to look at him.

"Fuck, are you alright? Are you hurt??" he reaches over and gently moves his hands over my arms, my neck, my face, checking me for injuries. I blink hard, trying to focus. The ringing finally fades away and I can hear him clearly again.

"Baby? Tell me you're alright."

I can tell he's panicked, but he's staying so calm and strong that I fall a little more in love with him. He's someone who will take care of me, always. I know it deep in my soul and I need that so badly in my life. I have no one else.

I do a mental check and I feel ok. I know that doesn't necessarily mean anything and that adrenaline can hide all kinds of things, but this isn't like before. I feel something wet and sticky on my cheek and reach up, wincing slightly when my fingers make contact with the cut in my skin. Must have gotten sliced by a stray piece of glass.

"I'm ok," I tell him. I take a shuddering breath and grip his hand tightly. "I'm alright. Are you?? What the hell happened?" I glance towards the front of the truck but the airbags make it hard for me to see much.

"Yeah, I'm good. A deer is what happened."

"I hit a deer?" I ask, aghast. I've never hit an animal in my life and tears spring to my eyes. "Is he ok?" My voice is wobbly and Bowen huffs out something between a laugh and a sob and a sigh.

"You're crying over a deer right now? Laney Thorton, what am I gonna do with you?" He leans over and kisses me on the forehead, careful not to touch my cheek. "No, sweetheart, you didn't hit the deer. The car in front of us did. It flipped over his car and landed in our fucking windshield."

"Whoa," I breathe. Well, it still makes me sad, but I'm glad that I wasn't the one who hit the poor thing. And maybe the damage to Bowe's truck won't be nearly as bad as if we'd been the one to get the full impact.

"Stay there, I'm gonna help you out, ok?"

I try to tell him that I really am fine and that I'm perfectly capable of getting out of the car on my own, but he's out of his seat and running around to my side before I can get a word out. He opens my door and hauls me out in his arms. He sets me on my feet and my legs nearly give out. Bowe holds me tightly while I take a few seconds to settle myself.

Eventually I feel steadier and give him a nod, telling him I'm alright. He eyes me, worry clear in his gaze, but I wave him off to go check out the other driver. I don't want to look at the poor animal on the hood, but I glance at it as I make my way to the other side of the truck to lean against the old fence that borders the McCarthy property. I'm willing to bet Mr. McCarthy will be out here any second to see what the commotion is about. He was my soccer coach a million years ago and owns the bagel place around the corner from the high school.

Maybe he'll bring bagels, I think, and then imagine him just walking around with bagels strapped inside his trench coat like a guy selling high-end watch knock offs in an old movie or something, and an almost hysterical laugh tries to bubble past my lips. I clamp them shut and put my hand over my mouth just to be safe. I can feel myself slipping and know I'm on a razor's edge of losing it.

Calm down, Laney. You're ok. Everything is ok. This isn't the same. You aren't back there. Everything is alright.

I take deep, calculated breaths, holding them each in for four seconds, before letting them out slowly. My second—no, third—therapist taught me that trick and it actually works wonders. I do it, over and over again, until I'm mostly calmed down.

Everything else over the next…half hour? Hour? I'm not sure how long—is all kind of a blur. Ambulances come and though I feel fine other than the cut, Bowe insists that we both go get checked out at the hospital just to be sure and the medics are in full agreement. The other driver was thankfully ok, Bowen's truck might be salvageable, and Mr. McCarthy had in fact come down to help, though, sadly, with no bagels.

"Laney, honey, are you alright?"

I look up to see Annie's mom bustling over. Of course, I should have thought to ask for her or even to call her directly when we got here. I'm admittedly not firing on all cylinders right now. I'm holding it all together pretty damn well, if I say so myself, but that doesn't mean I'm alright.

"Hey Dr. Conroy. Our truck got in a fight with a deer and lost," I say, giving her the best smile I can muster. She huffs out a laugh and picks up my chart, perusing it quickly, and then setting it aside, coming closer to look at my cheek.

"You're lucky that all you have is a scratch on your cheek then," she says and turns to look at Bowe. "And you, young man?"

"I'm fine, ma'am. Really," he adds when we both look a little dubious, "the impact was barely hard enough to set off the air bags really. I think it looked a lot worse than it was on account of the giant deer carcass in the windshield." He grins and Dr. Conroy and I both laugh. "I was just lucky and didn't catch a piece of glass like Laney did."

Even so, Dr. Conroy checks him out too and gives us both nods of approval.

"I think you can get away without stitches on this, Laney. We can glue it and you should be alright, but let me know if it opens up again and I'll put a stitch in, alright?" I nod, glad not to have to be sewn up, and she smiles. "Give me one second, I'll be right back."

In hospital time, a second means at least half an hour, but she does eventually return with what she needs and gets to work on my face. She's gentle and efficient and keeps my mind off of things with easy conversation that I know isn't just because I've known her practically my whole life. She has a reputation for being a fantastic doctor and having the best bedside manner in the whole hospital, and I hope that one day, that's the kind of doctor I'll be.

She's telling a semi-embarrassing story about the time Annie and I got stuck in her tree house and Bowe is chuckling quietly when I hear the all too familiar, demanding voice of Miranda Thorton.

"You called my mom?" I hiss at Dr. Conroy accusingly.

"She's listed as your emergency contact," she says quietly back as she finishes up my cheek. "I'm sorry." She sounds and looks like she really means it. I curse and exhale roughly as mom storms through the hallway until she finds us. I square my shoulders and prepare for the attack, but she goes after Bowen first.

"You," she sneers. "I knew something like this would happen if she kept hanging around you. Stupid, reckless—"

"Mom!" I cut in, sliding off the bed to stand. Though I'm much steadier than I was earlier, it still takes a lot of concentration not to tip over. But I always like being on equal footing when going head-to-head with mom, so I force myself to stay upright. She whirls on me, fire in her hazel eyes. "This isn't his fault."

"Do *not* try to defend him, Delaney," she spits. "I never should have let you see him."

"First off, you didn't *let* me do anything. I'm nineteen, or have you forgotten? I'm legally of age to make whatever decisions I want about who I see and what I do. And secondly, I'm not defending him, *I* was the one driving. Me. This is no one's fault but the deer who ran across the road."

She grinds her teeth at that, looking madder than a wet hen, like she'd just been waiting for an excuse to attack Bowe and is furious that I'd taken that away. She cuts her eyes back and forth between us, fuming, but eventually calms enough to speak. Part of me wonders if all of the anger is just a front for panic and worry. Is she reliving that day, the same as I have been off and on since the deer slammed into the windshield? Does she even really care about *me*, or is she just mad because it's bringing up memories of dad?

"Are you hurt?" she asks in a clipped tone.

"I'm fine. Just a cut that doesn't even need stitches." She seems to relax a fraction but I'm still pissed at how she came in here, immediately blaming Bowe and acting like this was inevitable, like I'm just destined to be hurt if I'm with him. I'll give him credit, he didn't say a word or rail back, just clenched his jaw and took it.

"Bowen is also fine, thank you so much for asking," I toss at her.

"Laney, it's fine," Bowe says, trying to diffuse the situation, though I can tell he's bothered by the whole thing. Shaken or angry or—God, he can't be thinking she's right, can he?

"No, it's not. You owe him an apology mom, and you know it." I cross my arms over my chest and am very aware of Dr. Conroy watching all of this from the other side of the bed, but she's no stranger to Thorton family drama. She's stepped into the motherly role for me on more than one occasion over the years when mine couldn't be bothered. Helping me pick my prom dress; holding my hair and gently scolding me when I'd had my first ill-advised evening with Jack Daniels, Annie right there hugging the porcelain beside me; coming to my rescue when my car blew a tire out on the highway when mom couldn't be pulled from a Foundation meeting—stuff like that.

Mom looks like she would rather walk naked through a bear's den covered in honey than apologize to anyone, let alone Bowen Wright, but she knows that I'm right. She turns to him.

"I am glad that you're alright," she says in a brisk tone. It isn't actually an apology at all, but it's as close as we can hope for. She turns back to me. "How much longer will you be?"

"We called Jared to come get us, you don't need to wait."

Her nostrils flare but she nods once and turns to storm out of the makeshift room. I let out a long breath and turn to Bowe, a little sliver of fear snaking up through my stomach and trying to curl around my heart. Will he get tired of dealing with mom? Will he decide it isn't worth it?

"I'm sorry," I tell him. He isn't the first person that I've had to apologize to for my mom's…well, her just being her. And I'm sure he'll be far from the last. He gets up from the chair he's sitting in and wraps his arms around me, pulling me into his chest. I exhale roughly and circle my arms around his middle, breathing him in. He kisses the top of my head.

"Don't worry about it, Lanes." As if reading my thoughts from a second ago, he adds, "It's going to take a lot more than that to scare me off." I sigh and give him a squeeze of thanks and love and too many other emotions to name. Tonight was…hard. And scary. And though the accident really wasn't bad at all now that we can look back at it, it could have been so much worse. It could have been like before…

My eyes water as memories threaten to drag me down again, but thankfully Bowe's phone goes off and he huffs out a laugh. I pull back to look at him and wipe my eyes.

"Jared is here but completely lost. He somehow wound up in the nursery and is now staring at cute babies."

I smile. "Why am I not surprised?" I turn back to Dr. Conroy. "Am I good to go now? And…sorry. For mom."

She gives me that sad, not-quite-pitying smile, and wraps me in a hug.

"You don't have to apologize for anything, Laney. And yes, you are free to go. Here are some aftercare instructions and call me if anything changes, alright? And please get Jared away from the babies. I'm afraid he might try to steal one."

She winks at me, and I smile despite the hell of a night it's been. She's probably right. Jared loves babies and it's actually really adorable to watch him with them. I think it stems from him having six younger siblings, so he was around babies *a lot.*

I thank her again and we go to rescue Jared.

* * *

THAT NIGHT, the nightmares come as bad as they had for a full year after the accident.

In reality, the car had flipped and they'd managed to get us both out and to the hospital. Dad had died on the operating table trying to fix his massive internal injuries. I didn't find out until two weeks later when I finally regained consciousness. He was already buried by then and not being at his funeral is something that I will never, ever get over.

But in the nightmares, it all happens right there in front of me. I'm dangling in the car and someone pulls me out but I'm screaming, screaming so loudly my throat feels like it's being torn open, for them to leave me alone, to let me get to him. They never listen. They pull me away and I watch as dad reaches towards me, pleading with me to save him somehow, but I can't. He dies stretching his hand for mine *every single time.*

I wake now, screaming and crying so hard I can barely breathe, but Bowe is there, pulling me into his lap and wrapping his arms so tightly around me that I would swear that he's the only thing holding me together at all. Without him, I'd just shatter into a million pieces and float out into the sky, disappearing forever.

"Shhh, baby, it's ok. I got you. I got you, Laney, it's alright." He strokes my hair gently and lets me fall apart. I can't stop it, even if I wanted to, but I learned a long time ago that stopping it doesn't help. So, I let myself feel everything. The hurt, the pain, the loss, the agony, the guilt, the despair, and the fear.

Because in this dream, at the very end, it hadn't been dad reaching for me, it had been *Bowe*.

He holds me, murmuring reassuring words over and over, letting me break for as long as I need to. After what feels like it could be hours, I finally settle. I let out a long, shuddering exhale and he sighs quietly.

"There she is," he says softly and pulls back, lifting my chin so that our eyes meet. He searches mine for a long time. I expect him to ask if I'm alright, but he doesn't, surprising me. Instead he asks, "Do you want to talk about it?"

"I…" I do. I'd gone to therapy for years after the accident, so it isn't like I've *never* talked about what happened, but this feels different. This feels like finally having someone I love to share in my pain, maybe help me shoulder some of it. I've never even told Annie everything. I've been completely alone in all of this for almost six years and now I finally realize just how hard that's been.

"Yes," I breathe, suddenly desperate.

So I do. I tell him about the accident, all the details instead of just the vague car wreck explanation that I'd given him before. I tell him about all of my injuries, how my spine had been cracked and they weren't sure that I'd ever even walk again. I know he's noticed the scars from the multiple surgeries, of course, but he's never asked about them, seeming to know that I would tell him about them when I was ready. *God, I love him.*

I tell him about the recovery process and how I worked my ass off, refusing to believe that this accident would take my dad *and* my life from me. I tell him how mom started to pull away almost as soon as I was mostly in the clear, how she just grew colder and harsher with every week that passed.

"When I finally went back to school, everyone looked at me differently. It was a small-ish private school, so everyone knew everyone, but after the wreck, I wasn't Laney Thorton anymore. I was the girl from the accident. I was the girl whose dad had died. Well, to everyone but Annie. She was the only one who didn't act even the slightest bit different, who didn't act like I was some fragile little bird that needed to be spoken to softly or coddled. She was a year ahead after that, of course, but we still had a handful of classes together, and I swear she was the only reason I stayed sane for that first year. It calmed down after that and everyone went mostly back to normal, but yeah, that first little stretch was not fun."

Then I tell him about dad, about how much I loved him and miss him and how amazing of a man he was. I find myself laughing as I tell him stories of the two of us up at the farm, stories that make my chest ache because they were so damned happy—and make me miss mom like a lost limb.

"I know I should cut her more slack," I sigh as he hands me a glass of water from the bedside table. "I mean…he was the absolute love of her life." I meet his gaze, hoping I'm not scaring him off or anything when I add, "I'm not sure that I'd be able to get over that either."

His face softens, a sad smile curving his lips.

"I don't know how I'd survive losing you either, Laney." It isn't those three little words, not exactly, but it's close enough. He reaches out and gently strokes my uninjured cheek, before leaning in to kiss me softly, but deeply, pouring so many unspoken words into that kiss that I feel like I might cry again. He pulls away and as much as I would love to expand on that kiss, I'm suddenly so exhausted that I can hardly keep my eyes open. He notices and laughs lightly. "Let's get you back to bed, darlin'."

This time, snuggled up against Bowen's side, head resting on his chest with his heart beating a reassuring lullaby in my ear and his arm wrapped protectively against me, the nightmares stay away.

LANEY

"SO, WHERE EXACTLY ARE WE GOING?" Jared asks from the backseat, hand out the window and the wind ruffling his almost-too long hair. He's going to have to start putting it in a manbun when they play shows soon if he keeps this up—I don't know how he can see with it all in his eyes.

"We call it the farm, and I guess it technically used to be one a long time ago, but we don't really farm anything now. I mean, there's a small apple orchard, but that doesn't really count. It's been in my dad's family forever," I tell him from the passenger seat. Bowe turns to give me a grin, one hand on the steering wheel, the other on my bare thigh, his fingers creeping slowly upward despite the audience in the backseat. The backwards hat and sunglasses combo is working for him and part of me really, really wishes that I'd made Jared ride in the other car. There wasn't *technically* room, but I'm pretty sure Jared would have been fine being strapped to the roof like luggage…

"And it's a great change of pace for a few days," Bowe adds. "Figured Kelly deserved a little break from taking care of our dumbasses for her birthday."

I'd actually been the one to bring up the idea with him when I learned that her birthday was coming up. I haven't been out here in way too long, mom is driving me crazy, I'm beyond stressed about my college decision and broaching the subject with Bowe—and then breaking the news to mom when I finally pull the trigger, which I need to within the next few days—so, it seemed like the perfect time for a little escape from the real world and birthday party all rolled into one.

So, we loaded up the cars with friends, food, and booze, and headed out into the country. With every mile, the shopping centers and corporate offices and restaurants start to fade into timberland and pastures as far as the eye can see, and my soul feels like I'm getting closer and closer to home.

"Turn right here," I tell Bowe, pointing out the private road that leads to the property. I sit up on the edge of my seat, practically bouncing with excitement. I nearly come out of my skin when I finally see the archway over the drive, the old plaque reading *Thorton Farm* swaying gently in the summer breeze.

Jared lets out a low whistle.

"You weren't kidding. It's like…a *farm* farm," he says, astonished, and I snort.

"What the hell did you think I meant when I said farm?"

"I don't know," he says a little defensively, and we all laugh, but then Bowe's brows fly up when we round the bend and he gives a low whistle of his own. I sigh in complete and utter relaxation when it comes into view: long, crushed oyster-shell drive; identical rows of towering oaks lining either side; beds of lilies and roses every dozen yards; and waiting at the end of it, like an old friend welcoming me home, is the house.

A big old farmhouse, white, with deep hunter green shutters and a huge wrap around porch, rockers lining the entire thing, fans turning lazily overhead, and oversized swings in each corner overlooking the wide front lawn, it's the epitome of picturesque. It's been remodeled a half a dozen times in the hundred plus years it's been around, additions built on to house larger generations, and dad added the four-car garage that stands off to the right, but it's still got that old southern charm to it.

The shutters and wide front door had originally been blue, but dad had changed everything to green because it's mom's favorite color.

Same with the lilies and roses: mom's favorite flowers. He tried so hard to make her love this place as much as he did, and for a time, she did. She used to love coming here too. She would never leave the comforts of the city to live here full time, but it had a special place in her heart too.

I think it still does, but now that place is too painful to reach.

For me, it's still heaven on earth. Sure, a pang goes through my chest at the thought of dad and all of our time here together, but I don't want to block that all away behind a wall like mom. I want to embrace it and open my heart to this place like dad did. It's what he would want, I know it.

I inhale deeply, letting the scents of home fill me: honeysuckle, lilies and roses, the faint smell of the apples wafting from the small orchard back behind the house.

"It's perfect," Bowe says as we pull the cars into the wide pad in front of the garage. Everyone piles out of the cars whooping and clamoring about the place, and the excitement is catching. Bowe meets my gaze and a slow, wide grin splits his face. A second later, he picks me up and tosses me over his shoulder. I let out a half-yelp, half-giggle and then he starts running around the front yard with Jared and Miles and Smith, like a bunch of little kids on the first day of summer vacation.

Kelly and Jessie look on, laughing and smiling as they start to pull stuff out of the backs of the two SUVs with Patrick.

I squeal as Bowe spins me around, laughing so hard I can hardly breathe, and I know that this is a memory that will never, ever fade. Here, with these people, at my favorite place, will forever be crystal clear in my mind, a memory that I'll pull up on a hard or rainy days.

* * *

I GIVE everyone a tour of the house and they all pick bedrooms. Aunt Shelby had been all too happy to get all of the rooms ready and necessities stocked for us. She's been taking care of the property for as long as I can remember and though she isn't technically my *real* aunt, she's always been Aunt Shelby to me. She and dad had known each other as kids. She'd joined the military and had a bad time of it overseas, losing a leg, but she's never let it slow her down. Like me and dad, life out here called to her, healed her in ways therapy and support groups never could, so they built her a cabin on the far side of the property right beside the stream and she looks after the place for us and keeps things running.

I smile when I see her note on the fridge.

Welcome home, baby girl. We've missed you. Come see me if you can.

    -S

By *we* she means her, her old German Shepherd, Mick—and the farm itself. She always says that it can tell when I'm here, that everything seems more alive whenever I'm around. It's silly, but I secretly allow myself to believe that it's true, that this place is somehow as connected to me as I am to it.

After everyone drops their stuff and settles in, we take out some of the ATVs so I can show them the property. We see the orchard, the big pond, and the well-worn trails through the woods that I've ridden a thousand times. The small pond is something I only want to share with Bowe and plan to show him that tomorrow.

We spend the rest of the afternoon swimming and lounging by the pool. The boys grill up some burgers for dinner, we pull out the cornhole boards and ladder golf, Bowe strums on his guitar beside a bonfire, and the whole day is practically perfect.

I go to see Shelby early the next morning, knowing that she'll be up and that the crew will almost all be sleeping in until at least eleven. We catch up, and I tell her about Bowe and my potential plan to switch schools—and make mom's head explode in the process.

"You have to do what's right for you, sweetheart," she says, her ash blonde hair pulled back in her customary braid. "I know it can be scary, but whether right or wrong, the choice for how you live your life has to be *yours*. Your mom will either get on board or she won't, but you can't let that steer you. You gotta let your heart do that."

I feel a bit of the tension in my chest ease at her reassurance, and wrap my arms around her.

"Thank you," I whisper.

She squeezes me tightly before kissing the top of my head.

"You're welcome, baby girl. You know I'm always here for you, no matter what."

I pull away and give her a watery smile. I hate how emotional something as simple as being hugged by someone who cares about me makes me. When was the last time mom hugged me like this? I snort inwardly: I literally can't remember.

I force the emotion away and ask her about Carlie, her niece. Shelby has never wanted kids of her own, but loves playing the doting aunt—to blood relatives or adopted ones, like me. She beams with pride.

"She's doing great—I was just about to tell you actually: she's going to come on as a second caretaker here at the farm while she takes some classes online and figures out what she wants to do with her life."

My eyes light up. Carlie is a few years older than me, but we used to play together when she came to visit Shelby and I know how much she loves the outdoors, just like her aunt. Living out here and taking care of the farm will be a dream come true for her.

"That's amazing! I know you've both gotta be so excited!" Shelby has free rein to hire whatever help she needs out here: landscapers, a pool guy, housekeepers, extra hands to harvest from the orchard (all of the apples go to local schools and food banks), maintenance guys—anything and everything to keep the place running, but I do feel better about her having full time help out here and some additional company.

She smiles and nods. "She's gonna do a little traveling over the next few months and start at the first of the year. She's got one of those tiny houses that are all the rage now—*loves* the damn thing, if you can believe it—and is gonna park it a little ways down the stream so she'll be close by, but we won't be on top of each other."

"Kind of hard to believe she parted with all of her shoes for tiny house living," I say with a laugh.

"I said the same thing!" she hoots, slapping my leg, and I grin.

Carlie had a slight obsession with shoes…and when I say slight, I'm talking *hundreds* of pairs lining her closet the last time we talked.

We catch up a bit more after that before I decide it's time for me to head back. I give her another big hug and pull out Mick's special treat: a brand new tennis ball. He will literally play fetch until he can't move, and I always bring him a new one when I come. Shelby sighs dramatically, but smiles.

"Well I guess I know what I'm doing for the next couple of hours."

"Why do you think I waited until I was leaving to give it to him?" I say with a grin as Mick whines impatiently, tail wagging like crazy as he eyes the bright yellow ball.

I make it back to the main house and start working on breakfast— really technically lunch at this point—and slowly everyone begins to rouse, whether just by the late hour or lured by the smell of frying bacon. Bowe is the first to come down, shirtless and in low-riding gray sweatpants, and my pulse races at the sight. He grins as he sidles up beside me, leaning in to kiss me. I kiss him back, meaning it to just be a quick, soft brush of our lips, but he holds me to him, shifting quickly and gripping my hips to lift me onto the counter. I gasp quietly against his mouth, but it transforms into a soft moan as he moves forward, pressing his hips between my thighs and sliding one hand to my nape.

Someone woke up ready and rearing to go this morning. I swallow hard and move my hands across his chest and down his stomach, loving the feel of his bare skin, the little jolts of electricity that seem to pass between us everywhere we touch. His muscles bunch and flex under my fingers and he groans against my lips.

"You drive me crazy when you touch me like this, Lanes," he whispers as he kisses across my jaw, reaching that sensitive spot just below my ear that he knows is my Kryptonite.

"Back at ya," I say, breathless. I can't stand it anymore. I need him in a way I've never needed anyone. I don't want anything else between us. We'd agreed to wait at first, but that was almost three months ago now. I love him more than I can even put into words. I know it in my bones that it'll never change. So, why the hell am I still waiting? I'm just about to tell him to take me upstairs right this instant, not caring if the bacon burns or if everyone else starves, when a throat clears from the doorway.

"Morning," Kelly says with a knowing smirk. I laugh lightly and Bowe nearly growls before stepping away.

"You are a moment ruiner, you know that right?"

"Words hurt, baby brother," she says, hand to her chest in mock pain.

I hop off the counter and finish getting breakfast ready with the help of Bowe and Kelly as the rest of the stragglers make their way into the kitchen.

But the look Bowe gives me as we start passing out plates tells me that he can't wait much longer either.

Chapter Twelve

BOWEN

THE FARM IS ABSOLUTELY AMAZING. I grew up on a couple of acres that are nothing to turn your nose up at, but it's *nothing* like this. The place is beautiful and freeing and something inside me sighs in utter contentment, like this is what I've been searching for, waiting for. I know that one day, I want a place like this. Space to spread out and grow with a family of my own—with Laney by my side. I blink then, realizing that that future could actually mean living *here*, in this very place. It's hers, after all. Her father had left it to her directly. I know how much she loves the place, but would she want to move out here full time one day? Could this be our little slice of heaven, our place to reset and recharge after what I hope will be country-wide tours?

I'm leaning my elbows on the railing of the front porch now, just looking out over the gently rolling pastures and the forest beyond, when she wraps her arms around me from behind. I smile and turn, leaning back against the railing and pulling her to me.

"Hey, you."

"I wanna show you something," she says and I quirk a brow. "Everyone else is either napping or swimming, so I figured we could sneak away." She gives me a look that's a mix of flirty, mischievous, and…nervous?

"Well then lead the way, darlin'."

I eye her with curiosity when she throws a duffle bag and an honest to God picnic basket into the back of the Gator, but I don't comment. She clearly has a plan and a surprise, so I just sit back and enjoy the ride. We take a different trail than we did yesterday with everyone, this one curving around to the left of the small orchard of apple trees and winding through the thick forest beyond it. Eventually we stop beside a large thicket of bushes—blackberries, maybe?—that stretches far out on either side, blending with the trees to make a thick, impenetrable wall.

"Come on," she says, grinning. I grab the bag and basket from the back and follow her to the right of the thicket where I see that there's actually a small, almost completely camouflaged opening. We slip through and my eyes go wide.

"Whoa," I breathe.

She sighs heavily in what seems to be utter contentment.

"This is my secret place," she says wistfully.

There's a small pond in the middle of a…a meadow is the only way to describe it I guess. Lush green grass swaying in the breeze and dotted with wildflowers of every color here and there, the thick trees and more of those blackberry bushes surrounding the outside of it creating an almost completely enclosed, hidden space. A gazebo sits to our right, just on the edge of the water beside a small beach-like area, and a giant weeping willow stands on the left, an old wooden swing hanging from one of its long, outstretched branches.

"Dad made it for me," she says, beckoning me forward farther into the grass. "Well, kind of. The pond was already here, but he worked to make the meadow and planted the bushes to make a living wall around the whole thing. Shelby keeps it looking perfect for me. Welcome to Laney Lake." She grins widely and gestures to a big sign nailed to one of the tree trunks that was clearly painted by little fingers.

"It's straight out of a fairytale or something."

She takes the bag from me and pulls out a big blanket, shaking it out a couple of times before spreading it in the grass. I sit the basket on top of it and grin. We're having a legit picnic it seems. But I guess it's not time to eat yet because she wanders towards the swing and I follow after her.

She sits down, and my heart skips a beat at the sight of long, tanned legs and a flash of black lace as her sundress rides up. *Mercy.* It's getting harder and harder to stop myself. I'll hold off for as long as she wants, I'm determined to let her make this decision, but it's like torture. I want Laney more than I've ever wanted another person and there are some days I feel like I might die if I can't have her in every possible way.

I shake off the thoughts and step behind her, pushing her gently.

"Thank you for bringing me here."

"I only share it with my favorite people. So, consider yourself special," she teases. I huff out a laugh and shake my head. She grins at me over her shoulder as she swings away from me. I glance up at the tree beside us.

"Ya know, I think you could make even a weeping willow smile*, Laney Thorton."

"That sounds like a song."

I hike a shoulder. "Maybe it will be."

She looks thoughtful. "Alright. Make a weeping willow smile. A little corny, but I'll take it." She meets my gaze over her shoulder again and I give her a dry look. She grins and continues on, swinging back and forth.

"What else can I do?"

I love that she plays along, that she doesn't take herself or anyone else too seriously, that I can be completely and totally myself with her and never feel self-conscious or worried about what she might think.

"Hmm...what about give me sunshine on a cloudy day?"

"The temptations already did that, silly boy, but I like the senti-ment. Hmm, what about...paint a gray sky blue?"

"Oh I like it. You might be a songwriter yet, Ivy League." She snorts. I say it as a joke, but the idea starts to take shape in my head,

---

* *Weeping Willow*

lyrics teasing the edges of my thoughts, melodies and chords bursting to life, and my fingers itch for a piece of paper and a pen.

"Make a sinner into a saint? Or…let's see…oh take the burn outta the tequila?" She laughs at herself on that one, the sound so carefree and warm and beautiful that my chest twists. I catch her on her next swing towards me, and hold her in place, leaning in close.

"I know you can sure as hell make the moon jealous of that sundress," I say, voice low and a little gruff. Something about this moment, in this special place, *her* song taking shape in my head, just makes my restraint snap. She inhales softly, eyes darting to my lips and back up again. The air crackles around us like a thunderstorm brewing.

"I love you," I blurt, tired of *not* saying it. She gasps quietly, but her eyes light up, the biggest smile spreading across her face.

"I love you too," she whispers and my eyes slide closed. I never would have thought hearing those words come out of her mouth would hit me like they do. It's like something in my chest cracks open and I know that I'll never be the same. I open my eyes and grin, leaning in and slamming my lips against hers. She tangles her fingers in the front of my shirt, gripping it like her life depends on it. I pull away just long enough to maneuver her out of the swing, immediately kissing her again as I lift her up and she wraps her legs around my waist. I grip her ass, fingers skimming over lace and soft skin. I walk us to the blanket, dropping to my knees and easing her down beneath me.

I settle my body over hers, capturing her panting breaths with my mouth. She digs her fingers into the small of my back and hitches her thigh up over my hip, making way for me to shift even more fully against her. The kiss burns hotter and hotter, all tangled tongues and searching hands and then, she says the words that make me freeze.

"Bowe, I don't wanna wait anymore."

I pull back, searching her eyes, trying to make sure that she isn't just caught up in the moment or thinks that's what I'm expecting after the L word bomb drops, but all I see complete and utter surety. Even so, I ask the question.

"You're sure? We don't have to—" She arches upward, cutting me off with a kiss.

"Bowen, I'm sure. I wouldn't say it if I wasn't."

My heart feels like it's about to beat right out of my chest and I'm so ready that it's painful, but even still, I study her for another minute before I sigh and slam my mouth to hers again. Things spiral after that, our clothes and all good sense disappearing in a desperate frenzy that neither of us can seem to control until we're closer than any two people have ever been.

"I love you," I whisper just before we cross that final line, the place we can never come back from, and she pulls me close, says she loves me, begs and pleads and demands and my entire body catches fire. Nothing has ever felt so right in my life and I know in this moment, nothing ever will again. Laney was made for me. Her body, her heart, her soul, it all fits with mine in a way I can't even explain. It completes me and I never want to be without her again.

I never will.

This is it. *She* is it for me. I know there are obstacles in our path, but I don't give a shit. We're bigger than any fucking thing the universe can think to throw in our way. We'll do the distance while she's at school. We'll talk every night and we'll visit each other during breaks, and we *will* make it work. Someway, somehow, we'll make it work.

What feels like hours later, we lie tangled up together on that blanket, both breathless and sweaty and blissed out beyond belief.

"Thank you for not breaking my nose," I murmur against her hair and she laughs loudly before turning to plant a soft kiss in the middle of my chest. She looks up at me and grins, and by the glint in her eyes, I know I'm in deep trouble.

"I make no promises. The day is young, Bowen Wright…"

Chapter Thirteen

LANEY

"ABSOLUTELY NOT!" mom roars at me, slamming her fist against the dining table the next day. I sit, unconcerned with her outburst. I came into this fully expecting her to lose her absolute shit, but I don't care. This is my decision and I'm sticking to it. I'm prepared for this to be the end of our relationship if it comes to that.

We'd come back from the farm this morning and after everything that had happened, I know without a doubt that this is what I want. Just like Shelby told me, I'm letting my heart steer me and make the choice that's right for *me*. I decided not to tell Bowe yet, though. I want to get this part with mom out of the way first and get everything sewed up before I tell him my plan. I want him to know that it's *my* choice. I don't want him to think that he's somehow making it for me. So, if I do it all before he even knows about it, there's no way he can say he had a thing to do with it.

"It isn't your decision to make, mom. I'm nineteen. I'm legally an adult."

"No. You will not throw your life away on some boy," she sneers the word like it's poison.

"I'm not throwing my life away, mom. *Jesus*. I'm changing colleges, that's it. I'm still going to school, then medical school. I'm still going to be a doctor, just like you always wanted. The only thing that's changing about the plan you've been shoving down my throat for the last six years is the location."

"Do you hear yourself, Delaney? You sound like a ridiculous child. You've only known him for a matter of months. You really think some musician is going to make you happy?"

"Yes, I do," I say, jutting my chin, not even bothering to bring up the fact that she and dad had supposedly known each other for *minutes* before they both fell.

"You can't really be this stupid," she spits, angrier than I've ever seen her. "You can't believe that he truly loves you, that this will last." Of course those doubts creep in the shadows of my mind. I think they do for anybody, in any relationship, but hearing her say them with her cold, biting surety makes my blood turn to ice. No. She's wrong. She's so fucking wrong. I know that he loves me. I know it in a way that I can't even explain.

I throw my napkin down and stand.

"Mom, this is done. I'm getting all of the paperwork taken care of this week. You can either support me in this, or not, I don't really care, but it's happening."

Her eyes blaze with fury. "And if I refuse to pay for this?"

"You aren't stopping this. If you want to cut me off, fine, I'll find my own way, but your threats aren't going to change my mind. You might say that I sound like a child, but this isn't a childish decision I made on a whim. I have thought this through, made plans, and backup plans and budgets. You should know me well enough to know that when I say I am prepared for this choice—including you and I being done—that I am one thousand percent *prepared*."

Her nostril flare and her jaw clenches and unclenches in tight pulses. She's pissed as hell but she knows that I'm not lying. I am completely and totally prepared for the decision that I'm making and her threats can't sway me.

"I'm going to go do this SAT prep session with the Walker twins. After that, if you want to talk more through my plans, I'll be available." I'm impressed with my calm and professional demeanor, honestly. Part of me wants to stick my tongue out and tell her she's not the boss of me, but I refrain. Barely. That would probably reinforce her whole *I'm-acting-childish* notion.

I leave the room and go to get changed, smiling at the small bouquet of wildflowers in the vase on my desk. I'd woken this morning to find Bowen already out of bed and getting things packed up in the cars, but the flowers and a note were lying on the nightstand.

TO THE GIRL WHO COULD MAKE A WEEPING WILLOW SMILE.
YOU'RE MY HEAVEN, LANEY THORTON.
I'LL LOVE YOU FOREVER.
—BOWE

Every time I read the words my stomach flutters. Thinking about yesterday sends shivers down my spine, warmth spreading through every inch of me. We'd finally crossed the line in the meadow—twice—and couldn't seem to keep our hands to ourselves for the rest of the evening and well into the night either.

I've had bad sex in my life and I've had decent sex and I've even had pretty great sex.

But nothing at all compares to sex with Bowe. It was…mind-blowing. Earth shattering. Life altering. The way he moved his body, the way we fit together, the heights he brought me to—it was all almost too much to take. I don't know how things can feel so, so different with him, but then again, I've never loved anyone else the way I love him. That must make all the difference. And here I thought that was all just sappy crap you see in romance novels and Hallmark movies.

But here I am now, Queen of the Saps, because it's true.

His last words before I'd drifted off to sleep echo through my mind:

"When I die, ain't no doubt I'm going to hell. Here, with you, that's my heaven, Laney. I'll never want another one."

I somehow smile wider, but shake myself and throw on some shorts and a t-shirt, toss my hair into a messy bun, and head back downstairs, half expecting mom to have slashed my tires or locked me in the house.

Of course, she hasn't done either, but I let out a small sigh of relief when I back out of the driveway. I won't see Bowen tonight—he going to a ball game down in Chesterfield with Jared and a few other guys and then fishing tomorrow morning—but he's supposed to meet me for dinner before their show tomorrow night, and I think I'm going to go ahead and tell him, even if everything isn't a thousand percent official yet. Now that I've told mom, it feels really real, and I want to share that with him.

Part of me wonders if he'll think it's crazy or that it's too much too fast, but I hadn't been lying when I told mom I'd come up with plans and backup plans. I have more than enough money in my trust fund to pay for tuition, or I can take out student loans for that piece. I've good a pretty decent amount saved up from my various tutoring gigs over the past two years, plus I can find a job once I move. So, I'll have enough that I can get my own place if he doesn't think moving in together right away is smart. And that's totally fine. I'm fine going slow with these next steps, but as long as we're together, in the same city, I know we'll be ok. We'll figure out all the rest of the details. Easy peasy.

I know distance can work, but I don't want to do it. Maybe that does make me a little childish, but I don't care. Why settle for being apart when we don't have to?

I call Annie and spill the beans about finally having sex with Bowen and the whole *I love you* thing on my way to the Walker's house. She screams so loudly that I wince, but laugh.

"I want details. All of 'em. Now."

"I'll give you *most* of them later after this tutoring thing, I promise." I can feel my cheeks heat at the mere thought of some of these details and I'm glad that we aren't FaceTiming right now.

"Ok, fine, I guess *most* is fair. How's Jare?" she asks, sighing a bit.

"He's ok. Misses you."

"Well, of course he does," she says breezily, but I can tell there's a bit of hurt there. They'd both decided that distance wasn't for them, so they aren't officially together anymore. No bad blood, no big fight, just a mutual understanding that whatever was between them had run its course. They were still friends as far as I could tell, but I know Jared still misses her even though she's only been gone a few weeks.

"Do you think this Nashville thing is insane?" I ask her.

"It is, but in the best way. There's just something about you two. It's obvious to anyone who looks at you that you have something different. Something special. So, yeah, it might be a little crazy, but isn't love supposed to be a little crazy?"

My lips curl into a smile, her words hitting the exact right spot in my heart. Dad had always said that love made you do all the crazy, but there was nothing else like it. It's like he's sending signs down to me, assuring me that I'm on the right path.

"Alright, I'm grabbing some coffee before I get to the Walkers, I'll text you later."

"Oh God, the twins?"

"Yep," I say with a laugh.

"You might want to switch the coffee to liquor with those two idiots."

"Be nice," I scold, but wrinkle my nose. They aren't the brightest crayons in the box, that's true, but I think I can get them where they need to be...eventually. "Ok, so maybe I'll add an extra shot of espresso into my order," I concede, suddenly deciding I'm going to need a bit more energy to deal with them. Annie snorts.

"You might wanna make it three."

Chapter Fourteen

BOWEN

I PULL up in front of the cabin after fishing with the guys and find a sleek Lexus waiting. I know who the car belongs to before she gets out, and I sigh and park the truck. It had cost way more than I'd wanted to spend to get it fixed after the deer, but at least it hadn't been completely totaled. It might put off the big Nashville move by a few months though since I had to dip into savings, but we're figuring it all out.

Jared gets out and eyes me as I come around the front of the truck.

"Uh…"

"I'll be fine," I say with a laugh. Miranda Thorton might not scare me, but she terrifies Jared. She'd caught him and a few other guys sneaking drinks from the bar at a Foundation event when they were seventeen, and she put the fear of God into him apparently. He claps me on the shoulder and glances over at the car where Mrs. Thorton stands with her arms crossed.

"Good luck, bro."

With that, he heads inside, giving a small, awkward wave to Laney's mom as he goes. I would swear that her lips curl into an amused smile for a heartbeat. I pull off my ballcap to run my fingers through my hair before tugging it back on. *Might as well get this over with*. I don't know exactly what *this* is, but I'm going to have to hear her out regardless.

She makes her way to me and I lean against the hood of the truck. She watches me with a cold expression, though her eyes are blazing with fury.

"Laney has decided that she is going to enroll in Vanderbilt," she snaps, like it's an accusation. I rear back, blinking in confusion.

"What?" I ask, completely blindsided and knowing I couldn't possibly have heard her correctly.

"She is giving up an Ivy League education so that she can follow you to Nashville."

"What the fu—" I stop myself and clear my throat. "What are you talking about?"

"She informed me last night of her decision. I take it by your reaction that you were unaware of these plans?"

"I…" I don't know what to say. Part of me wants to say that of course I was aware, feeling like I need to be on Laney's side in this no matter how confused and shocked I am, but the other part can't believe it. Of course I would love to have her with me, to be together, but I could never let her give up Princeton for me. That's insane.

"I won't let this happen," she says before I can think of something to say.

"It's not exactly your decision," I point out. My head is spinning, the two sides of my heart tearing at each other. I want the very best for Laney, I always will. I can't imagine her giving up something this huge for me. It's not right and I can't let her do it. The other part wants nothing but to have her with me, no matter what that costs, no matter the consequences. As long as we're together, that's all that matters. I know that second part is selfish and wrong and I grit my teeth trying to force it to shut up.

"No, you're right. It's not," she says, surprising me. Her voice is still hard, but it's lost some of the fire now that she knows I wasn't the mastermind behind this plan, swaying Laney to make this decision. My brows rise a fraction, and then she adds, "It's up to *you*."

I huff out a laugh and cross my arms over my chest.

"If you think that I make *any* decisions for Laney, then you must not know your daughter at all. She—" Miranda holds up her hand to stop me.

"I know that my daughter is in love with you, and…I believe that you love her back, despite how much I wish otherwise."

"I do," I say simply, still really confused by everything that's happening right now. Miranda takes a deep breath and squares her shoulders.

"I think that you love her enough to know that you can't possibly give her the life she deserves." A cold feeling settles in my chest. "How many years will it take before you find your big break, if ever? Hmm? How many low-paying gigs at dingy bars? How many dead-end jobs to make ends meet while you chase that dream? And Laney is doing what during all that? Supporting you? Living in a cheap apartment and making do? Using all of her trust fund to pay for everything? All while trying to finish her education and make something of herself? She has dreams of being a doctor, Bowen. Of helping people and being someone extraordinary."

I clench my jaw over and over, each word hitting me like a slap in the face. Of course I've thought all of these things before. Of course I know how scarily accurate they probably are. But I'd never let myself look at it straight on before, to really see the truth of it all.

"She is giving up a top-rated education at an Ivy League university for *you*, giving up all of the doors that could open for her for medical school and beyond—she's giving it up all up for this future with you that isn't even close to what she deserves."

My ribs feel like they're shrinking in and cutting off my air supply. I barely stop myself from rubbing my hand against my chest, where a sharp pain radiates through my heart. I want to tell her she's wrong. I want to tell her that I'm going to make it and that I'll be able to give Laney everything under the sun, but I…can't. Not with any surety anyway. I have no idea if I'll ever get to where I want to be, or if I'll always just be some guy who used to sing in some bars. I clench my jaw, hating that I have nothing to say, no assurances or denials.

"So, I'm going to make you a deal," she continues. "I'm going to give you a check right here, right now, enough to set you up nicely in Nashville for the foreseeable future and let you focus on this…music career of yours." I know the answer before I ask the question, my body suddenly feeling so fucking cold except for a burning in my chest.

"In exchange for what?" I grit, somehow forcing the words from numb lips.

"You will end things with Laney immediately." I knew it was coming, and yet I still huff out an incredulous laugh.

"You cannot be serious. You're going to *pay* me to break up with your daughter??"

"I am going to pay you to do what you know deep down is right. If you love her, you'll do whatever it takes to give her the life she deserves." She holds my gaze and I can't seem to look away.

I don't want to listen to this anymore. I don't want to have these thoughts in my head.

I don't want to accept that she's fucking *right*.

I try to control my breathing, clenching my hands into fists over and over. My eyes burn with tears of anger and denial, and I can see it the moment she knows she's won. She holds out a check. I stare at the paper like it's a venomous snake, but she eventually steps closer and lays it carefully on the hood of my truck. When she steps back, her features are softer than I've ever seen them, and she looks almost sorry.

"It isn't personal. I believe that you are a decent man and by doing this, you'll confirm my suspicions. You'll both be happier for it, in the end." She crosses the small gravel parking area that sits in front of the cabin and opens her car door. Just before she slides inside I call out.

"She won't accept it. She'll know it's bullshit." I try and fail to keep the desperation out of my voice, and I know she can hear the slight tremor. Maybe I can just tell Laney that I don't think moving in together is a good idea, that it's too much too fast and that we should just try distance, but I know that won't work. If she's made up her mind about this, there won't be any swaying her, and I know without a doubt that she'll have already thought about all of the options and possibilities. She'll say that we don't have to share an apartment, but can still be in the same place together. If I try to tell her I don't want her to give up Princeton, she'll tell me she isn't giving anything up at all.

But she is.

She's giving up *everything* for what might be a really, really hard life. One that may not ever amount to anything, not the way I hope. I won't be able to give her what she deserves, and she deserves so fucking much. She deserves everything.

I already know what Miranda Thorton will say when she gives me a sad, sympathetic smile. I already know what the only answer is, and I feel like I can't breathe.

"If you love her, you'll find a way to make her believe it. If you love her...you'll break her heart, Bowen."

PART TWO

Present Day

I YANK my hand away and stand, nearly turning the chair over from the force of it, and mom's hand falls limply to her side.

"Laney, please, I—"

I hold up a hand, an anger and hurt so icy that it burns filling my chest and stealing the air from my lungs.

A few days after she had that conversation with Bowen, I'd left for Princeton, abandoning the Vanderbilt idea and feeling so embarrassed that I'd almost made such a stupid decision that I've rarely let myself even think of it in all these years. The memory of that night tries to surface now but I angrily swat it away, forcing it deep down below the rage and fury boiling inside me.

He'd *destroyed* me that night…because she asked him to. Because she'd *paid* him to.

I didn't try to talk to Bowen again, didn't want explanations or to try to fix things. I just cut all ties and never looked back. And he hadn't tried to contact me either, not a single time. Kelly had tried, but I'd ignored her. I couldn't even talk to Annie afterwards either, feeling like she'd known somehow, even though she swore she didn't in the multiple voicemails and texts she'd left me. I'd ruined my friendship with her because of it, truth be told, but I wanted to forget that summer ever happened. I *needed* to forget about it and talking to Annie would just make it worse.

Years later, I'd had enough time and distance to look back with a little more clarity, the emotions not so raw, and realized how awful I was to Annie and how badly I'd handled things when she'd been completely innocent in it all. We reconnected a few years back, and I'd even set her up with her now husband. Alton and I knew each other from medical school and kept up with each other over the years, always ending up at the same medical conferences and doing rounds with *Doctors Without Borders* together. One thing led to another and I'd introduced the two of them when we were all in the same city for three completely unrelated reasons, funnily enough, and that was all she wrote. They were married within a year and now have two beautiful daughters.

But there has always been this unspoken rule between us that we never, ever talk about what happened or about Bowen at all. We just kind of pretend that summer never happened. It may not be the best way to handle it, but it's worked for us and I think we're both just so glad to be back in each other's lives again, that we're happy to ignore it.

After I left Riverbend, I threw myself into school, taking more than a full class load every semester and over the summers, not only catching back up to where I should have been if it hadn't been for the accident, but actually graduating a year *early*. Medical school, internship, residency—I filled my every waking hour with school or work or research or volunteering, *anything* to keep thoughts of him and that summer from my mind. I still loved him, even after everything, despite how stupid it was, despite how much he hurt me.

And to find out now that it was all...planned? That my mother had orchestrated the worst day of my life...God, I can't even wrap my head around it. My mind races, trying desperately to understand.

Does that mean that he'd lied that last day? I don't dare let myself believe it, a strange hope rising, but I smother it immediately. It doesn't fucking matter if it was an act or not. He still went through with it. He still ruined *everything* for some cash.

"You *paid* him to break up with me? You…you *asked* him to tear my heart in two?? Your own daughter?"

"I was doing what I thought was best for you, you have to believe that." She's crying and though part of me recognizes that it's the first time I've seen it in over three decades, the larger part doesn't fucking care. I'm so disgusted that I can barely stand to look at her. I've known for a long time that she was a heartless, broken woman, but *this*? This is beyond anything I thought her capable of.

"You saw how it destroyed me, how broken I was!"

"You deserved better than the life I thought he could give you." I huff out a humorless laugh and she winces. *Miranda fucking Thorton wincing and looking contrite? Pigs will be flying by the window any minute.*

"I realize now that I was wrong. Even if he wasn't a successful musician now, I was still wrong. It was your life to choose, and…he loved you. Laney, I'm so sorry, I know that he really loved you. It was the only reason I knew he would agree when I went to him that day. But I never should have—"

"But he took the money," I cut her off in a deadened tone, so completely numb and confused and angry and hurt and too many other things to name. I shake my head and back away. "I can't even look at you right now, mom. I can't believe you did this to me."

"Laney, wait, I need to tell you—"

"I've heard enough from you!" I yell, and she flinches again. I know it's probably wrong to scream at someone on their deathbed, but I don't care. It's too much. My head is pounding trying to make sense of it all, trying to sift through what was real and what wasn't and if it even fucking matters at all. I brace my hands on the dresser, feeling like I'm going to throw up or pass out or punch something.

"I love you," she whispers. The machines start to beep erratically and I whirl. "I'm so proud of you and…I love you. I've always…loved you," she says through struggling breaths, "even when I didn't…know how…to do it right."

I want to go to her. I want to tell her it's ok. I want to scream at her some more. I want to hug her. I want to tell her I hate her. I want to fix her somehow.

But I can't move. I can only stare, and a tear slides down my cheek.

My lips numbly form the words *I love you*, though no sound comes out, and her lips pull up into a soft smile. They're true. Despite the fact that I also hate her, she's my mom and I do love her. She closes her eyes, sighs in what seems like relief or contentment, and then, the all too familiar sound of someone flatlining fills the room.

Ryan rushes in but I stand there doing nothing. Not that there's anything I could do even if I want to. She's a DNR and I know beyond a shadow of a doubt, that she was ready. She took my last *I love you* as the tiny shred of forgiveness she needed and was done holding on. God, had she really waited to go just for me? Just to tell me this, even risking her going to her grave with me hating her?

Ryan turns off the machines and the silence in the absence of their beeping is deafening. I stare at my mother, looking like she could be sleeping peacefully. I look at the woman who, for better or worse, made me who I am. The woman who was judgmental and cold and rarely said a kind word to me since I was thirteen. The woman who was strong and formidable and did everything on her own after dad died. The woman who did so much good in the world through the Foundation. The woman who purposely broke my heart in ways that have never fully healed. The woman that despite everything is still my mother and…is dead.

I don't know what to feel other than hurt and sick and lost.

That's what it is. I feel completely fucking *lost*.

Ryan comes towards me.

"I'm sorry for your loss," he says in a soothing tone that he's probably used a thousand times. I nod absently, still staring, everything muted and far away. And then, quick as a snap, everything slams into complete and utter focus and can't fucking breathe and I don't know what the hell to think or say or feel. All I know is that I have to get out of here this instant.

I take a step away, and then another, and Ryan, God bless him, watches with complete and utter understanding in his eyes. He must be all too aware of the many faces grief can take. Sometimes it's sobbing so hard your body feels like it might break apart. Sometimes it's stoic acceptance. Sometimes it's rage-fueled screams and lashing out.

And sometimes, it's running the fuck away.

I turn and bolt from the room.

* * *

"HOW ARE YOU HOLDING UP?" Beth asks over FaceTime. She's rummaging through my fridge but I don't mind. In fact, it's the first thing that's made me smile in two weeks. Ever since mom dropped the bomb of all bombs on me and then…died—it still feels weird saying that—I feel almost like a walking zombie. Well, alternating between a zombie and a raging ball of fury who wants to smash things with a bat.

I'm still in Riverbend and being here is like torture. Everything is too fresh here, too raw and jagged with far too many memories haunting me like ghosts. Mom. Dad. Bowen. That summer. Everything that I lost here. All the pain. The good times and the bad. It's all coming at me from all sides and I can barely stand it. I mean, how much pain can one heart fucking take* before it just…gives out?

But I still can't quite make myself leave.

I tell myself that it's because wrapping up someone's affairs takes time, but that's a pretty flimsy excuse because of course mom had everything completely and meticulously planned out and taken care of. The funeral was beautiful—as far as I can recall anyway. I feel like I wasn't really there, like when I think back on it, I'm thinking about a dream that's just out of reach. I remember lots of condolences and hugs and shakes of my hand, though no clear faces of who I was talking to. I remember lilies and roses everywhere, but just blurry, out of focus pops of color and the scents filling my nose. I remember watching her casket lower into the ground beside dad's. That part is bitterly clear even though I don't want it to be.

Did I cry? I can't remember. Surely I cried. What kind of heartless daughter wouldn't cry at her mother's funeral?

Maybe one with a mother like mine, I think bitterly. Maybe it's wrong to speak ill of the dead, but what the fuck, mom? Finally telling me all of the things that she should have been telling me my whole life didn't

---

* *Can a Heart Take*

make up for all of the hurt and neglect and pain. And don't even get me started on what she confessed. I still can't decide if knowing the truth is worth it, or if I would have rather she just kept this a secret forever.

Some attorneys in a very fancy office downtown had gone through mom's Will and said lots of words like *bequest* and *sole heir* and *probate*. I didn't pay attention to much, but walked away with the vague knowledge that I'd been left a little over half of mom's insanely large estate, including the house in Riverbend and the one in Martha's Vineyard—which Jessa is already in the process of selling for me. I hate the Vineyard.

The farm of course was already mine, so that wasn't an issue, but she left me dad's old Jag and I'd admittedly curled up in the passenger seat of it and stayed there for hours, just staring numbly at the drivers' side, wishing he was there. Most of the rest had gone to various charities that mom loved and back into the Thorton Foundation.

Jessa has been a godsend through it all, handling all of the things that I was too out of it to take care of, or that I just didn't want to deal with. I don't know what would have happened if she hadn't been here and I was glad that mom left her something as well. She deserves it and more.

I still can't quite wrap my head around what mom did or the way it altered my entire life. I don't want to play the *What If* game, but it's hard not to. What if she hadn't paid Bowen off? What if I'd gone to Vanderbilt? What if I chose my own path and found something I was actually passionate about to do with my life? What if Bowen and I had gotten a real chance? *What if, what if, what if.*

"I'm…pissed," I tell Beth, honestly. "Really fucking pissed. And upset. And hurt. And confused. And—"

"Ok, ok, I get it. You're all the things. I'm sorry. Also, might as well go ahead and tell you: I did not, in fact, remember to water your plants, and three of them have sadly gone to the great garden in the sky."

I close my eyes and laugh. Despite everything, I fucking laugh, and a surge of love for this girl goes through me, momentarily easing the pain.

"You're the worst," I tell her.

"Gardner? Yes. Friend? Psh, don't lie to yourself and the world."

I shake my head, smiling, and dig through the shopping bags on my bed. Because of my scarily efficient packing that Beth had pointed out the day I left, I wasn't really prepared to stay this long. So, I'd done a little retail therapy, but it didn't really have the desired effect. I hang up the two dresses and a pair of jeans on the outside of the closet door.

It's still so weird being back in my old room after so long, but to my surprise, mom left it exactly how it had always been. All of my posters and trophies and medals and picture collages still cover the walls, my stuffed animals still reside in their hammock in the corner, even all my clothes are still in the closet. I refuse to make myself feel worse by going through those horrific fashion choices, so I just keep that door firmly closed. I purposefully ignore the pictures from that summer tacked up around my mirror and pretend they don't exist at all.

It doesn't really work. My eyes have traced over Bowen's smiling face far too many times to count. I have half a mind to have a little bonfire and toss them all in, but so far, I've talked myself out of it.

"So, I'm assuming you haven't really processed the big bomb drop yet since it doesn't seem you're really processing much of anything?"

"Hey," I protest, frowning at the screen.

"Totally *validly* not processing, don't get me wrong, but…still not processing," she says, not backing down.

Of course she's right. I'm not even remotely close to working through mom's confession, but I let out a long breath and give her the simple answer.

"I've decided it doesn't matter."

"What the fuck do you mean it doesn't matter?"

"Exactly what I said. It doesn't matter."

"Of course it matters!" she sputters.

"No, it doesn't. At the end of the day, he still chose to break my heart for money, Beth. Whether he actually loved me before that or not doesn't matter. If he's someone that can be bought off like that, he's not someone I give a shit about."

"Ok, yes, it's shitty. *Super* shitty. But he was twenty-two and just starting out and maybe…well, maybe he thought he was doing the right thing? Like, I don't know, letting you go because he loved you and thought he would be making your life easier or whatever?"

"Don't you dare try to justify it, Beth Evans," I warn, pointing an accusatory finger at the camera.

"I'm not, I'm not!" she says immediately, surrendering. "I promise I'm not…not *completely* anyway." My mouth pops open in outrage but she continues on quickly, "Look, it's just…I don't know, don't you want to know the full story? Your mom can only know *her* side."

Of course I want to know his side…while at the same time, absolutely fucking not. Going down that road again only leads to more heartbreak, because what are the options?

Option One: he admits that everything he'd said that last day was the truth, and that mom's offer had just given him an extra push to end things sooner—and gave him a nice little bonus in the process.

Option Two: he admits that nothing he said or did that last day was real, that it was all for show and that he had loved me as deep and as hard as I'd thought he had.

Option One would be horrible. But Option Two? To have him confirm that his feelings were real, they just weren't enough to outweigh cold hard cash? That would be so much worse.

"Even if I wanted to—which I'm not saying I do—it's not like I can just pick up the phone and call him, Beth. In case you forgot, he's kind of a fucking celebrity now."

She shrugs. "You could try sliding into his DMs."

I collapse onto the bed. I pinch the bridge of my nose with one hand, holding the phone above my face with the other.

"You did not really just say I should slide into his DMs."

"What?! It's a viable option these days. He might see your name and actually respond."

"Except he probably has someone who handles all that shit for him. He'd never even see it. *Not*," I add sternly, "that I'm even contemplating trying to get in touch with him. It was fifteen years ago. We were just stupid kids. He probably doesn't even remember…"

She gives me a look that says I'm an idiot and I sigh. I know he must. The song tells me as much. I'm still pissed that he turned that day, that special fucking moment between us, into a song that he shared with the world. It feels like almost as much of a betrayal as him taking the money from mom.

"Well, you're in luck because I've been doing some FBI-level deep diving through his social media ever since you dropped the casual 'I had an epic love story with Bowen Fucking Wright' bomb on me."

I roll my eyes. "You do recall that it ended horrifically, right?" I ask, rolling over onto my stomach and shoving a pillow shaped like a cupcake under my chin.

Ignoring me, she goes on. "So, one: his gym selfies should be illegal. Like seriously. *Jaysus.*" I huff out a laugh. She's not wrong. "Two: I totally forgot that he dated that one actress way back when! Whatsherface from that one show. You know the one, with the things?"

"And the stuff?" I add dryly, waiting for her to get to the point.

"Yep, the stuff. You know who I'm talking about. Anyway, three:" she bites her lip, "...he's playing a concert over in Charleston— tomorrow night."

Chapter Sixteen

BOWEN

EVEN AFTER WHAT feels like thousands of shows—hell, maybe it really has been that many if you count every gig at a dive bar or airport restaurant—I still get that tingle of excitement in my gut just before we go on. We go through our pre-show routines: set-list check, wardrobe check (which, isn't hard for me: jeans, boots, a t-shirt, and either a ballcap or cowboy hat), a FaceTime with mom and dad, and a shot with the band.

"Where are we tonight?" Kelly asks, shaking off her tequila shot with a grimace. "I can't keep any of it straight these days. This tour has been batshit."

I laugh, wiping my mouth with the back of my hand.

"It's almost time for a break, Kells. Just three more shows and we can rest for three whole months. And Raleigh, by the way. Charlotte last night, Raleigh tonight…and Charleston tomorrow." I ignore the dip in my stomach on that one. It's not like we haven't played there a time or twelve over the past decade, but every single time we get that close to Riverbend my heart seizes up a little. Not that she's still there, of course.

And not that she would ever be caught dead at a show after everything that happened, I remind myself, but there's always that tiny flame of hope in my chest when we're in that area that maybe, just maybe, I'll see her. Even just in a crowd or passing her on the highway or something. But I know she's up in Virginia now…because, yes, I've given in to temptation and checked up on her on social media a few times over the years. Every time I do, it cuts like a knife, but I remind myself that it was the right thing despite all the pain. She graduated top of her class from Princeton, same from Johns Hopkins, and became the amazing surgeon I always knew she'd be.

And she did it all without me.

And I'm happy for her. Really, I am. I'm happy that she moved on. I'm happy that her life is good and turned out the way it should have. I'm happy…but fuck if happy doesn't hurt like hell sometimes*.

Kelly, being the too-vigilant sister that she is, gives me a look.

"Charleston, huh?"

"Yup," I say in a tone that tells her there's nothing to talk about and that I'm fine. She isn't fooled, but lets it go like she always does. It's been fifteen fucking years. Why can't I just leave it in the past? This can't be normal. Maybe I should talk to a therapist or something.

"Alright, I'm gonna go pee out the jitters before this crowd gets too rowdy." She punches me playfully in the shoulder. "I'll see ya out there, Hot Shot."

Once she's gone, I take a deep breath and finish my own private pre-show routine. I take out my wallet and unfold the worn piece of paper. It's soft and wrinkled with age, falling apart at the edges from me manhandling it so damn much. I run my fingers over it and close my eyes, remembering.

The look on her face. The vomit I'd barely kept down at having any girl but Laney in my lap, having any girl's lips on mine but hers. The minute I could actually see her heart breaking and my own following immediately after.

I clench my jaw at the memory, and take a deep breath, letting it out slowly.

Bow-en! Bow-en! Bow-en!

I can hear the crowd chanting my name and it pulls me from the memories. The sound of it fills my entire body with excitement,

---

* *Happy Hurts*

temporarily erasing everything else. Every time it happens, I have to pinch myself to believe it's real. We actually did it. We actually fucking made it. It wasn't easy by a long shot, but we didn't give up. We'd lost Jared along the way when he got married and had his first kid, but me and Kells pushed on, even more determined.

After everything that happened that summer, I refused to stop. I'd lost almost everything that day, the whole future I'd seen for me and Laney together, so all I had left was this dream—and I clung to it like a madman. Laney had wanted this dream for me, and in some sick, twisted way, I've always told myself that I was doing it for her, that she would want me to keep pushing, to never stop until I got here.

After what I did, I'm sure she'd actually rather remove my balls with her dullest scalpel and hang them from her rearview mirror than have me succeed, but I delude myself into thinking she'd be happy for me. Proud, even.

I take one more deep breath, put the paper away, and head towards the stage, ready to sing my heart out to a girl who'll never hear it.

Chapter Seventeen

LANEY

"I CAN'T BELIEVE I'm doing this," I mutter to myself, still not completely sure how I ended up here. After my conversation with Beth, I *might* have gotten completely hammered, booked a hotel, and bought a ridiculously expensive last-minute ticket for the Bowen Wright concert in Charleston. At the time, I had grand, delusional, very drunken thoughts of storming in and confronting him, demanding answers and telling him he was a coward and an asshole and every other name I could think of—Beth had supplied lots of suggestions—maybe even throwing in a good slap before walking out in all my glory, leaving him dumbstruck and feeling horrible and stupid and crying.

Now that I'm actually walking towards the backstage area—a long hallway roped off about halfway down and with a large, very intimidating security guard standing sentry—I realize how completely ridiculous and stupid this entire thing is. I don't know why I even came. I told myself over and over again during the drive here to turn the hell around, that it was a horrible idea and that Drunk Laney was an emotional moron, but I kept on driving. I think maybe I'm still in shock of a sort, like adrenaline and a whole host of emotional stress are steering me more than rational thought.

So, here I am, at his fucking show, going all in on this insanity and approaching the security guard…only to realize that I have no fucking clue what I'm supposed to say. I hadn't really thought this far when I was drunk, but now the biggest flaw in my brilliant plan is obvious: they don't just let anyone waltz backstage. So, now I have to try to convince this man to let me through. What in the hell do I say to accomplish that? My palms are sweating as I make my way over, trying to come up with something. *Think, Laney. Think, think, think.*

Ok. I'm a doctor…maybe I lie and say there's a medical emergency back there and I was called in to help? An *is there a doctor in the house?* situation, and I just so happen to be in the house. It could totally work…except that feels wrong on too many levels, so I discard that plan pretty quickly. I could say I'm with the band…which is so clearly a lie that I immediately toss it in the trash pile too. Maybe I just flash the guy? That used to work, right?

"Can I see your pass, ma'am?" the security guard asks, holding up a hand to stop me as I get close to the rope. I crane my head up to meet his gaze. He's got to be every bit of six-seven, and built like a damn refrigerator. He has tattoos covering both arms and another snaking up his neck, and everything him about him says *fuck around and find out…* but his eyes are surprisingly kind and his smile is easy as he waits for my answer.

"Ok, so, see…I don't have one."

"I'm sorry, only people allowed back here are those with an access pass."

"I get that, I really do. But see…here's the thing…I…" I swallow hard. "I know Bowe—and I'm sure everyone trying to get back there says that, but I swear it's true. I'm a doctor, I took an oath." His dark brow furrows and I shake my head, realizing that I am spiraling and sputtering nonsense. "I mean, not an oath not to lie, obviously, but it's a very important oath and maybe that shows you that I have good character or…I don't fucking know. Forget the doctor comment— unless there's a medical emergency I can help with…?" I ask hopefully. Maybe that plan wasn't so bad after all, but he tilts his head, looking like he's torn between tossing *my* ass out and laughing *his* ass off. I shake my head, unbelieving that I really just said that. I pinch the bridge of my nose. "Nevermind. God, I sound crazy," I murmur. Bless him, he doesn't outright agree, but looks like he wants to. I exhale roughly, knowing that I'm spiraling the drain here.

"Look, I just…I need to talk to him. It's important, like fifteen years in the making important and I just…if you could maybe just tell him that I'm out here and see if he'll come…my name is…"

"Laney?" I hear a voice say from somewhere behind the security guard, blissfully interrupting my ridiculous rambling. A second later, I see her.

"Kelly?" I reply, somewhere between shock and relief. I don't know why I'm surprised to see her, really. The Outlaws had fizzled out after Jared got married and moved to Georgia from what I've seen on his Instagram, but Kelly stayed with Bowen, always part of his band even though he technically became a solo artist.

Her eyes fly wide and she runs a hand through her blonde hair, longer than she'd kept it back then. She looks fantastic, like she's barely aged a day, and a quick stab of a pain radiates through my chest. I hadn't just lost Bowen that day, I'd lost Kelly too, and I'd grown to care about her like my own sister.

"Oh my God, it really is you! Let her through, Chip, she's with me."

Chip nods, stepping aside to unhook the velvet rope.

"Good luck," he says with a smile. "Sounds like you might need it?"

I huff out an almost hysterical laugh, mutter thanks, and let Kelly drag me with her down the hallway a bit.

"I can't believe you're here," she says, hugging me so quickly that I don't even have time to return it before she's pulling me into what I guess is like a green room or dressing room or I don't fucking know what they call it—a place where the talent gets ready or relaxes before the show. She glances down the hall like she's making sure no one saw us come in here before she shuts the door and turns to face me. She studies me for a heartbeat and then her face pinches, her shoulders slumping.

"You know," she says softly. Simply. Not a question. I don't know what she saw on my face that made it so obvious, but there's no doubt in her words.

"And so did you?" I ask, trying to keep the accusation out of my voice. She got me backstage for this ridiculous plan, after all. I shouldn't attack her, but…well, fury rises in my chest, swift and scalding.

"Not until years later," she says and there's such sincerity in her voice that I believe her immediately. That quiets the anger a bit, but it's still simmering. "I'm so sorry, Lanes. I didn't know…that day at Johnny's, I had no idea…" She shakes her head. "I'm sorry."

I've been trying to keep the memory of that day from my thoughts, shoving it back every time it tries to break through the thin, desperate walls I've been trying to keep up ever since mom told me what she'd done. But now, being here with Kelly and being so close to Bowe again, it easily destroys the flimsy wall and slams into me so forcefully that it steals the breath from my lungs:

I kept telling myself that everything was fine. There was a perfectly good explanation for Bowen standing me up and not answering his phone. Worry had made it nearly impossible to breathe until I'd gotten a text back from Kelly telling me that he was already at Johnny's, hanging out before their show. So, he was alright. Physically, at least. I mean, he wasn't laying in a ditch somewhere or anything.

So, what the hell was going on?

I was half furious, half worried as I pulled into the gravel parking lot. I couldn't stop the ball of ice from settling in my stomach. Something was wrong, I just knew it, but I had no idea what it could be. Part of me assumed the worst, that he was freaking out over all the I love yous that had been exchanged out at the farm, but he hadn't seemed like he was weirded out. He was the one who'd said it first even. So, I pushed the unease away and headed inside, ready to have our first fight.

But then I froze in my tracks, my stomach dropping through the floor.

Bowen was lounging in the big corner booth with a group of people I vaguely knew. They were a few of the regulars that came to almost every show at the bar—and I especially recognized the blonde that was practically sitting in Bowen's lap, his arm thrown around her shoulder. What. The. Fuck. I could barely breathe around the sudden icy pressure in my chest. My brain was trying to tell me things that I refused to hear, but I couldn't focus on them over the roaring in my ears. The blonde—I couldn't remember her name. One of those double-first names, like *Lizzy Sue or Sarah Ann or something like that*—was always front and center during their sets, singing along and eye-fucking Bowe, but I'd never really paid it much mind. I hadn't been lying when I'd told him that I wasn't jealous of him on stage, of the flirting he did and the response the girls give him in return.

But, as I watched her lean into his side, smiling a coy, sexy smile, I thought that maybe I should have paid more attention after all.

He leaned over and whispered something in her ear, and she giggled, slapping him playfully on the chest. She left her hand there, running it downward and settling it on his stomach.

I couldn't possibly have been seeing what I was seeing. This had to be some kind of joke. A really fucking sick joke.

I walked over, torn between hurt and shock and rage.

"Bowe?" I said when I reached the table and he lazily turned his head away from the blonde.

"Oh, hey," he said breezily, like everything happening was completely normal. He grinned and based on the number of bottles and empty glasses littering the table, I assumed it was a drunken one. He didn't remove his arm from around the blonde's shoulders and she glanced between us, quirking a brow with a challenging look in her eyes. I ignored her and pulled my gaze back to Bowe.

"What the hell? I waited for you at The Hickory for an hour and you didn't answer my calls or texts..." I was trying so hard to find a reasonable explanation, one that wasn't the completely and totally obvious one, but with Blondie on his lap—God, what was her fucking name? Mary Ellen? Bobbi Lou?—*wiggling closer and him making zero moves to push her away*, it was really fucking hard. I knew the answer, but my mind wasn't quite ready to accept it.

"Oh, yeah, sorry, I got a little...distracted," he said, eyeing Blondie. She giggled again and I'd never wanted to pull someone's hair out more than I did in that moment. Absolute rage was warring with desperate agony in my chest. This couldn't be happening. There was some kind of mistake.

"What the fuck, Bowe? This isn't you." I wanted it to be true. I wanted the horrible feeling in my stomach to be wrong. I wanted to wake up from that awful nightmare.

"Look, Laney, this just isn't going to work out, alright?"

"What?" I asked, my breath coming out in a whoosh as if I'd been punched right in the stomach.

"You. Me. This whole thing." He gestured between us with the arm not coiling even tighter on…Fuck what was her name? I tried to tell my mind that it didn't matter what her name was, but it was latching on to this weird little detail to keep my attention off of the main attraction: my heart breaking. So, my mind went round and round, trying to think of the few times we'd all toasted a round with the regulars, hearing her name mentioned by the bartender…Lily Mae! That was her name!

He gestured with the arm not coiling tighter around Lily Mae's *fucking* waist.

"I'm over it." He took a swig of beer, eyeing me almost coldly. He'd never ever looked at me like that before. It didn't even seem like him. It was like one of those old movies I'd watched with dad what felt like a million years ago where aliens took over people's bodies.

"What the hell do you mean?"

"Jesus, do I really need to spell it out for you? I finally got what I wanted from you—took long enough, by the way. Fuck, I had to drop the L word to get those thighs apart." Lily Mae snorted and it felt like a knife had been slammed into my chest, the blade serrated and rusted and grinding against the bone. I wanted so badly to be pissed about it, to tell Lily Mae to shut the fuck up or fly at her across the table maybe, but I couldn't even breathe around the pain. I couldn't think, couldn't move, couldn't fully understand.

Or I could, but I really didn't want to.

"And now, we're done," Bowen added casually, as if he wasn't completely destroying me.

It was all a lie. He'd just wanted…

"No," I said, shaking my head, refusing to accept it. There had to be some other explanation. *"No. I don't believe you."*

He pulled out a cigarette then, and I watched numbly as he lit it. Smoking wasn't technically allowed inside but since it was before the crowd had really started to arrive, no one was going to say anything to him. The Outlaws kept this place packed every single Friday night, so Bowen could do pretty much whatever the hell he wanted.

He took a long drag before blowing the smoke out lazily, holding my gaze the entire time. I searched his eyes, desperate to find the guy I fell in love with, desperate to know that this is all some weird act, but...he wasn't there. I wondered if he'd ever actually existed at all.

If this was an act, it was Oscar worthy, and I tried to blink away the tears that burned my eyes as the full weight of it hit me.

None of it was real. Mom was right. I was so fucking stupid.

"Well, believe it, Ivy League," he said, stressing the Ivy League part, as if was an insult or something—before pulling the blonde in for a kiss. My breath caught in my throat and I took a step back, feeling like he'd slapped me. I wanted to vomit, seeing his lips on hers, seeing her hand cupping his cheek and holding her to him. I actually almost did, but I clamped my lips shut, forcing it down.

I hated him. I hated myself. I hated my mother for being right and for the way I knew she would gloat when I told her I'd been wrong, how she would never let me live this down. I hated that he made me love him. I hated that I was just a stupid, naïve, lovesick teenager like I'd kept telling myself I wasn't.

I hated that I still loved him.

Even as he shattered my heart into a million pieces and had his tongue down another girls' throat right in front of me, I still fucking loved him.

He pulled away from Lily Mae and turned back to meet my gaze. There was no remorse there, no pain, no sympathy—nothing. Just cold, empty, nothingness.

Tears slid down my cheeks and I hated myself for crying in front of him, for letting him see just how much he was hurting me. His jaw flexed once as I took another step back, then another, but he didn't try to stop me. I turned, running to get out of that place as fast as I could and never look back.

I ran right into Kelly.

"Whoa, easy there, Lanes," she said with a laugh, but then she took in my face. "Laney? Hey, what's..." Her gaze shifted over my shoulder to the booth and her brows drew down. "What the fuck?" She sounded completely surprised, but I couldn't be sure. She was his sister after all, they were so close...Another wave of pain hit at the idea of her knowing that he'd been playing me the whole time.

I flung her arms off of me and pushed past her, refusing to completely break down in this bar while Bowen Wright watched.

"Laney!" she called after me, but I didn't stop. I kept running. Away from the first man I ever loved. Away from the future I'd seen so fucking clearly in my head. Away from the pain and the loss and the embarrassment. I ran and ran and ran.

And I don't think I've ever really stopped.

LANEY

I RUB the heel of my hand against the center of my chest, trying to ease the sharp, stabbing pain there. I've tried to erase that day from my memory, or at the very least, never look at it straight on. In all these years, I've only allowed myself to see blurry snippets of it here and there—usually when I'm whisky drunk or having a really bad day and pain is welcome as a distraction. But even then, I never let the full memory in.

Now, it hits so hard I literally have to brace myself on the back of a nearby chair and I can hardly catch my breath.

"Laney, are you alright?" Kelly asks, coming forward and looking concerned. I nod and squeeze my eyes shut. I take a deep, settling breath, and pull on all of the emotional control I've worked so hard to hone all these years at the hospital. I always imagined it like a coat that I could pull on, keeping everything from touching me in order to think logically and scientifically. It sounds cold, but it's necessary to separate yourself from the personal side of medicine sometimes. I can't pull the coat completely around me now, I'm too raw and drained, but I tug it on enough to help me push past the memory. I open my eyes and meet Kelly's gaze, pulling myself together.

"I need to see him. I just…" I can't put into words something I can't even explain to myself. I need to see him. I need to make him look me in the eye and tell me if that day was a lie, or if *all* of it was. I need him to admit that money was more important than any feelings he may or may not have had. I need to hear the words from his mouth. I need him to see that I'm fucking fine, that he didn't break me beyond repair and that I've barely thought about him at all in the last decade and a half.

That last one is a lie, but I don't care. He doesn't have to know that. I pull the metaphorical coat tighter around me. I won't let him see me looking like a complete emotional wreck. I want him to believe the last bit about not thinking about him, and that won't hit quite right if I'm having a mental breakdown when I talk to him.

So, I straighten and shift my shoulders back, and am proud of how calm my voice sounds when I speak again.

"I just really need to talk to him, Kelly," I say simply. "Please."

Kelly chews on her lip, but then nods.

"He made his fucking bed, he needs to lie in it," she mutters. "Just sit tight, ok? I'll be back."

She leaves the room and I stand in the middle awkwardly for a minute before deciding to poke around. There's a fridge and a table full of snacks along one wall—chips and candy and protein bars, even a fancy-looking charcuterie board. On any other day, I would help myself to the goods, but right now the thought of eating anything makes my stomach roil. I can hear the rumbling of the crowd and the opening act already singing on stage.

"He really did it," I whisper to no one, taking it all in. I always knew he would, and of course I've seen the proof all over social media and heard it on the radio, but being here now, it really hits me: *he really fucking made it.* I wish that there wasn't a piece of me that was proud of him for it. That piece needs to fuck right off. I grit my teeth and keep wandering around the room because I physically can't sit still right now, so lounging on the couch is out of the question. I peek into one of the attached doors and find a small private bathroom. The other turns out to be a closet.

I wander back towards the couch and see what must be the set list on the coffee table. I inhale sharply seeing Bowen's familiar writing on the page. He's crossed out a few songs and written new titles in, and drawn a few arrows, rearranging the order for the night. I tear my eyes away quickly when I see *Weeping Willow.*

"Fucking asshole," I mutter, fuming again. God, my emotions are going to give me whiplash they're so all over the place.

Two guitars sit in stands beside the couch, one shiny and black and obviously expensive and the other—

"Oh my God," I whisper, moving to get a closer look. It's the same guitar he had that summer, the one he tried to teach me to play, the one he'd written countless songs on while I lounged beside him. The one… My breath hitches when I see it: the little heart next to the letter *L* that I'd drawn in sharpie on the neck one afternoon by the lake. I reach out and brush my fingers over the faded black ink. Why had he left it? Why not scrub it off or draw over it? Why—

I straighten and whirl when the door opens and I hear deep, rumbling laughter. A tall, lean figure in a tight black t-shirt, jeans, and a Longhorns ballcap steps over the threshold, still looking back out into the hallway, smiling and pointing at someone.

My heart starts to race and my limbs feel numb. A warm tingling starts in my chest and works its way outward, and my heart beats too fast against my ribs.

For the first time in fifteen years, for the first time since that night, I'm in the same room with Bowen Wright.

Fuck. Me.

Chapter Nineteen

BOWEN

RALPH SAID that Kelly was looking for me, so I decide to head back to the green room to wait. I need to finish getting ready for the show anyway, and I want to double check the changes I made to the setlist one more time. Bill makes some stupid joke about Kyle needing tighter jeans and I'm laughing when I step inside the room.

But the laughter dies when I turn and find Laney Thorton standing a few feet away beside my old guitar. I stop in my tracks, blinking several times. This can't be real. Am I hallucinating? My chest feels tight and I don't think there's enough oxygen in the room. A cold sweat immediately breaks out on the back of my neck and my entire body has a weird numbness spreading through it.

Her hair is darker now, subtle streaks of deep auburn in the strands now instead of the honey gold that they'd once been, and it's in big, loose curls flowing past her shoulders. Her hazel eyes are more brown than green tonight, and are wide and unblinking as they bore into mine. She's obviously older now, face leaner, cheekbones a bit more angular and defined—a woman, no longer a teenager—but she's still the same Laney. A lot of years have passed but damn they've been good to her. She's the kind of woman that makes you do a double take, the kind that draws every eye in the room without trying. Absolutely gorgeous.

God, it's really her. Against all odds and reason, she's actually fucking here. This is *real.*

Neither one of us moves or speaks. We just stand there, staring.

Then Kelly, ever the moment-ruiner, busts through the door.

"I couldn't find him but—Oh!" she gasps in surprise, skidding to a halt beside me and nearly falling over. If I wasn't stunned into complete and total immobility by the unreal situation I've found myself in, I would have laughed. "Here you are. So, uhhh…you have a visitor," she says, stating the obvious as she looks between me and Laney. She pats me on the shoulder, says, "Good luck," and bolts from the room like a dog with its tail on fire. She closes the door behind her with a deafening click that seems to echo through the room.

Leaving me all alone with Laney.

Fuck. Me.

I don't know how in the hell to start this conversation. I think about the last time I saw her, the pain and betrayal in her eyes as I forced myself to kiss that girl, as I made myself destroy everything we'd built in those few short months. It had been fast, but my God it had been strong and real and so utterly perfect—until I'd ruined it.

It was the right decision. It was what was best for her. I've told myself this over and over again since that day, so many times the words have lost all meaning, but it's been the only thing that kept me from trying to reach out to her, to explain everything and apologize and throw myself on my knees in front of her and beg for forgiveness.

I'd had no idea if I was going to ever really make it or not. It had taken almost a decade of clawing and scraping and fighting before we even really got a foothold in. Imagining putting Laney through all that makes me feel sick. That solidifies that I'd made the right decision.

But seeing her now…God, I wish I hadn't.

My heart is still racing in my chest like a stampede of wild horses, but I try to calm it. I need to think. I need to speak. I need to do something other than stand here staring like a fucking psycho.

Why is she here? After all this time, why would she come now? Past the shock in her eyes, I can see the pain and the anger, and with a sinking feeling in my stomach, I know that she knows. My chest clenches but I deserve whatever is about to come. I think part of me even welcomes it, feeling like I can finally let go of this secret sin that's been strangling me for fifteen years.

"Hey," I rasp and then have to clear my throat. I finally find my voice and the best I can come up with is *hey*? Real fucking smooth.

"Was it worth it?" she asks quietly. She doesn't yell. Her voice isn't laced with venom like I fully expect it to be. It's just...dead. Hollow. And this is so, so much worse. I want her to scream at me. I need her to yell and throw things and make me feel like shit. I deserve all of it and more. This emptiness guts me.

"Laney, I—"

"Was it worth it?" she repeats, cutting me off. "That's all I need to know, Bowen." I inhale deeply at the sound of my name on her lips after all his time. How can it still cut me right down to my core?

"She told you?" I ask instead of answering because the answer I need to give is *yes*. Yes, it was worth cutting out my own heart to make sure she had the life she deserved, to make sure that she had every opportunity that she could dream of. Ivy League education, top choices of medical schools, connections and contacts that she'd never have had if she'd changed all of her plans for me. But I can't imagine the look on her face if I give her that answer. I can't fucking do it.

"On her deathbed, yes."

I wince. I wonder if their relationship improved over the years, but by the way she says it, I don't think so. Even so, I can't imagine what she's feeling right now. Conflicted to say the least, I'm sure.

"I'm sorry," I tell her honestly.

"It's fine. I'm fine. I mean I'm not really but...it doesn't matter." She closes her eyes for a second and shakes herself. I'm moving towards her before I even realize I've taken a step, desperate to comfort her even though I know that's got to be the absolute last thing she could want. I stop when I'm a few steps away and she opens her eyes again.

I can make out more details now that I'm closer: a small scar above her right eyebrow that hadn't been there before, an even fainter one across her cheek from the wreck we got in after the gala, small smile lines fanning out from the corners of her mouth and eyes, more earrings lining the shell of her left ear, but so much of her looks just how I remember, I'm immediately transported back to that summer:

The night I first met her on the deck behind Johnny's; hanging out by the lake; the sight of her in that damned yellow bikini that nearly brought me to my knees; our first kiss on the dock; her sleeping while I wrote new songs, every damn one of them about the girl lying in my lap; movies and concerts and ice cream dates; the farm. Everything comes rushing back and I swear my heart twists inside my chest, recoiling from the pain, like it can escape it somehow.

The resolve she'd had before seems to be draining away with every breath she takes. Her eyes are glassy, her body trembling ever so slightly.

"Was any of it real?" she whispers, shoulders slumping. "I told myself it didn't matter, I told myself that I wouldn't ask, but…I have to know, Bowen. I have to fucking *know*." Her eyes water and God, it nearly breaks me. I barely stop myself from reaching out for her.

"Laney, I—"

"There you are!" a voice calls from the door and I curse to myself. I turn and find Piper coming through the door, smiling, and I immediately feel like a total jackass. Not that anything happened, of course, but from the minute I saw Laney, no one else on the planet existed. Piper's smile falters ever so slightly when she glances between me and Laney. Is the tension in the air around us that fucking palpable? Is it that obvious? But she recovers quickly.

"Oh, I'm sorry to interrupt," she says brightly, coming closer and wrapping her arm around mine. I don't think she's doing it to be territorial or anything, she just likes when everyone nearby knows we're together. She likes being Bowen Wright's girlfriend, no doubt about it. Sometimes I wonder if she actually likes Bowen Wright, though…but that's a thought for another time.

Laney blinks and it's like she's coming out of a trance. I clear my throat lightly.

"Piper, this is—"

"Just an old friend who was hoping to snag an autograph," Laney interrupts with an easy smile, that vulnerability from a moment ago completely erased like she's pulled on a mask. To anyone else, it would be convincing as hell, but despite all the years and hurt between us, I still know Laney Thorton better than I know myself, and I can tell easily that this is all for show.

"Right," I say, playing along because I don't really know what else to do. "We met the summer me and Kells lived in Riverbend and formed our first band."

"Ahh, ok. Wow, old friends is right," Piper says, smiling easier again. "What was that? Like a decade ago?"

"Fifteen years," Laney and I both correct at the same time, and there's a split second of awkwardness before Laney diffuses it with another easy laugh. She was always good with people, knowing how to put them at ease, the right thing to say, just the right timing of a laugh or a pat on the shoulder or a good-natured joke at someone's expense. I don't know if it was from years of being around Thorton Foundation events and seeing all the schmoozing, or natural bedside manner that I imagine has served her well with patients.

"A lifetime," Laney adds. "Laney, by the way." She reaches out to shake Piper's hand, making sure to move so that our bodies get nowhere near each other despite being only a few feet apart. The message is loud and clear and while I deserve it, I fucking hate it.

"Piper Waterford, Bowen's girlfriend. Fiancé one day if this guy will ever just pop the dang question." She rolls her eyes playfully and laughs, but do I imagine the tiny bit of strain there? "I swear I'm just about to buy myself a ring and make it official on my own. It's nice to meet you." The idea of being engaged or even married sends a spike of unease through me. Not quite fear but...dislike. A wrongness that I don't want to examine right now.

"You too. Well, I'm sure you need to get ready for the big show," Laney says brightly. "Thanks for the autograph," she adds, keeping up the ruse. She meets my gaze again for a heartbeat before turning away, but I don't miss the flash of pain and the thousands of unsaid words.

This wasn't how it was supposed to go. We didn't get to fucking talk. I owe her my side of the story. I owe her the full explanation. I owe her...something more than this. I turn quickly, desperate to...I don't know what, but I can't just let her walk away like this. I just can't.

"Here, let me walk you out," I blurt, even though she's almost to the door already. I cross the distance in a couple of long strides as she turns the knob and pulls it open. I grab the edge and pull it the rest of the way for her, attempting to look like I'm being gentlemanly and opening the door for a lady.

She doesn't look at me again, but just before she steps away and out of my life again, she mutters, "I hope that twenty grand was worth it."

I inhale sharply, but she's gone before I can say another word.

Chapter Twenty

BOWEN

"SHE SEEMED NICE," Piper says from behind me as I keep staring at the door long after Laney has disappeared through it. There isn't accusation in her voice, but there's definite curiosity. Could she tell that Laney and I were much more than just friends? Could you see the years of hurt and history and brokenness between us?

It had all happened so quickly, it's like a blur, and I honestly wonder for a second if I'd imagined the whole thing, but…no. Laney was here. She knows what happened all those years ago—well, some of it anyway. She knows what her mom told her, but she doesn't know the full truth.

And now, she never will. She's gone again and I know this time I'll never see her again. She came here in a state of grief and anger and confusion for answers. She didn't really get any, but whatever brought her here will disappear once the shock of everything that she just went through fades away.

I swallow hard and try to school my features and get my heart to calm the fuck down. It's still racing like I just ran a marathon. I turn back to Piper and force a smile, though I know I'm not nearly as good at hiding what I'm thinking as Laney is.

"Yeah, she was always nice to everyone. She grew up with our old drummer, Jared."

"Oh, that's cool. It was nice of you to get her a backstage pass and everything." I nod absently. "Well...you better get ready," she says, eyeing me like there's clearly something off. I need to get my shit together before the show. "I'll see you after."

"Yeah, see you after."

She leans in and kisses me quickly, barely a brush of our lips, and then she's off. The door closes behind her and I practically stumble to the couch, dropping down heavily into the worn leather. I rest my elbows on my knees and put my head in my hands, but the room feels like it's spinning or like I'm in some weird half-awake, half-asleep space where nothing is quite real or in focus.

The door opens again and I know it's Kelly without having to check.

"Jesus fucking Christ," she mutters. I don't look up and she comes to sit beside me on the couch. She reaches over and rubs my back in gentle circles, just like mom used to do whenever I got sick as a kid. "What happened? Did she slap you? I was kind of hoping she might slap you. What did she say? What did *you* say?"

"No slapping, though I really fucking deserved it. And neither one of us said much of anything, really," I groan, finally looking up at her. Her face is pinched with worry as she searches my eyes. I slump back against the cushions and exhale roughly. "I can't believe she was really here," I whisper.

"Are you ok?"

"No. Not really. But I never have been, so that's nothing new."

Kelly knows the whole story. *All* the gory details. I didn't tell her until years later, but I finally spilled it all when I was going through a really, really rough time. I got back into drinking pretty bad when we first moved to Nashville. Guess it was the way I was coping with losing Laney and everything, and things were even harder than we'd initially thought. We were playing any little gig we could find—any bar, any festival, any party. Even a wedding once. Literally *anything*— and barely eking out a name for ourselves. Then Jared told us he was gonna be a dad and he was gonna marry Ashton and move in with her parents down in Georgia. It had been a huge blow and I just spiraled right down the fucking drain. I went on a four-day bender, I guess deciding I'd try every fucking whiskey from every fucking shelf in that town if I had to, just hoping I could find one that brought her back* or erased the pain. Not a damn one of them worked.

When I finally came to, Kelly was sitting across from me on the bathroom floor where she'd been taking care of me after I'd puked my guts up for the umpteenth time.

"What the hell are you doing, Bowe?" she'd asked, looking at me like she hardly knew me. "This isn't you." The words had hit me right in my still semi-drunk heart. Laney had said those same words to me when I'd acted like an absolute bastard to get her to leave me in the rearview.

"I fucked everything up," I'd whispered brokenly.

She'd sighed heavily. "You didn't fuck everything up. We missed one gig, and you missed a shift at the bar, but I got Rick to cover, so it's alright—"

"No. With Laney." She'd blinked in surprise, brow furrowing. It was an unspoken rule between us that we never, ever brought Laney up. She'd of course wanted to know what the fuck that day at Johnny's had been about, what the hell I'd been doing, but I'd firmly—ok, maybe I'd screamed at her like only siblings can without destroying relationships—told her to let it go, and after that, she'd dropped it. I think she could see how hard I was trying to hold on and talking about it would push me over the edge, so she'd always just let me skate by on it, assuming I would tell her one day when I was ready.

I'd pushed myself up and scooted until my back was against the side of the tub.

"Haven't heard that name in a long time," she'd said cautiously, clearly confused but knowing that whatever I was going through, I needed someone to go through it with me. She met my gaze and something inside me broke. I couldn't hold it back anymore. I couldn't be alone in my guilt, in my pain. I told her everything. My conversation with Miranda, the deal, the act at the bar that day to make sure that

---

* *Some Whiskey*

Laney's heart was sufficiently broken enough to move on from me completely and forever.

"Oh Bowe," Kelly had whispered, scooting close and pulling me into her lap while I cried like I was five years old again and my pet frog had just died. She'd stroked my hair and I finally let myself feel all of it, everything that I'd bottled up and refused to let touch me since that fucking day at Johnny's.

Afterwards, she'd told me I was an idiot but that she understood why I'd done what I'd done and couldn't completely blame me. But she'd made me promise to cut back with the drinking and to get my shit together or we'd never stand a chance of making it.

Kelly is really the only reason we did. If she hadn't been there to help me pick up the pieces and really start pushing, we definitely wouldn't be where we are now.

"Her mom didn't tell her everything?" she asks after a few minutes, pulling me out of my memories.

"Apparently not. I don't know why. Or I can probably guess, but it doesn't matter either way."

"Of course it matters," Kelly objects. "Bowen, of course it fucking matters." She stares at me like I've lost my mind.

"No, it doesn't. She's gone, Kells. It's done."

I stand then, and though she looks like she wants to argue, she presses lips into a hard line. She sighs and shakes her head sadly.

"Get ready, baby brother. Pre-show call with the 'rents in ten."

Chapter Twenty-One

LANEY

"I'M FINE," I say for what feels like the thousandth time. I left Riverbend the day after my insane trip to Bowen's concert. What in the actual fuck had I been thinking? My medical diagnosis is severe emotional distress and a splash of temporary insanity. I had too much shit thrown at me at once and I wasn't making rational decisions whatsoever. In fact, it hadn't even felt like me making the decisions at all, it was like someone else was driving and I was just along for the ride in the passenger seat.

Seeing Bowen had been like a sucker punch to the gut by Connor McGregor. I had barely been able to breathe, barely been able to think or speak or do much of anything but stare at the man who had completely trampled on my heart...and somehow, despite that, still had a piece of it. I hated him for that. I hated myself for it even more. But there was no denying the fact that a part of me—a very stupid, ridiculous, sadistic part—would always love him.

The years had been better to him than he deserved, and he looked even better in person than in any picture on social media. He'd cut his hair since the performance on the morning show Beth and I had watched the morning before I went to see mom, the curls no longer reaching his shoulders like before. Which is probably for the best—no one should look *that* good with a manbun and it just seemed unfair to keep flaunting his perfection to the world. His scruff had been full but trimmed short, and his chest and arms were testing his t-shirt's limits, but God bless America, I wasn't complaining. I shouldn't have been appreciating anything about the asshole at all, let alone how good he looked, but I'd be lying if I said those thoughts weren't in the jumble with everything else.

The utter shock in his all too-familiar blue-green eyes would have been funny in any other situation. He'd stared at me like he was seeing a ghost...or maybe his worst nightmare come to life. I imagine that he never thought he'd see me again, let alone waiting in his dressing room before a nearly sold out show where he was about to perform for a hundred thousand people. Too many emotions had passed over his face when he'd walked into the room and stopped dead in his tracks like he'd been electrocuted.

It's all too fucking confusing to figure out. Every time I try, I feel like I'm wading through waist high mud, barely moving an inch forward no matter how much effort I put in. If mom had paid him off to leave me, and to do it in a way that ensured I'd never try to get him back again, then did that mean that everything *had* been real? That the last day at Johnny's was just an act to make sure I was broken and he got his check? Did he really love me the way he said he did, the way I was so completely sure he did?

Or was it *all* just bullshit and mom had given him a convenient out with a twenty-grand cherry on top? He'd been so cold that day, so callous and cruel, it's really hard to believe it was an act. He kissed that girl like it was nothing, had held her so tightly to him...The thought still makes me feel sick, even after fifteen years.

God, I am so pathetic.

I sigh, rounding back to the same conclusion as always: It. Doesn't. Matter. He'd chosen money over me. He'd seen mom's check as his ticket to Nashville, a tool to help pave his way to the big time. End of story. So, even if that last day had been an act after all and he wasn't that completely heartless, there was no possible way that he'd loved me the way I thought. So why am I still torturing myself trying to figure it out?

Beth eyes me dubiously—or, as dubiously as possible given the position she's in—and I give her a pointed look.

"I swear to God if you ask again, I will suture my initials into your forehead." She'd tripped in the law library and taken the edge of a book cart to the head. No real damage, just a superficial cut, but she needed a few stitches to close it up. She swears it was just a run of the mill klutz moment, but I think it's because she's working herself too hard studying for the Bar and is half-asleep on her feet most days.

"Sounds like something someone who is definitely *not* fine would say…ouch! You did that on purpose!"

"Oh stop it, you can't feel anything. Stop being a baby."

"It's only been like two weeks. Are you sure you don't want to take some time off?"

"Yes, I'm sure. I went. I said my goodbyes. I laid mom to rest. And I've moved on. End of story."

Almost every word is a lie. The truth is that I haven't dealt with shit, not really. I haven't dealt with mom's betrayal. I haven't dealt with her death and the whole host of emotions I'm ignoring because of it. I haven't dealt with seeing Bowen again. I know it isn't healthy, but I haven't let myself really think about any of it. I blocked everything out, came back, and immediately jumped right back into work like nothing happened. I haven't even cried, which is probably a huge red flag that a full-on breakdown is coming soon, but for now, I'm just trucking along until I can't anymore. Again, not healthy but, whatever.

No one seems to believe my *I'm fine* line, and it's really starting to get annoying.

"Laney?" Colt had said in surprise when he'd seen me my first morning back. He'd done a legitimate double take, clearly not expecting me to be standing there with a chart in my hand.

"Hey, Colt," I'd said with a bright smile. "How are ya?"

He'd looked at me with a worried expression, coming close and talking in low, soothing tones like I was a trapped animal he was afraid was going to bite him. Maybe I would. Who knew anymore.

"I'm good...how are you?" he'd asked slowly.

"Great. Already knocked out an emergency appy this morning and patient is doing fantastic, not to toot my own horn but," I'd shrugged and given a little *toot toot* motion with my hand.

"No, I mean...I thought you'd be taking some time off with... everything?" He knew about mom but had no idea about all the other drama, of course. Colt and I are good friends, but the only person I'd told everything to is Beth, and even though they're dating, I knew she wouldn't spill all the tea.

"Nope, no need. Everything is all good. I went and said my good-byes, the funeral was very classy as per Miranda Thorton standards, the estate is all in order. So I'm back and back in the saddle."

His dark brows had furrowed as he studied me. Colt knows me better than almost anyone and I knew that he wasn't buying my *happy-go-lucky-I'm-totally-fine-that-my-mom-is-dead* act.

"Thorn, come on, be real with me."

I smiled—a real one that time—at his old nickname for me. We'd been rivals when we'd first come to the hospital, both vying to prove ourselves to be the top dog, and had kind of hated each other actually. He'd called me Thorn, both as a sort of play on shortened version of Thorton and because I was a thorn in his side, for a full year before we'd ended up hate fucking after a night out with all of the Residents. We woke up the next morning, hung over as hell, looked at each other with *what the fuck did we do?* expressions, and then laughed so hard we couldn't breathe. The animosity disappeared after that, but the nick-name stuck around.

My façade cracked just a bit, and in that moment, I wished so badly that I could love him, that we could have found a way to work. We'd tried to date once or twice over the years, but it was never more than a week or so before we both realized we were made to just be friends. And now, of course, he's with Beth and they're perfect for each other, but I can't help but think that maybe if I had someone else, all of this shit with Bowen wouldn't be so fucking hard.

But, admittedly, there's *never* really been anyone but him. I dated casually over the years, and never had any problem scratching an itch when needed with no-strings-attached fun, but I've never let myself really be with someone. I blamed it on school first, then medical school, then the stress of just starting out as a doctor, then focusing on my career…but really, they were all just excuses. Valid ones, to an extent, but deep down, I know that there was more to it than that. I don't know if it's because I've been scared of getting hurt again, or if I'm just too jaded and my heart is closed off completely, or…or if maybe I had my one great love story and I'm not supposed to have another.

And I'd rather have nothing than settle for less than the kind of love that I felt for Bowen.

"I'm dealing the best I can for now," I'd told Colt honestly. "I can't take time. I just…I can't do it. Not yet. I need to be here, busy and working and keeping my mind occupied, C."

He'd sighed, pulled me into a hug, and kissed the top of my head in a friendly way.

"Alright. Then consider this a sympathy bone: I've got a ruptured spleen coming in from a construction accident. He's all yours."

So, yeah, I've thrown myself into work full force, taking extra shifts and as many surgeries as I can, refusing to let myself stop for long enough to really think about any of it.

I haven't looked too closely into mom or her death or how I feel about it. I haven't let myself really feel the depths of hurt and betrayal for what she did with Bowen. Save my temporary insanity of going to confront him, I haven't even come close to dealing with the Bowen situation at all.

It isn't that I don't *want* to deal with it all, it's just that I don't know how. I don't know how to even begin unpacking everything. And, truthfully, I don't know how to survive it once I do. I'm terrified that I won't be able to come back from it, that I'll spiral somewhere so deep and dark that nothing and no one will be able to pull me out again.

So, for now, I'm not ready to go there.

"Ok, you are all set," I tell Beth as I finish the last stitch and get her bandaged up. I take off my gloves and toss them into the bin. "And I'm officially off the clock, so we're going to get tacos and you're going to take a night off from studying or even so much as thinking about the exam." She starts to argue but the look I give her lets her know I mean business. She sighs and I know that she knows that I'm right.

"Yes, mom," she grumbles and I punch her in the arm. I'm only eight years older than her, but she likes to pretend it's closer to twenty.

"Let's go, asshole."

Chapter Twenty Two

BOWEN

IT'S BEEN ALMOST a month since Charleston. A month since Laney Thorton walked back into my life before disappearing all over again. A month since I've slept more than a few hours a night.

It's like seeing her finally ripped off the fifteen-year-old tourniquet that I've kept tied around my heart, keeping all of the feelings and thoughts about her bottled up. But now, there's no stopping them. Of course she's never been *completely* erased. In some way or another, she's always been on my mind, but not like this. Never like this. It's like everything with her has been muted, but now it's bright and vibrant and so in my face that I feel like I'm being suffocated.

We finished up the tour a week after Charleston, and have been on a much-needed break since then, with another almost two and a half months left before the next thing—a fundraising concert, I think? Or maybe an awards show of some sort? It's so hard to keep it all straight and our manager, Tully, is a miracle worker getting us everywhere we need to be, and on time to boot.

Piper wanted to jet off to some festival in California and then the Maldives, and then I can't even remember where after that during this break, but all I wanted to do was relax and do *nothing*. I love this life. It's all (well, *mostly* all) I've ever wanted, and I know how lucky I am to have it, but I still get burned out sometimes. And now, I feel restless on top of exhausted, and I just needed to get away from everything. No festivals. No vacations. No social media posts or interviews or any of it. I just wanted to try to breathe for a fucking second, because to be quite honest, I feel like I haven't been able to since the second I turned around and saw Laney standing in that room.

It's so ridiculous that seeing her for five minutes has me torn up this badly, but there's no denying it.

Piper had gone off with some of her girlfriends instead, and I honestly don't even know if she notices I'm not there. She wasn't upset that I didn't want to go. She just called up some friends, gave me a quick kiss goodbye, told me to have fun, and took off.

I don't know what's going with us. Not just right now, but for the past year or so. Things haven't been bad, exactly. I mean, we don't fight or anything, but I feel like we're just kind of...there. She's supportive and sweet, but there's not any passion or fire between us. I don't know if it's just that everything has been so insane between tours and making albums and promoting and more tours, that we've both just been too tired to put the effort into us.

Or if neither one of us really *cares* enough to put the effort into us.

The thought makes me a little sad, but it isn't heartbreaking or devastating and I realize now that I've been putting off thinking about all of this for a while now. Things with Piper have always just been... comfortable. And I needed that. In all of the hectic, amazing crazy that's been my life for these past few years, comfortable was good. It was soothing and reassuring and calming when everything else was the opposite.

But can comfortable really be all there is? Am I just overthinking things after drudging up all of the memories of Laney? Maybe the kind of love I had for her isn't sustainable. It's that potent, crazy, young love kind of feeling that's so insane and all-consuming. Maybe it isn't supposed to last.

Then why does every fucking inch of me, every single fiber of my DNA, *yearn* for it? Why does everything inside me scream that it wasn't just crazy young love, that it's what real love is *supposed* to feel like?

I groan and sit heavily on the haybale beside the barn. I decided to do what every successful, sort of famous country music star does when life gets confusing and a little scary: run home. It's so damn good being back. I'd forgotten how nice it is to be where things just move a little slower and I feel like I can take a full breath. I was blessed enough after our first couple of years of real, steady success to be able to pay off mom and dad's mortgage completely. It was the least I could do for all of their endless support over the years.

Now they've finally been able to do some of the upgrades they always wanted to: overhauled the barn to accommodate more horses, gotten a couple more to fill the stalls, put in a pool, and added a big deck around the back of the house. This stuff had been mom's dream for years and years, but teacher salaries aren't much, especially on top of keeping up with the land and all the animals, and they always, always put Kelly and me over everything else. I know just how lucky I am and the fact that this is the first place I want to go when I need to feel safe and whole speaks volumes.

"Time for a ride," Dad's deep voice rumbles from above me. I hadn't even heard him walk up. I glance up and see him eyeing me in that way of his. He's always been able to tell when I've got too much going on in my head or if something isn't sitting right with me. The answer is always *time for a ride*. The two of us would head out together —sometimes Kelly would try to tag along when she was feeling extra bratty—for hours, just letting the world fall away around us. Sometimes we'd just trot and have some of the most meaningful conversations of my life, learning how to be a man and accepting when I'd failed at it. Others, we'd ride like the devil was on our tails. No words said, just letting the wind rip away whatever I was going through, like when Grandpa Larry died. I'd ridden my poor horse nearly into the ground that day.

I nod and without another word, we got the horses, Cash and Waylon, ready. I know, I know, but we're a musical family—every animal we've ever had was given a country music legend's name. Mares named Dolly and Reba, a goat named Hank, kittens named Loretta, Garth, and Shania, and our old golden retriever, King George.

Cash has been with us since my senior year of high school, and he gives me a loving nudge as we walk out towards the pasture and the woods beyond.

"I've missed you too, buddy," I tell him quietly, running a hand down his neck.

As always, dad lets me set the pace, letting me decide what kind of ride it's going to be. This one starts in a wild sprint. I need the feel of Cash beneath me, practically flying as he builds up speed, the rush of the wind around me. I need the safety that this place has always given me to feel anything that I need to feel.

So, as we run, I finally open myself up and let everything in, *really* feel it for the first time in damn near fifteen years:

The pain. The guilt. The loss. The longing. The love.

It all hits me like lashes of a whip, over and over and over, and with each strike, I feel the walls I've built around myself crumbling away brick by brick. Tears sting my eyes but I don't give a shit. I let them come, let myself feel it all.

Eventually, I slow Cash to a walk and dad and Waylon follow our lead.

"I'm assuming this all has to do with a visit you got before the Charleston concert?" dad asks knowingly and I roll my eyes.

"Kelly is such a tattletale."

He laughs, loud and hearty and it's so nice to hear it in person again. They've come out to concerts and awards shows here and there, of course, but they have their own lives too, and it's been almost four months since I've seen them. My lips curl into a small smile, despite how horrible I'm feeling.

"She is," he agrees easily. "So, Laney Thorton, huh?"

"Yep," I say on a long exhale.

"I've never pushed you on it, but I think there's much more to that story, son. And I would bet a pretty penny that it's the reason you're so torn up now from seeing her again." As usual, he sees everything. I've never been able to pull one over on the man. Every white lie, every sneak in past curfew or sneak out when I was grounded—he *always* knew. Sometimes, he let me get away with it, thinking I was clever. Others he'd call me on my bullshit. He always seemed to know which I needed at the time. I guess that's part of being a good dad, and he's the absolute best. I hope one day I get the chance to try my hand at it and make him proud, that my kids feel as safe with me as I do with him, that they know they can come to me with anything.

"You would be correct on all counts," I sigh and then I tell dad everything about Miranda's deal and what I'd done to Laney, how I thought I'd been making the right decision, the best decision for her and her future. I tell him about her showing up at the concert—though Kelly's big mouth already clued him in on some of that.

"And how did it feel? Seeing her again?"

"It was terrifying and shocking and felt like I'd been punched right in the stomach, the kind of shot that knocks the breath right out of you. But it also felt…" I take a deep breath. "It felt like coming home, dad. It felt like I was finally back where I was supposed to be. Like I could breathe for the first time in too damn long."

He looks thoughtful for a long minute before he answers, taking everything in.

"But you didn't tell her your side of the story?"

"We got interrupted and then she left. The way she looked at me…" I shake my head. "I know she never wants to see me again. Rightfully so, of course, but…yeah. So, it's done. It's over."

"It's not done until it's done, son. There's no over until one of you takes your last breath. If you think you owe it to her—and yourself—to give her the explanation she never got, then you need to find a way to do it. I know you did it for good reasons, but you broke that girl's heart, Bowe. And your own in the process. Maybe you both need some closure."

I exhale heavily and know that he's right. I do want to talk to her. I don't have any delusions of any kind of future or friendship on the horizon with her, have no reason to think that she'll forgive me, but the fact that she came to see me at all makes me think that she needs to hear it too. I'd hoped that she'd moved on and forgotten about me completely, but I don't think that happened. I'm ashamed that a small part of me is happy about that.

And thinking about her never knowing the full truth feels like a knife twisting in my gut. So, I decide that I'm going to find a way to talk to her. Doctors' medical credentials are public record, aren't they?

Maybe we can find the hospital she works for and conveniently schedule a visit to the kiddo's wing? Spread some joy and maybe happen to run into her...

I shake my head. That's a terrible idea, really, and I'm sure I can think of a better one. But I do feel better. I smile at dad and his answering one makes the nearly unbearable tension in my chest ease ever so slightly. I don't know what I would do without him in my life, without either of my parents, and my mind again circles back to Laney. *God, will it ever stop?* I wonder how she's dealing with the loss of her mom. Their relationship was the definition of complicated, but even so, a parent dying can never be easy.

"Come on, your momma's probably got supper ready."

"Race ya," I say with a grin, and Cash and I shoot off.

Chapter Twenty-Three

LANEY

"WHAT DO WE GOT?" I ask as EMTs rush in through the Emergency Department bay doors. Colt and I are both at the ready, falling into tandem rhythms that are as familiar as breathing after so many years together.

"Forty-year-old female, GSW to the abdomen," one of the guys says. We get her shifted over onto the bed and start the standard initial checks that are all but second nature at this point in my life. I could probably do them in my sleep. During second year, I think I *did* do a few in my sleep. I hardly notice anything in particular about the woman, not out of callousness or indifference, but because it's just part of treatment in these situations. In these vital, precious initial moments, she isn't a woman, or even a patient, she's simply a sum of her injuries that I need to analyze and assess.

But then I notice the birthmark on her left wrist and suddenly, I can't breathe.

Something as innocuous as a fucking birthmark, and I am completely and totally *broken*.

Mom had one in the exact same spot. A slightly different shape—this one is more of a simple circle and mom's looked almost like a lopsided star—but it's enough to tear down the walls inside myself that hold back all of the pain and trauma and repressed feelings for the last month.

My mother treated me like little more than a burden for most of my life. She didn't show me the love I know I deserved. She altered the entire course of my life and betrayed me in ways I can barely even understand.

And she's…dead. She's gone, forever.

My ribs start to pull inward, squeezing, squeezing, squeezing. I blink away black spots from my vision and everything sounds like I'm underwater, all of the sounds muffled.

"Thorton?" I vaguely hear as I take a step away. I try to fight against it. I know this woman needs my help, I know I need to be there for her, but I just *can't*. "Elliot, get over here, now!" Colt's voice still sounds so far away, like he's shouting down a long tunnel, as I take another step from the bed, clawing at my chest.

"You got this?" Colt asks someone. Elliot, I guess. He must say yes, because a second later, Colt is guiding me away. I can't feel my legs and mostly just stumble beside him until I'm in a room on the next hall.

"Thorn? Thorn, look at me."

"I…I can't…" I'm gasping for breath, clinging to Colt for dear life. My eyes water, but the tears still don't come. He wraps his arms around me and pulls me tight into his chest.

"Breathe, Thorn. You're alright. It's ok, but I need you to breathe. Come on, breathe for me."

I try to speak, to explain everything going on inside my head, but no words will come. So, I just clutch him, clawing at his back and trying so desperately to breathe around the physical pain and the emotional. I can't even completely understand what's happening, though a small part of my mind whispers the answer: panic attack.

"Come on, *breathe*," Colt says again, and I know if I can't get myself together, he's going to have to sedate me. "Focus on my chest. Follow my breaths. In and out, come on."

Somehow, I focus on tangible things around me to help ground me and pull me out of this spiral: Colt's white coat with the scent of Beth's perfume all over it; his St. Christopher medallion hanging around his throat; the *Paw Patrol* watch his beloved nephew Jackson had given him for his birthday the year we started at the hospital.

Slowly, my heart rate slows and my ribs start to recede again, allowing air into my lungs. I take a shuddering breath.

"That's it. Another," he encourages. "Good. One more."

By the third big inhale, I'm feeling better, but I'm still so far from alright. It's like now that the dam is broken, I can't stop the deluge and I'm just being swept along in the raging water, barely keeping my head above water.

"I think I need to take some time off," I finally tell him in a hoarse voice.

"I think you might be right." He chucks me under the chin and I try for a small smile but don't think I succeed. "What was it?" he asks quietly.

"Hmm?"

"What was it that finally broke down the walls I know you've had up," he clarifies. "For me when my dad died, it was finding one of his old hats in the back of his truck that I inherited. I rode in the truck every day for months and I was fine, but then one morning, I looked back and saw that old Yankees cap stuck under the seat, and I lost it. Everything came crashing down."

I suck in a relieved breath. Having someone understand exactly what had just happened means more than I can even say.

"The birthmark," I say quietly. "The patient had a birthmark in the exact same spot as my mom." Colt nods in understanding.

"I'd like to promise that it won't happen again, but..." He shrugs, telling me that this is far from over and grief is weird as hell.

"I know," I sigh. "Sometimes it still happens for me with my dad and it's been...hell, twenty years now?" I shake myself. "Thanks, Colt."

I give him another hug and assure him I'm alright enough to make it to the Chief's office by myself. He eyes me suspiciously, but finally relents.

"Hold on!" he calls. I turn and find him scribbling on his prescription pad. I roll my eyes when he slaps a piece of paper in my hand, but thank him. Valium probably. And probably not the worst idea he's ever had.

Chief Wellford urges me to take as much time as I need and to let her know if I need anything at all. I thank her, get my stuff from my locker, and head home.

Colt of course let Beth know of the incoming emotional shitshow, and she's waiting in my living room when I step inside the front door. She holds up a bottle of tequila in one hand, and an entire cake with bright pink and purple balloons iced onto the middle in the other. On the counter is a stack of horror movies and also a pair of slutty heels.

I quirk a brow.

"So, this was the only cake I could find on such short notice, but I figure this is half mourning, half celebrating anyway, so it works," she says with a hike of her shoulder. "We also have tequila, because—duh, of course we have tequila." She nods to the counter. "You can choose a slasher-fest or a night out on the town, or none of the above. I am at your disposal for however you want to deal."

I huff out a laugh and rush forward to wrap my arms around her. I've never been more thankful to have her in my life.

"I love you," I tell her honestly and she manages to slide the cake onto the counter behind me before hugging me back tightly.

"I love you too, Laney Waney. Now, let's drown your sorrows, curse your mom, and have some cake."

"HEY BABE," Piper calls when she walks into my place in Nashville. I've thought about selling it a handful of times since I spend so little time here lately, but I haven't gotten around to it. I'd rather have a place like mom and dad's, or like…no. I cut the thought off before it can form. I'd rather have a place out in the country with some land and some animals, a place I can go to unwind and relax and escape. This penthouse apartment in a downtown metropolis ain't it.

"Hey," I say as she comes into the living room and gives me a quick kiss before heading into the kitchen to grab a drink. "Did y'all have fun?" I call over the back of the couch.

"Great time! I wish you would have come with."

"Do you?" I ask and she frowns as she comes back into the room.

"What do you mean?"

I nod for her to sit down and she settles on the edge of the couch that sits at a right angle to mine, so we can face each other.

"What's going on, Bowen? You're acting like something's wrong…" she says apprehensively.

I sigh. Since my talk with dad, I've been *really* thinking about everything, not just Laney, and looking at things that I've been avoiding for a long time.

"Do you love me, Piper?"

"What? Why would you ask me that? What a silly question." She sounds like she's somewhere between offended and confused and... nervous?

"Come on, Piper. I'm serious. I'm not mad or upset or trying to hurt you or start a fight. I just...I need to know. I know you love this life and the idea of me, but...do you love *me*?"

"I..." She blinks, and to my surprise, she doesn't answer immediately or burst into tears or start screaming. She studies me for a long minute, blue eyes searching mine. Eventually, she lets out a soft, what sounds like *relieved* breath.

"No, Bowen, I don't. I'm so sorry." It jolts me a bit, I won't lie. And it hurts a little, too, but I'm not completely shocked by her answer and I'm glad she feels like she can be honest. She shakes her head and reaches out to grip my hand. "I think I did, at first. Or loved you as much as you'd let me." My brow furrows at that.

"What do you mean?"

She gives me a sad smile. "I knew I wasn't getting a white picket fence future with you*, Bowen. I might have wanted it, might have even gotten a version of it if we kept this going, but it wouldn't have been real. Your heart is locked away behind some very, very strong walls and I don't think anyone can touch it."

I blink at that, completely thrown for a loop. She thinks that I couldn't love her back? Couldn't love *anyone*?

"It's alright, I didn't mean it to sound harsh or anything, it's just...I knew I'd never get *all* of you, and I was ok with that. Some of you was better than none." She looks pensive, brows drawing down a bit. "And I think we *did* have love, actually, just not quite the right kind. I knew pretty early on that I would never get the right kind from you, and I told myself I was alright with that. We had fun and things were good, and I figured I could deal with it for...well, for forever, I guess."

"You deserve a lot better than that," I say. I'm still shocked by her admission. I knew that things with us were just kind of...safe or meh or whatever you want to call it, but I never thought it was because I

---

* *Stone's Throw Away*

apparently can't let myself love anyone. Is that true? I've never really thought about it…never really *let* myself think about it, I guess. But now I do and…

Fuck. She's right.

Since that day almost fifteen years ago, I've closed myself off from ever *really* feeling anything, from ever letting anyone all the way in. Maybe I'm broken and unfixable and I really never will love anyone again. I run a hand through my hair, frowning slightly when the strands slide through my fingers so quickly. I guess I'm not used to the cut yet.

I feel like a complete and total asshole—and idiot, for never connecting the dots.

"I'm sorry, Piper. Really. God, I never…I didn't realize…" I shake my head in frustration.

"Hey, it's alright." She squeezes my hand and I can't believe this is the direction that this conversation went. I thought maybe she'd agree that things had just gone a little stale with us, or maybe she'd get mad and throw a lamp at my head or something. But not this. And she really does seem relieved, like she's been wanting to have the conversation too.

"It's not your fault. I made the choice to stay, knowing what I knew. I'll admit, part of it was just the lifestyle and the idea of you, like you said. I liked traveling around to all these big shows and getting fancied up for red carpets. I liked being Bowen Wright's girl." She shrugs and I huff out a laugh. "But I was happy. Maybe not happy *and* completely in love, but just happy isn't nothing."

I give her a small smile.

"No, just happy isn't nothing," I agree, squeezing her hand. I let out a long, shaky breath, not really sure where we go from here. I know that this is for the best, and while I may not have been madly in love with Piper, I do care about her a lot.

"Hey, there can be plenty of love in letting go, B*," she says softly, giving me a sweet smile, and my chest twists. She's right. I force myself to smile back at her, nudging her knee with my own.

---

* *Love in Letting Go*

"Thought I was supposed to be the wordsmith around here." She huffs out a laugh and waggles her eyebrows.

"Turn it into a song and give me writing credit?"

"You got it." We both chuckle a bit at that, but I won't lie that it's got my mind working in the background, a melody already playing softly on repeat, but I'll come back to that later. After a few seconds I nod and look down at our joined hands.

"So…that's it then?" I ask.

"Yeah," she sighs. "I think so."

"And you're alright?"

"I am. I really am. I'll miss you, miss *us*. Even if we weren't crazy in love, we were still…us, ya know? Safe. A comfort, like a security blanket or something." My lips curl upward. Hadn't I described our relationship as comfortable too?

"I know what you mean."

"I should have said something sooner, too, I know. But I just thought I was ok…settling for less than the crazy, all-in kind of love people talk about—the kind you sing about," she adds with a smile. There's a small, knowing edge to it that I don't quite understand. "But," she takes a deep breath but then squares her shoulders. "I've been talking to Casey a lot lately—you know, Luke's lead guitarist? Nothing's happened between us or anything," she assures me quickly, "but…well, I think it *could*, and feeling that connection with him has made me realize just how much has been missing with you and me, and how much I don't want to settle. I want the fire and the passion and the can't live without the other person kind of feeling."

"I hope you find it, Piper. I really, really do. Maybe with Casey. He's a great guy, you should give it a go," I tell her honestly. She smiles and eyes me, looking like she wants to say something, but before she can, I let out a long exhale and shake my head. "Well. Alright then, I guess. You can stay here for as long as you want. I can go to Kelly's." We don't *officially* live together, but most of her stuff is here and she hardly ever stays at her place.

She nods in appreciation, still looking like something's on the tip of her tongue. I arch a brow in question, telling her to spit it out. She rolls her eyes with a smile.

"Can I ask you something?" she finally says.

"Shoot."

"The girl who was at the Charleston show. Laney. She's the one, isn't she?"

"The one? What do you mean?" I try not to let my shock—and maybe a little bit of panic?—show.

"The one you write all your songs for," she says with that knowing smile again, and then I understand. "I knew damn well they weren't about me, though it was fun to pretend," she adds with a laugh. "But the way you looked at her in that room that night..." She shakes her head. "Well, you've never looked at me like *that*, Bowen Wright."

She leans forward and kisses me softly.

"I'm gonna go call Stacey and grab a drink."

I nod a little numbly, my mind spinning like a top, and she rises from the couch. Just before she leaves the room, she stops in the doorway, hand on the frame.

"Hey, Bowen?"

"Hmm?"

"I don't know what happened between you two, but whatever it was...I think she still loves you too, for what it's worth."

Too. My breath hitches. *She still loves you too.* Could Piper possibly be right? What had she seen between us that would make her think that, or that made it so obvious that I was still in love with Laney?

With that, she walks away and I'm left with pain ricocheting through my chest. But even worse than the pain of my relationship ending, worse than the pain of remembering Laney and wondering if my heart really is closed off forever...is hope.

A tiny ember of hope that maybe, just maybe, Piper is right begins to burn in the center of my chest. Maybe Laney could still love me after all this time and everything I put her through.

I don't want to hope. Hope is a dangerous, vicious thing and only leads to more pain, because I know—I fucking *know*—that she can't possibly love me anymore.

But that ember won't snuff out no matter how desperately I try to smother it.

Chapter Twenty-Five

MY HEART IS POUNDING and my palms are sweating as I make my way up the front steps. I'm not sure that this is a good idea. Actually, scratch that, I'm completely sure this is a terrible fucking idea, but between dad and Piper, I pretty much had no choice. I *have* to do this, and then it will be done, finally, one way or another.

Even so, I stand on the small porch for what's probably a creepy amount of time, not ringing the bell or knocking. Just standing and staring and trying to remember how to breathe. It's a really nice townhouse, all brick and colonial charm, with window boxes overflowing with flowers and only one adjourning neighbor. I've admittedly always pictured Laney living out on the farm, not in an upscale townhouse surrounded by a bustling city on all sides, but this makes sense. The hospital where she works isn't far and I can only imagine how busy her schedule must be, so I'm sure the convenience of a short commute and very little lawn maintenance is a big draw.

Even still, it's hard to imagine her here.

I shake my head, feeling like an idiot. I don't even fucking know her anymore. She could be a completely different person than the one I knew fifteen years ago. She could absolutely love city life now, could have sold the farm and never looked back, could have changed in a thousand different ways from the girl I knew. The girl I loved.

I blink as the thought sends a jolt through me. Of pain. Of apprehension. Of fear.

Fuck.

Maybe this was a mistake. As much as I want her to know my side of the story and as much as she seemed to need some sort of closure, maybe this was a big fucking mistake. I shouldn't be here. I should just let it go and move on like a normal person. I take a step back from the door, ready to bolt and pretend this never happened, when someone speaks from behind me.

"Hi, can I help you?" My entire body freezes for a heartbeat before I realize that I don't recognize the voice. *Not Laney.* I turn to find a pretty redhead with her hair piled up in a messy bun and those cute thick-rimmed glasses perched on her nose standing at the bottom of the shared stairs to the two townhouses, a wrought iron railing separating the two halves.

"Oh, hey, I'm looking for—"

Her eyes fly wide and her mouth pops open, and her keys fall to the ground with a loud clatter.

"Holy shit, you're Bowen Wright. Holy shit, holy shit, *holy shit!*" She runs up the stairs towards me, keys forgotten. "I cannot believe you're standing on my porch." She looks down at the railing separating us. "Ok, technically you're not on *my* porch, but still, I'm counting it. I'm a big fan, by the way."

"Thanks, I appreciate that."

"I'm Beth, neighbor and best friend extraordinaire."

"Nice to meet you," I say, holding out my hand to her. She shakes it, shaking her head while she does as if she can't believe it's happening.

"This is batshit. No one is going to believe me when I tell them that Bowen Wright was on my porch...ok, again, not *my* porch but...Oh shit." She bites her lip, looking upset. "Laney's not here, she's..." Her brow furrows and she tilts her head, a look of suspicion narrowing her bright blue eyes. "Hey, how did you know where she lives anyway?"

From Miranda Fucking Thorton of all places. I still can't quite believe it.

When I'd made the decision to track Laney down, the first place I'd gone was her old house in Riverbend. I had no idea if she would still be there or not, but it seemed like the logical place to start. I figured if Laney wasn't there, maybe whoever answered the buzzer at the gate— a housekeeper or security guard or something—would at least hear me out and maybe take a little pity on the guy trying to track down his old flame. Of course, there was always the chance that whoever answered had been around fifteen years ago and knew what a fucking asshole I'd been to Laney and would send me packing immediately, but it was a chance I was willing to take.

But to my surprise, when I'd told the man my name over the speaker, he'd almost immediately opened the gate and told me to come on up. I figured it was either because Laney was there and had miraculously agreed to talk to me, or because of my sort of celebrity status that I'd admittedly been ready to use as leverage to grease the information wheels.

Jessa, Miranda's executive assistant, greeted me at the front door and invited me in with a big smile. Stepping over that threshold had been like stepping right into the past. Everything still looked exactly the same as it had fifteen years ago: travertine tile floors, twin grand curving staircases winding their way up to the second landing, giant crystal chandelier hanging high above.

Memories flooded my mind as I looked around the space: picking Laney up for that first date; Miranda appraising me and apparently finding me lacking; Laney looking downright sinful in that black dress before the gala…

I'd clenched my jaw and forced the memories to recede like waves on the beach. I knew they'd just wash back up again soon, but for the moment, they were out to sea, giving me a few minutes peace to figure out how I might get Jessa to tell me where I could find Laney.

But before I could say anything, Jessa held up a finger.

"One second," she'd said and hurried over to a side table. She thumbed through a pile of papers, and then came up triumphantly with an envelope. She came back and handed it to me. My brow had furrowed in complete confusion.

"Uh…"

"Mrs. Thorton left this letter for you."

"You're shitting me," I'd said before I could stop myself. She's huffed out a small laugh.

"Not at all. She said that you would probably come looking for Laney, after…" She swallowed hard, looking sad, but then shook herself and continued, "That you might come after Mrs. Thorton was gone, and when you did, to make sure you got this letter."

What the fuck? I blinked several times, trying to make sense of what Jessa had just said, what I was holding in my hand. Miranda Thorton had been…expecting me? She'd known I'd come here looking for Laney? So, that meant that she must have known that there was a good chance Laney would have tried to contact me after their conversation before she passed away. I was reminded all over again at just how smart and formidable Miranda Thorton was. And it seemed that despite never really acting much like a mother, she actually knew her daughter pretty damn well.

"Uh…thanks." I'd tried not to sound as confused as I felt, but based on Jessa's quiet laugh, I knew I hadn't succeeded.

"She said you would probably be extremely shocked by the whole thing, but it was important. I'm just glad you showed up."

"Why's that?" I'd asked.

"Because if you didn't—though she seemed certain you would—I was to make sure this letter got to you somehow and I really wasn't sure the best way to get a letter directly to a famous musician." She'd smiled and I couldn't help but return it. She knew exactly who I was but either didn't really care, or was doing a fantastic job of acting nonchalant.

"Well, I'm happy to make your life easier." She laughed again but then her phone went off. She glanced down and gave me a contrite look.

"I'm so sorry, I have to take this. Laney is selling the house in Martha's Vineyard and this is the realtor with what I'm hoping is good news."

"Oh of course, I'll get out of your hair." I waved as I slipped out of the front door, the envelope seeming to burn in my hand. What in the hell would Miranda Thorton have had to say that was so important that she'd tasked Jessa with tracking me down if necessary. Another warning to stay away from Laney? An extra bonus as part of her Last Will and Testament for doing such a bang up job of making Laney hate me for fifteen years? A promise that she'd haunt me forever just for shits and giggles?

I sat in my car just staring at the envelope for a long time, turning it over and over in my hands. No one came out to shoo me off the property, so I guessed they didn't mind me sticking around for a while. I realized after a few minutes that I probably should have asked Jessa for Laney's address, but the whole letter thing had thrown me completely off of my game. I'd decided to read whatever it was that was so important, and then go back inside to try to weasel information out of Jessa…but it turned out, that wasn't necessary. Once I finally got up the courage—because yes, I was nervous as hell to see what Laney's mom could have needed me to see so badly—to tear open the envelope, I'd had to read the whole thing three times before I could believe what I was seeing.

Dear Bowen,

If you're reading this, then I'm gone. I'm a coward for never finding a way to say the things in this letter to you myself before the end, but I'm hoping that reading them now will be enough.

I'm sorry, Bowen.

I realized much too late that though my intentions were only to give my daughter the best life possible, I made all the wrong decisions. Decisions that didn't just hurt her—they hurt you as well. You loved her enough to let her go. You are a far better man than I ever could have guessed and someone I would be proud to have my daughter be with. I know that you are the life and the love she deserved.

Hindsight really is 20/20, and when you're looking back over the expanse of your life, all of your mistakes stand out in perfect clarity. I was never the mother Laney deserved, but I did love her with all of my heart. I know that you (and she) will find that hard to believe, but I promise you that it's the truth. It wasn't the way that she deserved to be loved, but it was the only way

I could after I'd been so completely broken. It's no excuse, and there is no forgiveness to be found, but it is the absolute truth.

I don't know what your situation might be, but I know what it's like to lose the love of your life. I had no hope of getting mine back again, but if there's even a chance that you still love her, then you'd be a fool not to at least try.

1440 Sunflower Lane
Arlington, VA

I KNOW *that she never stopped.*

GOOD LUCK, *Bowen. I hope that you find your happiness, and, maybe, just maybe, help my daughter find hers.*

MIRANDA

I'D LET OUT A LONG, long exhale, my chest feeling tight.

I know that she never stopped.

I read that line over and over and over. Laney never stopped loving me? Is that what Miranda meant? I didn't want to let myself hope, but that damn ember from before grew into a small flame every time my eyes scanned over the words.

She never stopped.

With that line echoing through my mind like the beating of a drum, I'd said a silent thanks to Miranda Thorton, and booked it to the airport like a bat outta hell.

I pull myself from the memory now and tell Beth about the letter, making sure it doesn't sound like I'm just being a crazy stalker or something.

"Whoa, she really was trying to make amends on the deathbed. Damn."

"So, uh…Laney told you…about…" I rub the back of my neck. I

suspected that she knew at least some of the story since she knew that I was here for Laney, but I was kind of hoping maybe she didn't know all of the sordid details. Like the part where I looked like the biggest asshole in history.

My hope is wasted.

"Oh yeah, Loverboy, she told me *all* the dirty details. As someone drowning in debt from student loans, I definitely get the appeal of twenty grand but…" She shakes her head, and it says clearly the words she isn't saying out loud: *but I would never destroy the love of my life for it.* I open my mouth to explain, but she immediately holds up her hands, palms out. "No judgment though, really. It was a long time ago. People do all kinds of dumb shit when they're young. Seriously. If I showed you a picture of the guys I dated when I was in my early twenties, all of your mistakes would seem like Nobel Prize-winning decisions, trust me." She shudders and I laugh. I can see why Laney likes her.

"So, you said she's not here—do you know when she'll be home?" I saw a coffee shop around the corner, maybe I can hang out there until she gets back, or go to my hotel and come back tomorrow if she's working all night or something.

"No, actually. She took some time off from the hospital after…well, after everything. She kind of bottled it all up and wasn't really dealing whatsoever, and then just a few days ago it just sort of imploded." She looks worried and my chest clenches. Was Laney alright?

"Shit," I whisper, imagining Laney breaking down over everything.

"Yeah, shit is right. It wasn't great. She's ok, or she will be, but she needed some time. She went to the farm." My brows fly up and Beth quickly adds, "I mean, like the *actual* farm that she has out in the middle of nowhere back in South Carolina. Not like when your dog dies and your parents tell you that he went to 'live on a farm'," she says, doing air quotes with her fingers.

I can't help but laugh and she smiles.

"Do you know where the farm is? Laney left me the address if you need it."

"I've been there before." Memories of that weekend rise to the forefront of my mind and they're so bittersweet that I taste acid in the back of my throat. I shake them away and wonder how quickly I can get on a flight. I'm sure racking up the frequent flier miles in this crazy chase, but I couldn't care less.

"Well, go get her then, Romeo," she says with a simple shrug, grinning.

I tip my ballcap to her and grin. "Yes ma'am."

She blinks several times and a blush spreads across her cheeks.

"Well, *that* should be fucking illegal," she says. I chuckle low and she fans herself. "Seriously. Don't do that to people, man. It isn't fair."

"I'll try my best," I tell her with another smile.

"I would say I hate to be that girl, but I really don't give a shit—" She holds up her phone, quirking one brow in question, "—would you mind?"

"For the neighbor and best friend extraordinaire? Of course not."

I lean in beside her over the railing and she snaps a few selfies, muttering *I can't fucking believe this* the whole time.

I thank her for the help, and head back down the stairs.

"Good luck!" she calls as I'm sliding into my car. "You're gonna need it."

Chapter Twenty-Six

LANEY

GOD, I've missed this place.

Once I pulled myself together from my little breakdown, I'd decided that the only place I wanted to be was out here at the farm. It's where I feel closest to dad. It's where I feel closest to *myself*. When I'm back in Virginia, I feel like I'm playing a part. I go through the motions and do all the things I'm supposed to, and it isn't like I'm miserable or anything, but I don't feel like *me* there—at least not the full, real me. I've been feeling it for a long time, but now with mom and everything, I know it's finally time to take a good hard look at my life and figure out what *I* really want. The farm is the only place where I can do that.

I'd be lying if I said my chest didn't splinter a bit when I first arrived, the memories of that trip here with Bowen and everyone slamming into me like a freight train. I could practically see the boys running around the yard, whooping and hollering, Kelly laughing by the back of the SUV, that perfect weekend just getting started.

Aunt Shelby passed a few years back, but Carlie still runs the place and was all too happy to get things set up in the house for me when I'd told her I was on my way. We'd grabbed dinner my first night here and it was so good to see her that I felt something in my chest ease a fraction, like I took my first full breath in…God, I want to say just since the day mom died and a huge part of my world crashed down around me, but in actuality, it's been far longer than that.

I love Carlie, but I wish so badly that Aunt Shelby was still here. She would know exactly what to say now. She would know how to help me navigate all of this. And I sure as hell could use some help because I feel completely lost.

I don't know how to feel about mom and her passing. I'm sad, but also a little relieved, and disappointed, and pissed, and resentful, and about a thousand other things too. I try to tell myself that she really did try at the end, and that shouldn't count for nothing. I could say it was too little too late, especially in light of what she confessed, but I don't want to be that person.

And in the end, *I* get to decide how to feel about this, don't I? I get to choose how I want to look at this situation, and I want to look at it as her trying to right wrongs. At least I got that. She could have gone to her grave with the same old anger and hostility between us, this secret forever buried with her, but she chose not to.

I've been by the side of many people on death's doorstep over the years. I've seen the regret in too many eyes before they slipped away forever, never getting the chance to try to make things right.

So, I'm going to be thankful that mom wanted to try. I'm going to be thankful that she told me the truth, even knowing that I might hate her forever because of it. I'm going to be thankful that, in the end, I did feel like she loved me in the only way she could. That doesn't mean it was enough or what I deserved, but I do believe that there was love there, and she wanted to try harder at the end to show it.

Does it make up for everything else? Absolutely not. But I'm not going to completely discount the end just because it doesn't erase the beginning.

I'm still working through all of the emotions I have about mom, but I'm getting there. I don't know that I'll ever work through all of the ones I have about Bowen. I don't even know where to start, so I've mostly just been focusing on mom and my future and allowing memories of him to float in as they will and not forcing them away.

I'm lying on the oversized porch swing that dad had built for us— it's really more of a porch bed, to be honest, big enough for two people to lounge and swing lazily—listening to the thunder rumbling far off in the distance. I eye the gray clouds beginning to churn overhead, and a smile actually pulls my lips upward. Sitting on the porch listening to a good southern storm sounds like perfect form of therapy to me right now. Maybe when the flood gates open up above me, it'll finally open my own, because I *still* haven't fucking cried. A few stray tears here and there, sure, but I haven't *cried* cried, and that honestly worries me a bit. I'm afraid that when it happens, I'm never going to be able to stop.

I hear a car coming up the drive and turn my head to watch the black truck making its way closer. I'm assuming it's one of the folks Carlie employees or maybe a delivery or something, but push myself up on the swing to check it out.

The car pulls around the circular part of the drive that curves right in front of the porch instead of to the garage or taking the turn off that leads to the outbuildings and the rest of the property, so I definitely think delivery of some sort. I left this address with the hospital in case they needed it while I'm out, so maybe someone sent flowers. Ooo, or maybe Beth decided to DoorDash me some cheese fries. My stomach growls at that exact moment and I realize that I have no idea when the last time I ate anything was. So, I'm really hoping for the DoorDash option when a tall figure gets out of the driver's side door.

But it isn't a delivery guy.

And it isn't food.

Bowen Fucking Wright steps around the front of the truck.

For a long time, I'm completely frozen, barely able to pull enough air into my lungs. This is different than when I went to see him before the concert. That time I knew what I was getting myself into, at least to an extent. This is a complete surprise. I never thought I'd see him again. Ever.

And I was ok with that.

Mostly.

I think.

Fuck, I don't know anything anymore when it comes to this man. But still, I can't seem to move or speak. Thankfully, he does it first.

"I'm sure you don't want to see me, but I need to tell you my side of the story, Lanes. Please."

The use of the old nickname snaps me out of my frozen state, and to my utter shock, it isn't pain that rushes through me at seeing him here. It's *rage*. I'm pissed as hell and it feels good to feel something other than sorrow and despair for a minute. I stand and walk to the railing, crossing my arms over my chest.

"Well fucking come on then. Justify what you did. I'm all ears," I spit, the sarcasm so thick it could choke him.

"I'm sorry," he says first and it makes me see red.

"Don't you fucking dare," I all but snarl quietly. Somewhere inside my mind, I know that this much anger probably isn't completely justified, but I don't care right now. "Don't you dare apologize. I don't want your fucking apology, Bowen Wright. I don't want anything from you."

"Then why did you come to the concert?" he asks, pushing back ever so slightly as he studies me.

"Temporary insanity. It's a thing. Trust me, I'm a doctor," I say in a mocking voice.

"Bullshit," he tosses back, surprising me. Most guys in his position would be walking on eggshells right about now. But not Bowen. "You came there for a reason."

"You're right, I did!" I yell. "I came there to make you look me in the eye and tell me it was worth it!" I slam my hand against the railing and try my best to ignore the vibrating sting it sends across my palm and up my arm. "Tell me, Bowen. Tell me it was fucking worth it to completely shatter my fucking heart! Tell me it was worth it to destroy everything we had for a big fat check from my mom!" He flinches and clenches his jaw. "Or was that last day not the lie at all? Was the *entire fucking thing* the lie?? Were you using me the whole time? Just killing time? Just trying to get in the little rich girl's pants?"

I pretty much already decided that that wasn't the case. I think all the terrible things he said that last day were just done in an effort to make sure I ran away and never looked back, just like mom said, but I can't help throwing them at him now. I know I'm lashing out. I know only part of it is really directed at him, but everything else going on is getting thrown in too and I can't quite stop it from happening.

"Come on, Laney," he says, voice low and hard.

"So what's the fucking answer, huh? You came here to tell me your side, so tell me!" He stands there, staring, and I'm breathing hard. "Fucking TELL ME!" I scream so loudly that a few birds that had been picking around the grass take flight.

"She was fucking right!!" he yells back, throwing an arm out towards the driveway as if he's pointing towards mom back in River-bend. "I couldn't give you the life you deserved. There was no fucking guarantee I was ever gonna make it, and you deserved so much better than to tag along through years of bullshit just for the tiny sliver of a chance that it would all pay off! Your mom was fucking *right* to tell me to break it off when you'd decided to give up Princeton for me," he finishes more quietly, and though I can hear the pain lacing his words, I don't let it penetrate this haze of anger.

"I wasn't giving up Princeton for *you*, you selfish fucking prick! It was *my* choice, *my* decision, *my fucking life*! I was choosing my own path for a future that *I* fucking wanted! Don't you get it?? Deciding to change schools and be with you was the first decision I ever made for my *own* future. It wasn't for you. It was for *me*. There's a big fucking difference and the fact that you couldn't see that tells me everything I need to know."

His blue-green eyes are blazing with too many things now and my fire is starting to fizzle out. I want to keep it roaring because I know when it goes, the pain that will remain will be nearly unbearable, but I honestly don't have the energy. I'm so fucking exhausted.

"Like what?" he asks in a low voice, holding my gaze.

"That you aren't the man I thought you were. That you never loved me the way I thought you did. That regardless if you thought you were doing the right thing for me, you still took away my choice in the matter. That in the end, money was more important than anything else. Take your fucking pick, Bowen." He clenches his jaw and thunder rumbles above us ominously. I don't want to say the next words, but they come out anyway.

"Do you think I just ran off to school and was completely fine?? That I just got over you like it was nothing?"

"I hoped you did," he said quietly. "I wanted you to."

I huff out a humorless laugh.

"Sorry to disappoint because I never fucking did, Bowen. Never. Even when I hated you…" I shake my head. "What did you do with them, huh? All the pieces of me you kept all these years? Because as much as I fucking hate it, you've had them all this time. You took them with you and I've never been able to get them back. Did you even notice? Did you even care??"

"Laney, I…" He trails off, looking…stricken, his chest rising and falling in quick bursts. Thunder rumbles again and he clenches his jaw. "Damn it, this isn't how I wanted this to go." He pulls off his hat and runs a hand through his hair before tugging it back on in frustration.

"Look, I'll make this easy for you, ok? You broke my heart, but you did it for what you thought were the right reasons, so now you're absolved. There, is that what you needed to hear? We can both move on." My voice sounds dead, all that fire completely snuffed out now, the pain starting to pull me down into a deep, dark abyss that I'm not sure I'll ever escape. I shake my head and take a step away from the railing.

I don't know why I say the next words, but they just come out.

"Want to know one of the most pathetic parts? I still have that note. *To the girl who could make a weeping willow smile,*" I recite. I laugh a sad little laugh. "I shouldn't have been surprised when I heard you put it in a song like it was just another lyric, but…I thought maybe that was one thing you wouldn't take from me."

He clenches and unclenches his jaw, his entire body rigid. I run a hand through my hair and shake my head just as the first drops of rain start to fall. He doesn't seem to notice at all, just stands there as he gets pelted.

"Just go, Bowen," I say so quietly I'm not sure he can even hear me, but I don't care. I'm done.

I turn around and walk inside without looking back. The rain is coming down in sheets now, so loudly that I can't hear his truck when he leaves. I head to the fridge and grab a water, taking a long drink before leaning my elbows on the island and putting my head in my hands. Tears threaten to spill, but there's no reason to try to hide them now. I don't feel any better even after yelling at him. Why the hell had he come here? How had he even known where to find me?

The screen door screeches over the sound of the rain and I jerk my head up to find Bowen storming through the living room towards the kitchen. I straighten and blink, so completely confused. I thought he'd left. What the hell is he doing? Why is he still here? I don't have it in me to fight anymore. He's soaking wet but doesn't even seem to be aware of it. There's a blazing determination in his eyes as he takes the final steps to stand across from me at the island, pulling his wallet out of his pocket as he does. My brows knit together.

"What are you—"

He slams his palm down on the counter and holds my gaze.

"The song was for *you*, Laney. Every fucking one has been for you. Some are how I feel about you—how I *still* fucking feel, even after fifteen years, how I never stopped feeling. Some are how I figured you probably feel about me." A few songs about lies[*] and betrayal[†] spring to my mind. "Some are about how I wish we were, together and happy. But make no mistake, Laney Thorton: *Every. Fucking. One* is for you." I inhale sharply, unable to do much more than that. "You say I've kept pieces of you all this time? Well, you haven't kept just pieces of me, Lanes. You've kept *all* of me. Every last piece of me has been yours for fucking fifteen years."

He keeps his eyes locked on mine for a heartbeat longer, and then turns and strides back out into the storm, letting the screen door slam shut behind him. I stare after him, trying to process everything he'd just said, before shifting my gaze downward.

My heart twists and I gasp quietly.

There on the counter, looking like it's been folded and unfolded a thousand times, is a check for twenty thousand dollars from my mother.

---

[*] *Lies*

[†] *Betrayal*

WELL THIS WENT FUCKING GREAT. Nothing happened the way I wanted it to. I couldn't say the words I wanted to, my mind was too wrapped up in being here again and seeing her and her anger and hurt and I fucked everything up. Again.

Must be Tuesday, I think angrily as I walk back out into the rain towards the truck. This really is it then. This is the last time I'll ever see her and though I didn't really get to explain everything right, at least she knows the whole truth of it, or the important parts anyway.

Just as I'm opening the driver's side door, she calls out above the roaring of the rain and the low rumbles of thunder.

"Bowen!"

I jerk my head towards the porch and see her running down the stairs out into the downpour. I come around the front of the truck and we stop a few yards apart. She's drenched within seconds, dark hair plastered to her temples and blinking raindrops out of her eyes.

"You didn't take it?" she yells over the din.

"Of course I didn't take it," I call back.

Our gazes lock for an endless moment and I swear to God I don't fucking breathe the entire time. And then, something snaps and she's rushing towards me, closing the distance in a few long strides. She grabs the front of my shirt, and my entire world shrinks to this tiny space around us, this one, perfect moment.

She tugs me down and slams her lips to mine. Electricity shoots through my entire body as we kiss, sparks flooding every inch of me. I cradle her face between my palms. I've been waiting fifteen fucking years for a kiss like this. Her lips feel like coming home, like I'm finally back exactly where I'm supposed to be. She tilts her head and opens her lips in invitation. I take it, rolling my tongue against hers, moaning at the contact and the absolute fire it sends through my veins.

I can't quite believe that this is happening, that she's actually in my arms again, kissing me like she would rather die than stop. I slide one hand to her nape, holding her to me as I deepen the kiss, thrusting my tongue harder against hers, capturing her moans with my mouth and using my other hand to grab her hip and tug her hard against me. She snakes her hands under the wet, clinging fabric of my shirt and I groan as my muscles tense under her scorching touch.

God, I haven't felt this in so long. This fire, this burning, this unquenchable want. The rain pelts down, soaking us both to the bone but neither one of us could care less, but then a clap of thunder booms so loudly that Laney jumps, gasping. I pull her lips back to mine almost immediately, but know we need to get out of this storm. I reach down and grip her hips, lifting her easily. She wraps her legs around my waist like we've practiced this move a million times, and I walk us back up the porch steps and into the house. I turn and press her against the wall, rattling the frames, and she grabs my hat, tossing it to the floor behind us. She tunnels her fingers through my hair like she's been wanting to do it for years, and I roll my tongue and my hips hard against hers, needing more, more, more.

I groan and shift away from the wall, heading for the kitchen a few yards away through the living room. As much as I would rather be tossed into a pit of vipers than stop whatever's happening between us, I know there's a few things that need to be said. I sit her gently on top of the island and run my hands up her sides, fingers clenching with barely contained need to rip this flimsy tank top from her body.

We're both breathing like we've just run a marathon when I finally force myself to stop kissing her. I can't seem to make myself put any real distance between us though, wedging my hips between her thighs when she makes room for me, and leaning my forehead against hers.

"Why not?" she whispers, breathless. I take a deep breath, knowing that we need to talk. *Really* talk, finally after all this time. No more secrets between us, no more lies. I pull away so that I can meet her gaze, but she locks her heels behind my thighs, making it clear she doesn't want me to go too far. *Thank fucking God.* She rests her hands on my stomach, clenching the wet cotton in her fingers.

"Why not?" she asks again, searching my eyes.

"I never, ever wanted me leaving you—or making you hate me so that you would leave me, I guess is more accurate—to be for something as fucked up as money, Laney. I know that sounds stupid and there's no excuse for what I did regardless, but no amount of money could ever be worth hurting you. Ever. I really thought I was doing you a favor. I wanted you to have the best of everything and I was convinced I couldn't give that to you."

"But that money could have changed everything for you, could have made things so much easier."

"I don't care. There were times we were literally surviving on the dollar menu and a fistful of fucking hope, Lanes, and I still never even thought about cashing that check. That's blood money, the money I sold my soul and cut out my own heart for. I'd *never* fucking touch it. What happened that day, what I did, it had nothing to do with the money, I need you to believe that. I thought—I *knew*—that you deserved better than me. You always will."

"You're an idiot," she whispers, and my lips quirk.

"No objections there."

"Oh God," she says, suddenly looking worried and pushing me away ever so slightly. "What about Piper? Shit, shit, shit. This was a mistake. I can't do this to someone, Bowe, this was—"

"We broke up," I cut her off. She gives me a skeptical look and I nod in reluctant agreement. "Ok, I know that sounds like something a guy would lie about in this situation, but it's true. It happened about a week ago." She studies me and I guess decides that I'm not lying.

"Why?"

I sigh heavily. *In for a penny, in for a pound, right?*

"Because apparently I can't love anyone but you," I say honestly. It feels good to say the words, to finally stop lying to myself after all these years. "It's always been you. It will *always* be you. And I'm not saying that with any hopes or expectations, but I just…I needed to say it. I needed you to know the truth, all of it, finally. I've loved you every second of every day since I watched you walk out of that bar and out of my life. Breaking your heart was something I'll never forgive myself for, but breaking my own was a price I was willing to pay if it meant giving you the life you deserved, but make no mistake: I never, ever stopped loving you. Not for a single fucking heartbeat."

She reaches up to run her palm along my cheek, holding my gaze, and I wonder what she sees there. The soul deep ache for her to believe me? The unyielding, undying love I have for her? The intense, desperate need?

Her eyes are almost completely green today, streaks of gold standing out brightly as a flash of lighting illuminates the entire room. Thunder cracks almost immediately, shaking the dishes on the shelves, and then she's kissing me again and I'm practically fucking melting at her touch.

It's both familiar and new at the same time. I know her better than I know myself, and yet, she's also a stranger. It's been so long, we've both grown up and changed so much. The idea of spending hours learning each other all over again makes my cock throb in anticipation.

She tugs at my wet shirt and though it's a little difficult, we manage to get it off. I toss it aside and lean in to kiss her again, nipping gently at her bottom lip as she runs her hands over my bare chest and stomach, her fingers gliding over my rain slicked skin. God the feel of her hands on me after all this time makes it hard to breathe. I kiss along her jaw and she shudders when I run my tongue over the spot just below her ear.

I smile and whisper against her skin, "Good to know that hasn't changed."

She digs her hands into my hair and I kiss the spot again for good measure before running her ear lobe between my teeth.

"Bowe," she half moans, and the sound of my name on her lips nearly destroys the tiny shred of self-control I have left. I'm telling myself to go slow. I'm telling myself to let her lead and steer this where she wants it to go, but I've never wanted anyone the way I want Laney in this moment.

"I've been dreaming about you saying my name like that for fifteen years, Laney," I tell her as I kiss down her throat. She rocks her hips forward against me and I grip the edge of the counter so hard I think I might break the damn thing. "Been dreaming of you *screaming* it."

She inhales sharply as a small shiver runs through her entire body.

"God, I've missed you. Missed this," she pants.

I kiss her lips again, unable to stay away for long. Everything is starting to burn hotter, and I know that before too long, it'll be completely out of control. A wildfire with no hope of containment. I can't quite believe this is really happening, that I actually have Laney back in my arms after all this time. I've dreamed of it. I've yearned for it. I've written too many songs to fucking count about it. But I never, ever imagined it would be possible. But here she is. Real and warm and clinging to me like her life depends on it.

Sure enough, the kiss becomes more frenzied, more desperate with every lap of her tongue against mine, every roll of her hips on the edge of the counter, every breathy moan against my lips. I need more of her skin against mine. I need *nothing* between us. I reach down and grip the hem of her shirt, and she immediately puts her arms up in invitation for me to yank it upward. It joins my own somewhere on the floor, and I quickly unclasp her bra with one hand. She laughs lightly.

"Learned a few new tricks, have we?"

"Oh darlin', you have no idea," I rasp against her lips and she shudders before a soft moan escapes as I palm her breasts, kneading and pinching her nipples *just* hard enough. She bucks her hips forward again, grinding against my cock and I swear to God the damn thing is about to burst right through my zipper. I quickly tear her shorts open and tunnel my hand beneath her panties, not waiting to push a finger inside her. She gasps and moans and *fuck* she's so wet and tight, I have to grit my teeth to keep control of myself. I move my head downward to lave my tongue over her breasts, to lick and suck and drive her wild.

The sounds she makes, the feel of her, slick and ready and demanding, it's enough to make me lose my mind.

I'd love nothing more than to tear my own jeans open and sink my cock so deep in Laney that I lose myself forever, but I won't. Not yet.

I've got fifteen years' worth of groveling to do.

And the best way to grovel is *on my knees.*

Chapter Twenty~Eight

LANEY

I CAN'T BELIEVE this is happening. Maybe it isn't. Maybe I finally collapsed under the weight of it all and took a little grippy sock vacation in the psych ward. Maybe Dr. Lamb has me on a really great cocktail of meds right now and this is all just some blissful escape that my mind conjured.

But no. No, I don't think even a drug-induced mental time out could have come up with the perfection and intensity of this moment.

This is no dream. This is no hallucination. This is *real*.

All of it is real: Bowen's soft lips on mine, warm and giving, yet demanding at the same time; Bowen's hands on my body, setting every place he touches on fire; Bowen's fingers deftly unbuttoning and unzipping my cut offs and maneuvering inside before—

"*God,*" I moan loudly as he sinks a finger inside me. I dig my fingers into his shoulders and rock my hips forward, desperate for more as he slowly thrusts.

"Jesus Christ, Lanes," he groans against my throat, kissing and nipping his way downward. A heartbeat later, he ducks his head and swirls his tongue around one peaked nipple before closing his lips and sucking hard. I cry out something intelligible, the pleasure sending shivers through every inch of my body, like tiny sparks. The sensations are almost too much to handle.

Jesus, how long has it been since I've been with anyone? I…can't even remember? Even if I could, I don't think it would matter. No one can hold a candle to Bowen. No one ever has.

I keep one hand tunneled in his hair, holding him to my breast and begging him silently to keep going, and brace the other on the countertop beside me, using the leverage to rock my hips harder in time with his thrusts, demanding more. He moans around my nipple, biting gently before moving to the other side and flicking his tongue over the hardened peak. It sends a jolt through my body like I've been shocked, and I'm nearly fucking whimpering with how badly I want him.

Without warning he pulls his hand away, but before I can demand to know why he would do such a horrible fucking thing, he lifts me from the counter with one hand while he yanks my shorts and panties off with the other. I gasp when he sets me back onto the cool counter, but I barely even notice. Oh no, my full attention is on Bowen as he holds my gaze and sinks to his knees in front of me. *Oh God is this really happening?*

I swallow hard and try to control my breathing as he quirks a brow in question. I lick my lips and give him a slow nod. I don't think I've ever wanted anything more than I want him to do this now.

He smiles and leans forward, settling my knees over his shoulders. He grips my thigh and leans in, and my entire fucking world explodes at that first lap of his tongue.

"Oh my *God*," I moan, gripping the counter on either side of my thighs so tightly I would swear I could break right through the marble. It's absolute ecstasy and I never, ever want it to stop.

"Fuck me," Bowen rasps before licking me again and again, alternating between long, slow laps of his tongue and deep thrusts. "God you taste good, Laney," he says in a low rumble and I make an admittedly embarrassing sound that's somewhere between a whimper and a moan. Soon enough, I'm slicked with sweat, my whole body trembling from the force of the pleasure as he continues to lick my pussy like no one ever has. He adds his fingers and sucks on my clit as he thrusts, curling them in just the right spot when he's so deep inside and I swear to God I see stars.

He wasn't lying when he said he'd learned some new tricks because where in the fuck did he learn *that* and who do I have to thank for teaching him? I'll be sending flowers in the morning because *Jesus. Fucking. Christ.*

"Oh my God, Bowen, don't stop. I'm close. *Fuck, fuck, fuck.*" He makes an entirely sexy almost growling sound that sends a shiver up my spine.

"That's it. Come for me, Laney. Come on my tongue, sweetheart."

Fuck. Me. When did he become a talker? And how did he know that I love it? I want to laugh, thinking it's some cruel joke that the universe is playing—*or maybe just fate?*—that even apart all these years, we somehow grew *together*, fitting together perfectly just like always.

I feel like I'm at the very top of a rollercoaster, just cresting that hill…and with one more hard suck on my clit, I'm done for. I'm careening down that first drop, freefalling into nothingness. I scream out his name as I collapse backwards onto the counter, back bowing as wave after wave of pleasure rip through me. Bowen removes his fingers but doesn't move away.

No, instead he replaces them with his tongue, licking furiously, spreading me wide and taking everything I have. I try to tell him to stop, try to push him away, but I can't quite form the words because I don't actually *want* him to. It feels so fucking good, I never want him to stop. So, I don't tell him to. Instead, I force my thighs to relax from what was surely a strangling grip on his ears, and let myself feel every little sensation; every tremor that still echoes through me from orgasm; every lap of his tongue; every caress of his fingers over my thighs and stomach and breasts as he reaches upward.

"That's it, Lanes. God, you're perfect. Let me make you come again." His voice is low and raspy and sends a violent shiver up my spine. I don't know what the future holds, but I do know that I will never, ever get Bowen Wright's dirty talk out of my head for as long as I live. It seems really unfair that someone can look as good as he does, have the voice he does, and be this fucking sexy and skilled in the bedroom.

Or kitchen counter. Whatever.

Seems like the universe would wanna spread out the blessings a little bit more instead of heaping them all on Bowen, but he seems to have gotten them all. In the moment, I'm not complaining one damn bit.

"Yes," I beg. "Please, Bowen. Don't stop. It feels so fucking *good*." He doesn't stop, but he does slow down now, seeming to want to relish every touch and taste and it feels so good that I'm writhing soon, panting and climbing up that hill all over again. Lighting streaks across the sky, illuminating the room every few minutes, thunder crashing around us moments later, but the storm raging outside has nothing on the one coursing through my body, the one that Bowen and I are caught in together.

I reach down to palm my breasts, pinching my own nipples as he begins to pick up the pace again. Not frenzied like before, but a controlled increase in tempo and pressure. God, he really knows what the fuck he's doing, that's for sure.

"I'm close again," I whisper. "Don't stop...just like that...fuck!" I scream as I come again in a rush. I bolt upright, sitting straight up and gripping his head, grinding my pussy against his tongue as the waves hit me all over again. He digs his fingers into my outer thighs as he keeps licking, not stopping until the last of my shudders subsides.

This time, I do push him away. He turns to kiss my inner thigh before resting his forehead there. He's breathing hard, a sheen of sweat beading his forehead. His hair is an absolute mess from my fingers, but he looks all the sexier for it.

He looks up at me again and my God the look in his eyes is enough to set me on fire. He slowly stands up and I slide off of the counter to stand in front of him. I quickly go up on my toes and wrap my arms around his neck, pulling him down for a soul-crushing kiss. He makes a little sound of surprise, but then returns the kiss with deep sweeps of his tongue against mine. I turn to walk backwards, keeping him close as I guide us into the living room. His hands rove over my body, up my sides and cupping my breasts before skimming back down and around to grip my ass.

He kicks his boots off as we walk and, somehow, he also manages to get his socks off, thank God. If there's one thing that will kill the mood for me, it's socks. I undo his belt and tear it free from the loops, dropping it to the wood floor with a loud thud, but I can barely hear it over the storm and my heart thundering in my ears. I unbutton his jeans and get the zipper down just as we reach the couch. I shove him backwards and he sits heavily with a laugh. I follow him down, straddling his lap and he groans when I settle myself down. I can feel how hard he is, only the thin fabric of his boxer briefs between us now. I rock my hips, moaning loudly into his mouth at the feel of him beneath me.

"Fuck, Lanes," he mutters before I suck gently on his bottom lip and he bucks his hips upward, gripping my waist to pull me down hard at the same time. "We…we don't have to…*fuck*, I can feel how wet you are," he groans with a shudder and I smile against his lips. He reaches up to cradle my cheek with one big palm. He holds my gaze and it seems to take a great deal of concentration for him to say, "We don't have to do anything else if you don't want to."

I lean into his hand and know that there's no hope of ever stopping this, of ever recovering from it if—*when?*—it goes south. I'm still in love with him. I've never stopped loving him. Despite all of the hurt and the years, I've loved him for every minute of every day since the night I met him. And now, he's here and I'm here and I'm going to enjoy every fucking second until reality comes crashing back down and we have to figure out what this all means.

So, I turn and kiss his palm and he sighs heavily.

"I don't want to stop, Bowe. Make me forget. Erase the last fifteen years without you. Remind me how much you loved me."

He lets out a shuddering breath, as if the reminders hurt him. He slides his hand to my nape, long fingers tangling in my hair as he pulls me gently towards him again. He kisses me slow and deep, and there are so many unspoken things in that kiss that it breaks my heart. *I'm sorry. Forgive me. I can't forgive myself.*

Though still slow and measured, the kiss takes on a fiery desperation that neither of us can deny. It's like we suddenly both need to convince ourselves that this is real, that we're both somehow really back here together after all this time and everything we've been through. He shifts so that I'm beneath him and I shove his pants and underwear down his hips. He maneuvers out of them with impressive efficiency—wet denim is nearly impossible to get out of it—and kicks them to the floor, but leans down and fumbles with something for a second. I don't understand until he comes back up with the little square and I shake myself. Thank God one of us is thinking clearly because contraception was the last thing on my fucking mind. I'm on birth control, but still.

He eyes me as he shifts to his knees between my thighs.

"You sure?"

"Beyond sure," I promise. I need him more than I can even put into words, some bone-deep longing that I can't even really understand. He rips the package open with his teeth and don't ask me to explain why it's hot. I reach out and run my fingers over his abs while he rolls the condom on, his muscles bulging and flexing as he works and I'm squirming beneath him by the time he's ready. He grips his shaft and runs his fingers gently over my clit and between my lips before pushing them inside. I gasp and arch as he pumps, stroking his cock while he does, watching raptly. I bite my lip. Watching him, while he watches himself finger me, is insanely sexy and I can't even completely explain why.

"Mmm, so wet for me again already, darlin'?" he says in that raspy voice that makes me even wetter.

"Bowe," I say, half warning, half plea. He laughs lightly, but removes his fingers and positions the head of his cock, hissing quietly as he slowly pushes forward. My back bows off of the couch as he slowly, oh so slowly, slides forward.

"*Fuck*," he whispers through gritted teeth, muscles tense as he finally slides the last couple of inches until he's seated so fully inside that there's no space between our bodies. He closes his eyes and stays completely still for a heartbeat, like he's utterly lost to the moment, or trying to convince himself it's really happening maybe.

His eyes snap open, and his pupils are blown wide, the black nearly overtaking the blue-green that I've been seeing in my dreams for fifteen years.

"Alright?"

"Yes," I pant. He's big and it's a tight fit, but not in a painful way. In a *holy-fucking-shit-how-did-I-forget-how-good-this-felt* way.

He holds my gaze as he slides back before shifting his hips forward again, slamming back in to the hilt. I moan loudly, gripping the edge of the couch so tightly my knuckles turn white. He does it again, and again. Slow, measured thrusts that rattle my brain and drive me crazy. It feels so fucking good.

"Harder, Bowe," I beg. "More." I reach out and splay my fingers over his stomach, needing to touch him.

"You're sure?"

"YES," I groan, moving my hips to chase his cock as he withdraws again. He smiles then, a crooked, mischievous, sexy, heart-breaking smile, and my stomach twists in anticipation. He hooks his elbow under my knee and spreads me wider.

"Then hold on tight, sweetheart."

Chapter Twenty-Nine

BOWEN

THIS CAN'T BE FUCKING real. I've got to be dreaming. I never would have thought I'd be here again, cock buried so deep in Laney that I think I might die from the sheer fucking bliss of it.

She gives me a sultry, challenging look and my cock throbs. Laney is game and that thrills me. I wasn't sure if we would still be on the same page after all the years, but it seems like we fit perfectly in all ways, just like we always have.

I start to move in earnest now, shifting her thighs so that she's spread open for me and slamming my hips forward so hard that her breasts bounce with each thrust. She cries out in pleasure, moving her hands over her head to push back against the arm over the couch, making each thrust hit that perfect fucking spot with her resistance.

"Ah, fuck, Lanes. You feel so good," I pant, unable to stop myself. I reach down and palm her breasts, never letting up in my relentless rhythm, but she's meeting me thrust for thrust, head whipping back and forth, dark hair spread over the white couch, nails raking across my stomach. God, this woman will be the death of me. I know it right here and now. Whether from pure fucking pleasure, or from a broken heart, I'm not sure, but either way, I know I'm done for in this moment.

"Don't stop," she begs. "Please, Bowe. *Don't stop.*" I move so that

I'm lying on top of her and pin her hands above her head with mine, intertwining our fingers. She hikes her thigh over my hip and we move together until what feels like hours later, she's screaming my name and coming apart beneath me. I can feel her coming and it's almost too fucking much, but I'm not done yet.

I shift up to my knees again, moving back to sit so that she's straddling my lap once more. I reach out and brush sweat-soaked hair from her temple, caressing her cheek then across her jaw, finally trailing just my index finger beneath her chin to make sure she holds my gaze. Her eyes are blazing, her lips red and swollen, cheeks flushed, and she's never looked more fucking beautiful or sexy.

"Yeah?" I ask, making sure she's alright, that she wants to keep going.

"Yeah," she says, breathless. She drapes her arms over my shoulders and I grip her waist. She starts to move, slowly gliding up and down, up and down, and *fuck me* it feels better than anything should. I let her set the pace, my fingers gripping her hips but not guiding. She picks up the pace, starting to ride me harder, her fingers digging into my skin as she moves. I gnash my teeth, trying so hard to last, but I'm not sure that anything has ever felt this good.

"Just like that, Lanes. Fuck, *look at you,*" I whisper. She whimpers and slams her lips to mine, kissing me hard and deep, tongue rolling against mine, teeth clashing as she moves her hips in a punishing rhythm. I hold on for dear life, desperate not to come until she does.

"Bowe," she rasps against my lips. "Fuck, I'm going to…come… feels so…good…" She cries out as she comes hard again, and I can feel her body clenching all around me. Her muscles tighten and I can't hold back anymore. I use my grip on her hips to wrench her down as I buck my hips upward. Once. Twice. Three times. I bury my face in the crook of her neck and yell out her name as I come harder than I ever have, hips arching off the couch, toes digging into the floor, stars bursting behind my eyes. She keeps rocking her hips above me even after I'm spent, her body still shuddering gently.

I pull out of her and twist so that she's lying on the couch again. I take a heartbeat to commit this image to memory: Laney, gloriously naked, body slicked with sweat, eyes closed and a soft, blissful smile on her lips. *Fuck me.*

I quickly get the used condom off, tie it and toss it aside before I move down her body, kissing over her breasts and stomach before settling my shoulders between her thighs again.

"Bowen?" she asks, craning her head to look at me, clearly confused and more than a little dazed. "Wh-what are you doing?" She's breathless and her pupils are completely dilated as she watches me in fascination. How much time has passed? Hours maybe?

"I'm not done with you yet, baby girl. I have too much to make up for. I'll worship you all fucking night if you let me." I plant a soft kiss just above her clit and she inhales sharply, her hips arching of their own accord.

"I...I can't...I don't know if..." She cuts off with a low, quiet moan, as I gently run my tongue along her pussy, giving a low moan of appreciation. I keep things slow and gentle, lapping and sucking softly, making her groan and whimper and writhe lazily. Another orgasm eventually rushes through her, and only then do I move to collapse beside her on the couch, pulling her into my side. She drapes one arm over my stomach and settles her head on my chest.

We lay there in silence for a long time, the only sounds our heavy breathing and the rain still beating on the metal roof. No more thunder though, so the worst of the storm must have passed on at some point.

And then, I feel the wetness on my skin and look down to find tears streaming down Laney's cheeks. I stiffen, worried about what this might mean, if I've hurt her or did too much or rushed too quickly, but she tightens her grip on me and I know that she doesn't want me to move. So, I hold her closer, stroking her hair and letting her cry for as long as she needs to. They aren't great, racking sobs, just quiet tears that fall in a soft trail over my chest. I'd be lying if I said that a few tears of my own don't escape down my cheeks as we lie there together. It's just too fucking much. Everything that happened fifteen years ago, everything since then, the hurt and the pain and the longing and the regret. So much fucking regret. It all comes out and we just hold each other for what feels like an eternity.

Eventually, she pulls away and pushes up so that she can see me. She wipes away a tear from my cheek and gives me a soft smile.

"Big baby," she mutters and I huff out a laugh. Lightly at first, but then it comes louder and soon, we're both laughing so hard we're crying again, but for completely different reasons. When we've both regained some composure, I shift off of the couch, pulling a blanket from the stack beside the table and wrapping it around her shoulders.

"Water?"

"Yes, please."

I scoop up the discarded condom to toss in the trash and head into the kitchen.

"You should be illegal," she calls, watching me walk away. I laugh and look over my shoulder.

"Admiring my ass, are we?"

"I'd be a fool not to."

I grin as I find the glasses—still in the same place as before—and fill one up from the fridge. I come back and swat at her thigh so she'll move enough for me to settle back down beside her. I hand her the glass and pull the blanket around us again while she takes a few deep sips. She hands it to me and I finish it off before setting it on the table. She sighs heavily.

"Is this the part where we figure out what in the fuck this means?"

I think about that for a minute. I know that it has to happen and as much as I want it to be an easy, simple answer, I know it isn't going to be. But with everything we just did and how fucking content I feel with her cuddled up against me, more at ease than I can remember being in years, and the rain falling in a soft, lulling rhythm on the metal roof, I want to hold onto this weird little limbo we're in for a while longer.

"I think this is the part where we catch up on the last fifteen years," I tell her instead. She turns to look at me, lips curling into a soft smile. Her hair is an absolute mess, but she's never looked more beautiful to me.

"Alright then," she agrees, clearly happy to hold onto this moment for a little longer too.

So, we take turns telling each other everything that's happened in the years since we've been apart. I tell her about the first few years in Nashville, how hard we had to scrape tooth and nail for every inch. I tell her about the tiny apartment we rented when we first got there, and the even tinier one Kelly and I moved into when Jared left, where I slept on a couch for a full year. I tell her about the horrible gigs and the great ones, the horrible jobs and the alright ones. I tell her about the crazy people we met and the lifelong friends we made and the ones we lost along the way. I tell her about the night I finally broke down and spilled the truth to Kelly. I tell her about how when I finally started gaining some ground and getting a good following on social media, I constantly had a heavy feeling of despair in my stomach, like it was all going to fall apart any second.

"I think I still have that to an extent," I admit, tracing lazy circles on her thigh. To my delight, she's been perfectly content to stay completely, blissfully naked during our talk and I've taken full advantage. I've behaved—mostly—but I'm taking every opportunity to touch every inch of exposed skin that I can. She doesn't seem to mind at all and returns the favor without even seeming to realize she's doing it, running her fingers over my chest and shoulders and stomach, pausing sometimes to arch a brow in question at some new scar that she's never seen before. I tell her the stories, most of which are pretty boring: appendectomy; cat; a piece of glass on a field during a game of pick up football; Roman Candle to the shoulder on Fourth of July.

"I get that," she says now. "I still feel like a terrified first year sometimes, like everyone is just waiting for me to screw up and fall flat on my face."

She tells me about college and medical school, the ups and downs and how she thought about giving up more than once. She tells me about how her relationship with her mom only got worse as time went on until they got to the point where they only saw each other once a year, sometimes not even that. She tells me about her first few years in the hospital, her rivalry and then friendship with Colt Donner, who is now dating Beth, the neighbor I met. Which reminds me.

"She didn't warn you I was coming?" I ask, surprised.

"No, the little shit," Laney mutters. "But it's probably because she wanted you to have a fighting chance and if she warned me ahead of time, there's honestly no telling what you would have rolled up to." My lips quirk.

"A shotgun?"

She hikes a shoulder. "It's a possibility. Dad's is still in the closet up front." She laughs lightly and then sighs. "I really don't know what I would have done if I'd known you were coming. I've spent so much time caught in the middle between hating and loving you*," she tells me honestly.

"I deserved all the hate. None of the love."

She turns so she can look at me and reaches out to run her palm along my cheek, smiling at the stubble. She leans in to kiss me, shifting so that she's straddling my lap again. I groan quietly against her lips, already getting hard again beneath her. She tilts her head and deepens the kiss, wrapping her arms around my shoulders and toying with the hair at my nape. Things spiral quickly after that and what feels like hours later, we're somehow sprawled on the floor in front of the fireplace.

"How did we end up here exactly?" I ask with a frown. Everything is a bit of a blur, to be honest.

"Well, you couldn't really get behind me very well on the couch…"

"Ah, that's right," I say, grinning at the memory of Laney on all fours in front of me, gripping her hips and slamming her back, watching as my cock buried so deep inside her…I clear my throat, trying to keep my thoughts from running off the rails. I don't think Laney could go again right now even if she wanted to. I'm pretty much spent myself, but my tongue and fingers work just fine even after the three…no, four? rounds we've gone.

She goes to scrounge up some food from the kitchen and it's my turn to admire the view. My God, every inch of her body is fucking perfect. And I don't mean that it's flawless, but even the flaws are nothing but perfect to me. My chest twists as my eyes track over the scars from her accident. They're fainter than they were fifteen years ago, but still there. Eternal reminders of everything she's been through, everything she lost. I clench my jaw, wishing so badly I could take all

---

* *Loving and Hating You*

the hurt away, but I know I can't. And maybe, she wouldn't really want me to. Scars make us who we are, whether they're on the outside or inside. They shape us and remind us of what we've survived. Her scars remind me how fucking strong she is, and I wouldn't wish them away even if I could.

She settles back down with me and we actually start a fire. The storm must have brought in a bit of a cold front because the temperature is definitely colder than it was…fuck, was it this morning that I showed up here? I don't even know what time it is, but I would guess early evening by the fading light outside. We have a little floor picnic in front of the fire and talk almost the entire night. Dawn is breaking by the time we're both so tired we can barely keep our eyes open. I think I've been up for almost forty-eight hours at this point, hardly being able to sleep since I read that letter and started this whole chase.

We settle back on the couch, neither of us having enough energy to make it all the way to the bedroom, and I pull her hard against my chest, wrapping my arms tightly around her. I can feel her breaths evening out almost immediately and I'm not far behind. Before sleep can pull me under, though, I kiss her temple and whisper against her skin the words that I've longed to say out loud for fifteen years:

"I love you, Laney Thorton."

Chapter Thirty

LANEY

I WAKE with late afternoon sun streaming in through the windows in the living room, still wrapped up in strong, warm arms.

Bowen.

I'll admit that a part of me thought that maybe it had been some insanely good—and vivid—dream, that none of it could possibly have been real. But he's really here, and based on the pleasant aches in various parts of my body, we most definitely really did do all of the things I think we did. A small shiver runs through my body at the memories.

I reach up and put my hand on his chest, feeling the steady beat of heart beneath my palm. Once upon a time I thought that beating was the center of my universe. It was the thing that grounded me, that made everything else finally make sense. It was the thing that I clung to when I had hard days with mom or nightmares. Feeling it beneath my hand or hearing it while I lay on his chest calmed me in a way nothing else could. Even in the short time we were together that summer, the reassuring *thump thump* of Bowen's heartbeat became something I never envisioned my life without.

But I had been without it. For fifteen years I'd been without it. And not just without it, but hating it and wishing I could forget it and yet still stupidly clinging to it, never able to get it fully out of my head.

Reality comes crashing in and though I hadn't realized he was awake yet, he responds like he can read my mind.

"Not yet," he whispers without opening his eyes. "Don't make us leave it yet."

The perfect bubble we've been in for the past…I don't even know how long. Twenty-four hours at least, maybe more. The bubble that doesn't ask any questions about the *hows* or the *whys* or the *what happens nows*. The bubble that doesn't acknowledge anything beyond this room and these moments together.

I lean my head into the crook of his neck and allow myself one more minute to just be here with him in the bubble. I kiss his throat and sigh heavily before pushing myself up. He opens his eyes and watches me warily, like he's preparing for the axe to fall. I move to run a hand through my hair and grimace when I can barely make it an inch before encountering a rat's nest. I scrunch my nose.

"Shower?" he asks with a sleepy grin, and I can't help but laugh at the hopefulness in his voice. Ok, so maybe a few more minutes in the bubble won't hurt.

"Shower," I confirm. He leaps off the couch and I squeal as he lifts me bodily and tosses me over his shoulder, carrying me down the hall to the master bedroom like a caveman.

* * *

THE SHOWER TAKES TWICE AS LONG as it should because I have to show him that he isn't the only one who's learned a trick or two over the last decade and a half, and as amazing as it is, we decide it really is time to get dressed.

"Put your underwear on at least!" I cry as he waltzes outside to his truck to get his bag. He struts back up the porch, even stopping to strike a pose like a bodybuilder while I watch from the doorway, snorting with laughter.

"You know there are plenty of people who work out here, right? What if one of them had seen you?"

"Then they'd have gotten the show of a lifetime, I'd say." He leans in and kisses me playfully and I try and fail to hide my smile. How are things so easy with us again? Like the heartbreak and the time and distance never happened? Maybe it's just because we haven't fully come out of our bubble yet.

Or maybe it's because this is how your life is meant to be, a small voice whispers in the back of my mind. Laughing and being stupid with Bowen, being happier than I can remember being in so long it's actually kind of pathetic, feeling like everything is finally *right*…

No. It can't be that easy…can it?

I watch—a little reluctantly, I'll admit—as he gets dressed and I make coffee. He slides into one of the chairs at the oversized island and I stand on the other side, leaning my elbows on the counter and holding my coffee cup in both hands. I hadn't expected the cold snap to come in with the storm yesterday, but it actually feels like fall today. Normally real fall doesn't show up in this part of the state until at least November.

I'd put on an oversized sweatshirt that droops off of one shoulder with some leggings, and thrown my hair into a sidebraid, so I don't look anything close to glamorous…but with the way Bowe keeps looking at me, you would think I was about to walk a red carpet. I force myself not to get distracted by that look.

He takes a long drink of his coffee and then takes a deep breath, letting it out slowly. He squares his shoulders and nods.

"Alright."

"Alright," I repeat, agreeing that the bubble is officially popped and we have to have a real conversation about what in the actual fuck just happened and, more importantly, what comes next.

But neither of us seem to know how to start or what to say. Eventually he just shakes his head.

"I'm just going to cut right to the heart of it, alright? Bottom line for me is that I love you, Laney. I've been in love with you for fifteen years and I'll never stop. You're it for me. You always have been. I know I can't expect your forgiveness and it might be too late for you to even think about giving this a real chance again, but…I want to be with you and I'm willing to do whatever it takes to make that happen. When it comes to this, to *us*, Laney, I'll never stop fighting. I'll die on that battlefield fighting like hell for us*, whatever that looks like. If you need time to figure out how you feel or if you can ever forgive me, then I'll wait as long as it takes. If you need to go slow, I'll go slow. If you want to move in together tomorrow, then I'm down with that too." He smiles and I huff out a small laugh. His smile fades and he swallows hard.

"And if you can't do this, or…or don't *want* to do this, then I understand that and will respect that decision too."

My pulse is racing and my heart thunders loudly in my ears.

"I…"

I don't know what the hell to think or say or do. The logical part of me knows that this really is insane, that there's too much hurt and history between us and we can't possibly just jump into…whatever the hell this is, without a second thought. But the other part of me, is so damn tired of not being happy and having what I want.

And what I want, is Bowen. Despite everything, despite the time and the hurt and the distance and the thousand other obstacles in our path, I want him. I've always wanted him, and no matter how much I've tried to tell myself otherwise all this time, that is never going to change.

Yes, he hurt me.

No, I'm not just forgetting that or overlooking it.

Yes, I believe he thought he was doing it for the right reasons.

No, that doesn't make it ok (but I understand it at least).

Yes, we have a lot to figure out.

Yes, we need to have some big conversations.

Yes, it's crazy.

But my mind goes back to all those years ago, and Aunt Shelby's voice echoes in my head.

I know it can be scary, but whether right or wrong, the choice for how you live your life has to be yours. Your mom will either get on board or she won't, but you can't let that steer you. You gotta let your heart do that.

Of course, the part about mom doesn't apply like before, but the

---

* *Fight Like Hell*

rest is spot on. It is fucking scary, and I don't know if it's right or wrong, but I know where my heart is steering me. As stupid as it is, my heart is steering me right to Bowen Wright. It always has been. I may have taken a long ass detour to get here, but he was always my destination.

If there's anything mom's death has taught me it's that I don't want to be at the end of my life looking back with regrets. Almost my entire life has seemed to be someone else's. Someone else's plans, someone else's dreams, someone else's ideas of what my life should be. And I'm done with that.

I'm finally going to live the life *I* choose, and if it's complete and utter insanity, well I don't really give a shit. I'd rather take the reckless chance. We might have lost time we could have had, but it's our choice now whether we lose another second.

I come around the counter and he turns on his stool. He widens his legs so I can stand between them and he settles his hands on my waist as I wrap my arms around his neck. I lean in and kiss him, sighing quietly as the feeling of contentment washes over me. One simple kiss with Bowen and I'm happier than I've been in years. I'm sure that says enough—or it does for me anyway. Everything else can be figured out and worked through. If being with him like this again feels right, then I'm not going to fight it. I've put my own feelings and happiness aside for so fucking long, I'm not going to do it anymore.

I eventually pull away and trail my hands downward to rest on his chest. My lips curl at the feel of his heart beneath my palms. *Thump thump.*

I'm not losing it again.

"Does that mean what I think it means?" he asks, barely more than a whisper, and the hope in his voice breaks my heart a little. He reaches up to trace his thumb across my bottom lip, his forefinger resting beneath my chin. I barely suppress a shiver, but then sigh, suddenly knowing exactly what I need to do.

"It means we need to go see my mom."

Chapter Thirty-One

BOWEN

WE HEAD BACK towards Riverbend and riding with one hand on the wheel and the other on Laney's thigh, just like old times, has too many emotions roiling through me.

She didn't say no. She didn't turn me away. She didn't tell me that last night was just the closure she needed to finally put us behind her. She didn't tell me that she could never forgive me or love me again.

She didn't say no.

Technically, she didn't say *yes*, either, but I'm taking the non-no as a good sign. She wants to go visit her mom's grave, and while I can't even begin to pretend I understand the road she's trying to navigate with all of the grief and hurt and anger between them, I think this is something she needs. So, I'm all too happy to take her wherever she wants to go.

I'd never really thought of a cemetery as being a place of beauty before, but Twin Oaks Cemetery certainly fits the bill. Sprawling and meticulously landscaped, with ornate gates and stone paths winding throughout with gleaming white and deep gray headstones dotting the lush, green expanse. Bursts of brilliantly colored flowers show where loved ones have come to visit, and stalwart stone mausoleums and columbariums are spread throughout the rolling acres, some with intricate carvings on the pillars and doors.

"These belong to some of the oldest families in Riverbend," Laney explains as we walk past them, hand in hand.

"And by oldest, you mean richest?" I ask and she laughs lightly despite the tension I can practically feel radiating from her.

"Yeah, that too," she says with a small smile. She nods towards one of the biggest buildings with an ornately carved iron fence surrounding it and a full garden on either side of the path leading up to it. "That's the Greenfields. They founded Riverbend way back when. There aren't any of them left, but we're related somewhere along the way. I think their last heir married into our family like three generations back or something like that? I can't quite remember."

She points out a few other notable names as we walk: a semi-infamous bootlegger with supposed mafia ties; a poet; a federal judge; her kindergarten teacher.

Finally, the path we're on curves around a small rise, and I'm actually surprised by the understatement of the Thorton Family plot. No giant mausoleum or ostentatious statues like some of the other plots around, just simple but elegant white marble headstones denoting a whole host of Thortons through the ages. Laney guides me to the far side of the fenced area, to an oversized headstone beneath a weeping willow of all things. She catches me noticing and turns her head to give me a small smile, but it fades as we get closer.

She stands and stares for a long time, and I try and fail to imagine what this would be like, to have to stand here and see my parents' names carved into a stone, to know that they're gone forever. I squeeze her hand reassuringly but feel utterly helpless. I have no words to ease her pain. There is nothing I can do to fix this.

But I know that's not why we're here.

"I don't even remember her funeral," she says finally, running her hands over the top of the stone. "Not really. I was in shock I think. I have a fuzzy picture, but nothing really concrete other than seeing the casket lowered into the ground. That part is so weirdly vivid. I don't even know if I actually cried. Isn't that messed up?"

"People grieve in different ways," I offer. She nods in understanding.

"I still haven't."

"That's ok, Lanes." I try to sound reassuring, but I feel like I'm adrift at sea here. I'm hoping that just being beside her is all she really needs from me right now. She stares at the stone for a long, long time, and I can see a thousand thoughts running through her mind.

"When she told me what she'd done, I was so angry," she whispers, voice shaky, her hand trembling softly in mine.

"You had every right to be." She nods absently and her eyes turn glassy.

"I—" She cuts off suddenly with a strangled sob, one hand flying to her mouth. I blink in surprise, but wrap an arm around her as she finally breaks apart, really experiencing losing her mom for the first time from the sound of it.

"I didn't let her finish," she gasps out. "She told me about the bribe, about giving you the money and telling you to make me hate you and I was so, so mad. I walked away and I wouldn't let her say another word. She wanted to tell me, I know it. She wanted to tell me that you didn't actually take the money, to make me understand that you didn't betray me the way I thought, but I wouldn't let her." She starts to cry harder, the words coming out in between racking sobs. "That's what she was trying to tell me and I screamed at her not to say another word. I spent her last moments on this earth *furious* with her."

Her knees give out and I sink down to mine on the soft earth with her. I pull her into my chest and hold her as she cries and cries and cries. I know this is years and years' worth of emotion finally coming to a head, not just the loss, and everything is hitting her like a freight train.

"My mom is dead," she rasps as the sobs finally slow.

"I know, sweetheart," I say softly as I rock her gently in my arms. "I know."

"They're both gone and as much as I hated her for so long, she was still my mom. I feel so alone now."

"You're not alone, Laney. You're never alone," I promise her.

"Part of me is sad, but there's a part that isn't. Is that horrible?"

"Hey," I tell her, pulling away and tilting her chin up with one finger to meet my eyes. "You're allowed to feel however you want about this. Your relationship with your mom was…difficult. I'm not saying her trying at the end isn't worth something, because it definitely is, but that doesn't mean you have to let it erase all of your very valid feelings from all of the time before that."

She lets out a shuddering breath, seeming relieved that I've given her some kind of permission to feel the things she's feeling. Maybe permission isn't the right word, but validation that what she's feeling is ok, probably healthy even.

"I feel like a weight has been lifted off my chest. I never realized until she was gone how *exhausting* it was trying to navigate our relationship. I dreaded every call, every meeting. As much as I told myself over and over that it didn't matter that I would never live up to her expectations, it still did. It mattered so fucking much." She runs a hand over her braid, eyes watering again, but there's anger flashing now too, and hurt. So much fucking hurt, and it guts me. I need to do something to take the hurt away, but I know that I can't. I have to let it run its course and as much as that kills me, at least I can be here beside her while it does. For now anyway. I try not to think too far past the next few minutes. She hasn't given me a real answer yet. I have no idea what tomorrow might hold for us.

But even if this is all the time I get, I'll be grateful for it. It's way more than I ever thought I would be blessed enough to get again.

"I wanted her to be proud of me," she says quietly. "I wanted her to tell me I was good enough. I wanted her to tell me that she would be happy no matter what my life looked like as long as *I* was happy."

She sniffles and wipes her eyes with the back of her hand.

"She did tell me she was proud at the very end, so I guess that's something."

"It is," I agree, rubbing her back in soft, soothing circles. "And I think she always was, she just didn't know how to show it or say it. I think…" I frown, trying to figure out how to word it right. "I think that she loved you very much, but she did it in the only way she could after losing your dad. I think trying to control every little thing and keeping herself walled away was the only way she could give you the best life she could, maybe even keep you safe, without taking a chance of her heart breaking again." I shake my head. "I'm not saying it was right. I just…I think all of the anger and control and coldness did come from a place of love."

She studies me for a long moment and then turns to look at the headstone.

"I think you're right," she sighs. "Her last act on this earth was to try to give me what she took away all those years ago." She turns back to me. "You," she clarifies at my confused expression. "A second chance."

"She gave that gift to both of us." I take the letter out of my pocket and hand it over. I'd told her about going to the house to try to find her and being given the letter, but I hadn't told her exactly what it said. She gently unfolds the paper and I watch as her eyes scan the page.

She finishes and her lids flutter closed. She takes a deep breath and lets it out slowly. When she opens her eyes again, they're brighter, and I can see a lightness settle over her, like she's put down the weight that's been hanging around her neck all this time. She gives me a smile that makes my stomach clench.

"Let's go. I've finally said my goodbyes." I nod and stand, helping her up and kissing the top of her head when she's on her feet. She leans over and rests a hand on the center of the headstone, in between her parents' names.

"Love you," she whispers to them both, and a soft breeze circles us, rustling the leaves of the willow standing guard above us all.

She looks up at the branches and then to me, lips curling. Was it just the wind? Maybe. But do both of us think it was a sign from her parents, them telling her they love her in return and saying goodbye? Absolutely.

"You can still make them smile, ya know," I say, nodding to the weeping willow as she reaches out to grab my hand and lace her fingers with mine. She huffs out a laugh.

"I was so mad when I heard the song," she says as we walk away from the family plot and back through the cemetery towards the truck.

I snort. "I can see that given the circumstances at the time."

"I think my exact words were 'that mother fucker,' but Beth can confirm." We both laugh lightly.

"And now?" I ask when we reach the truck. I turn and lean back against it and Laney stands between my legs, resting her hands on my chest while my own settle on her hips.

"Now," she says quietly, and we both know we're talking about much more than just her feelings about the song. I'm not going to rush her. I'll give her as long as she needs to figure out what she wants, but I need to know at least a hint of what direction she wants to go here. Does she want me to leave and never speak to me again? Does she want to start trying to be friends and see what happens? Does she want to jump all in and freefall off this cliff with me?

"Now," she continues, leaning up to kiss me softly, "it's time to finally start living the life *I* choose."

My heartrate kicks up, but I don't dare let myself believe it. Not yet. I clear my throat.

"And, uh, is a certain country music singer a part of that life by chance?"

"Kelly? She *has* aged like a fine wine now that you mention it…"

I bark out a laugh and give her ass a playful smack. She giggles and then sighs, shaking her head.

"Of course you are, Bowe." My chest lights up like a fucking Christmas tree, every cell in my body jumping for joy and sighing in utter contentment at the same time. She wants me. She wants this. "I have no idea what that life looks like, but I know that I want you beside me in it. That's all I've ever wanted. I know it's crazy and fast and we should probably—"

I cut her off with a kiss, unable to hold myself back any longer. She laughs lightly against my lips, but kisses me back fiercely, clenching the fabric of my shirt in her fingers. I cradle her face between my hands, deepening the kiss and pouring so much into it that my eyes water. I've wanted this since the night I met her. To finally hear the words after so long, when I thought I'd broken everything between us beyond repair, is almost too much.

Eventually I pull away, hands still on her face and my thumbs gently stroking her cheekbones. I hold her gaze for a long, long moment.

"You're still my heaven, Laney. I never wanted another one, and I never will."

Her eyes are glassy and she gives me a big smile, reaching up to put her hands over mine. A glint of sexy mischief sparks in her eyes before she leans up to kiss me softly again.

Against my lips, she whispers, "But you bet your ass I'm going to make you grovel for *years* to come, Bowen Wright."

She bites gently on my bottom lip and I groan from the sensation and the thousands of ways I plan to do just that running through my mind.

With the biggest smile I've worn in my entire fucking life, I say, "Yes, ma'am."

Chapter Thirty-Two

LANEY
ONE YEAR LATER

"ALRIGHT, READY?" Kelly says. "Three, two…"

Everyone in the huge circle has their shot glass raised in the air as we wait for her count. Bowen's arm snakes around my waist and pulls me tight against his side, and I look up to find him grinning like a fool. I can't help but return it.

"One!" Kelly yells and we all down our shots. Whoops and cheers and even a few sounds of disgust follow as everyone in the band finishes the preshow tradition. Kelly winks at me and holds out her hand for my glass. I hand it over and yelp when Bowen picks me up and tosses me over his shoulder. I giggle and wave as he strides off towards the green room.

"Be ready for show time in forty-five!" Kelly calls. The opening act is just starting up and I can feel the vibration from the bass even down here below the amphitheater stage. Bowe waves in acknowledgment and ducks into the room, kicking the door closed behind him. He turns and slides me down his body and presses me against the door in one smooth, fluid motion. His lips find mine and I rip his hat off and toss it away, tunneling my hands through his hair.

"This is my new favorite preshow tradition," he whispers against my lips before kissing along my jaw and down my throat. I moan quietly and arch my hips against him as he hits that spot he knows is my Kryptonite. He laughs lightly and I tug hard on his hair in retaliation, which only makes him laugh harder. He runs a hand down my side, over my waist, and grips my thigh, yanking it up to hitch it over his hip. He presses forward again and I curse quietly when I feel him hard against me.

I still can't quite believe I'm here. Not just backstage making out—and most likely about to do much more—with Bowe before another sold-out show on the first leg of his new tour, but *here* in the grander sense. Sometimes I can't believe that we're together, that our lives somehow curved back around to intersect again after we both thought they were on different paths forever. It was a bit of a whirlwind at first when we'd decided to throw caution to the wind and just jump in.

It was crazy.

It was reckless.

It was amazing and perfect and everything we could have dreamed.

We'd lost so much time already that neither one of us wanted to waste another second. I decided to step away from life in the surgical field for a while so I could really focus on me and what I wanted out of my life, and Bowen and I had spent every second of the rest of his break together.

We'd spent another couple of weeks at the farm where he did a lot of work on that groveling he'd promised, and we'd rarely gotten dressed at all. After that, we went out to visit his parents in Texas with Kelly and her husband, Tyler. The Wrights had welcomed me with open arms, acting like I'd always been a part of their family, and the kindness and love had hit me harder than I'd expected. I hadn't felt that kind of paternal love since my dad died, and I'd be lying if I said I wasn't kind of addicted to it now. I talk to them almost every day, and they are honestly the most salt of the earth, kindest people I have ever met.

After that trip, we'd escaped to one of those private bungalows that sit right out over the water in Bora Bora and *dear God* I blush just thinking about all the ways Bowe groveled there…

"How would you feel about living on the farm?" he'd asked on our last night there while I'd laid, sweaty and so blissed out I could barely move, on his chest.

"What do you mean?"

"I mean...would you want to make that our home? Live there together?" I'd pushed myself up and blinked at him. "Or we can buy something completely new, or we don't have to live together at all yet if it's too soon, I was just thinking...The farm is so special to both of us, and I know it's where your heart is, so I just thought..."

"You'd be ok with that? Living there?"

"Of course I would. I've always pictured myself there, if I'm being honest. All the time we were apart, there was still always this vision in my head of the future I wanted, the one I knew I gave up when I gave you up, but it never left me, regardless. And that future is you and me and our family on the farm. I'd want to get a few horses, of course, teach you and our kids to ride like I did growing up...what? Is that stupid? Or creepy?" he'd asked, grimacing a bit when I'd just stared at him in response.

"Kids?" I'd finally said quietly, as a smile spread across my face and warmth filled my chest. A family with Bowe out on the farm. It's the future I'd always pictured in the back of my mind too, even when I was too embarrassed or angry to admit it to myself.

"Hell yeah. I mean, if you want them..."

I'd leaned down to kiss him, slow and deep.

"I want that future too, Bowe. All of it. Even the smelly old horses," I'd told him, wrinkling my nose and he'd laughed.

Spoiler alert: turns out, I fucking love horses. We'd officially moved out to the farm a month later, bought our first two horses—keeping the musical pet name tradition going and naming them Tim and Faith—and there's been no looking back. Though of course Bowen still has to travel a ton, the farm is home. It always has been, really. It's the safe place he can come when everything else becomes too much, and it's the one place I've always felt like myself.

Being back close to Riverbend again, I started working more with the Foundation. I'd started an offshoot of it to provide medical care to low income areas, and though sometimes I do miss actual surgeries and treating patients directly, I get such an intense joy and sense of purpose from the Foundation work that I know in my heart that this is what I'm meant to do. I'm still licensed to practice medicine, of course, which has come in handy a few times on tour with rowdy musicians running around, and who knows, maybe one day I'll get back into it, start my own practice to serve the smaller communities out by the farm, but for now, I'm immensely happy where I am.

I honestly didn't know what was going on the first time the feeling swept over me. The total, all-encompassing feeling of contentment and joy that made my heart feel like it was swelling in my chest was so foreign to me that I'd apparently looked confused as hell.

"You alright, babe?" Bowe had asked one night as he'd worked on plans to turn the second floor of the detached garage into a home studio with all the bells and whistles.

"Yeah, I'm just...happy, I think."

He'd snorted and put his pencil down, rising from the table and striding over to me. He'd lifted me onto the counter and leaned in, wedging his hips between my thighs and gently running his hands up them as I draped my arms over his shoulders. He'd leaned in and kissed me softly.

"You think?"

"I mean, I *know* I'm happy, asshole, but...this is the first time that everything in my life has just felt...right, ya know? Like I'm exactly where I'm meant to be and where I *want* to be, and everything is just so perfect I kind of want to cry."

"I'm glad you finally found it, Lanes. You deserve it more than anyone I know."

Beth passed the bar with flying colors just like I knew she would, and actually moved to Riverbend to serve as in-house counsel for the Foundation. She'd earned the spot completely on her own without any help from me. I'd only casually mentioned that we were looking and she took it from there. It's been absolutely amazing having her and Colt so close. Colt and Bowen hit it off immediately, thankfully, and we're actually hosting their wedding out at the farm in just a couple of months.

So, yeah, life has been amazing and hectic and crazy and scary and perfect and a thousand other things all at once. But my God, it's *mine*, the life I chose for myself and I wouldn't have it any other way.

I pull myself back to the present when Bowe kisses along the top swells of my breasts above the dip of my tank top and I gasp, writhing my hips against him.

"We don't have much time," I remind him, digging my fingers into his hair harder and wondering if they could really say that much if he's a little late. I mean, he's the headliner…they'll wait for him, right? But no, that's wrong and I know it, and we have things to discuss before he goes on stage. So, I smile and decide to change the direction this is going, knowing just how to have some fun with time to spare. I lower my leg and he makes a sound of annoyance against my neck, but I yank his head back up to mine and kiss him hard as I tear his belt off and his pants open.

"Lanes," he says, half warning, half begging, and I grin against his lips.

"Time me," I whisper. "Bet I can have you coming and thanking me in ten minutes flat."

He tries to protest, maybe saying he'll definitely last longer than that, but whatever he's going to say dies in his throat as I sink to my knees in front of him and pull his cock free. The sight of him hard and ready only makes me wish we had all night to play, but I remind myself that we can revisit after the show.

I don't waste any time, just lean forward and twirl my tongue around the crown, making him groan. His head lulls backwards as I slowly take him deep, sliding his shaft between my lips until he hits the back of my throat and, not for the first time, I'm glad I've never had a gag reflex to worry about.

"Ah, *fuck*," he hisses.

I suck him hard and his hips buck, a low moan rumbling through his chest. I glide one hand upward, beneath the hem of his shirt, and splay my fingers over his stomach, loving the way his skin feels beneath my palm, the way his muscles flex at my touch. I take him deep again and again before moving to suck on just the tip, using my hand to stroke his slicked shaft.

"Jesus Christ," he rasps. He tangles his hand in my hair and uses his grip to tilt my head back. My entire core clenches, knowing what's coming. I fucking love when he does this. I meet his gaze, his eyes dark and burning.

"Eyes here, darlin'." I moan softly around his cock, but don't dare pull my gaze from his as I slowly take him deep again. "*Ah fuck,* that's my girl."

My stomach clenches, his words making me melt. He keeps his hold on my head and then starts to gently guide it forward as he moves his hips. He waits for a second after the first slow thrust, arching a brow in question. I nod emphatically and he shudders. And then he's moving his hips again, harder now, and I dig my nails into his stomach, the other clenching his thigh.

"Ah, God, just like that. You look so fucking pretty when I fuck your mouth, Laney."

I whimper, nearly combusting. He reaches over my head with his other hand and leans his palm against the door, needing the support, I think. He keeps arching his hips, keepings guiding my head, and slides deeper and deeper down my throat. I can tell he's getting close by the sounds he's making. Little part moans-part grunts-part growls, and they drive me fucking crazy in the best way.

"Don't stop…"

I don't dare. I add my hand again, stroking in time with the bobbing of my head, and his breathing becomes harsh and ragged.

"Fuck, fuck, *fucckkkk,*" he groans loudly in a hoarse voice as he comes hard. I keep going, taking everything he has to give, drinking him down and preening at the way his body trembles. "Jesus Christ, Laney."

I pull away, grinning, and place a soft kiss on his hip bone before pushing to my feet. He leans in and kisses my forehead before leaning his against it, still breathing hard. I lay my open hand against his chest, that reassuring *thump thump* slamming against my palm.

"You are gonna be the death of me, you know that?"

My smile widens and he kisses me softly before sighing and pulling away to fix his pants.

"Was that ten minutes?"

"Just remember payback is a bitch," he says with a mock scowl. I quirk a brow in challenge, but can't wait for him to give me my payback as soon as humanly possible. *The things that man can do with his tongue...*

"So, you like having me on tour with you then?" I ask as I saunter to the couch and sink down, tracing my fingers over his old guitar and smiling at that little heart from so long ago. He comes over and flops down beside me, running his hand through his hair.

"Oh you have *no* idea, sweetheart," he tells me with a grin as he trails his hand up and down my thigh. We both glance to the door when someone bangs on it.

"Five-minute warning!" Kelly calls. "Gotta call mom and dad!"

Well, I guess it's time. My heart starts to beat double-time, and I take a deep breath to settle myself. I put my hand over his where it rests on my leg and intertwine our fingers.

Here we go.

"It's a shame I'll have to miss the second half of it then," I say casually and his brow furrows.

"What? Why are you missing the second half of the tour? Did you decide to go back to the hospital?" he asks, eyes zeroed in where he gently runs his thumb in slow circles along my inner thigh. I love that that's his first thought. I love how much he's always encouraging me to do whatever I feel in my heart is right and supporting me a thousand percent no matter what direction that takes me on any given day.

"Nah," I say breezily with a shrug. "I just think touring with a newborn will be a little difficult."

He freezes completely for a heartbeat before he whips his head up to meet my gaze.

"Did you just...are you saying...are we...?" I bite my lip and nod, and he jumps up from the couch and throws his head back, yelling to the ceiling. "Whooooo!!!! YEAH BABY!!" He pulls me up and I can't help but laugh through the tears welling as he lifts me into his arms and spins me around and around. I wrap my arms around him and he buries his face in my neck. His shoulders shake gently and I can feel his tears tracking down my throat.

"Hey," I say softly. "Are you alright?" He sets me down so that he can pull back and meet my gaze. He puts one finger under my chin in that way that makes me melt and tilts my head back.

"Alright? Baby, I've never been happier in my life." His blue-green eyes are shining with tears, his smile so big and genuine that my heart breaks a little from pure happiness. "I'm gonna be a dad," he says in an awed whisper. "We're gonna have a baby."

"Yeah we are," I agree, smiling so big my cheeks hurt. He leans in then and kisses me in a way he never has before, a new kind of love and gratitude and devotion flowing into it that I'm breathless by the time Kelly bursts into the door.

"Did you tell him!?" she asks, rushing forward. Bowe and I pull apart and Kelly holds her hands to her chest. "You did! Ahhhh!!!" I step out of the way as she barrels towards her brother, and the two of them lock in a fierce embrace. Both of the Wright children are crying when they finally break apart.

"I'm going to be the best fucking aunt," Kelly says, wiping tears from her eyes.

"Wait—you knew?" Bowe asks her, looking between the two of us with a bit of accusation.

"Well, I kind of had to tell her to explain why she needed to make my shot apple juice before all the shows recently instead of bourbon," I say with a shrug.

"Do you know how hard it's been to keep this secret for the past month!? I've been literally dying," Kelly says dramatically before pulling me into a tight hug. She pulls away and yanks her phone from her pocket.

"And now, we finally get to tell the grandparents!"

I'M GONNA BE A DAD.

Laney and I are going to have a baby.

I really didn't think life could get better with as blissed the fuck out as I've been with Laney for the last year, but this news fills my entire soul with a new kind of joy that I hadn't even imagined was possible. I've always wanted a family. I hadn't been lying when I'd told Laney that I'd imagined our future at the farm together, including kids running around. A little boy with hazel eyes like his momma, a little girl who loves to ride horses with her daddy. I could see it all so clearly, despite the knowledge that it was all just a dream that would never come true.

But now, it is. Now it's real and I don't even know how to contain the happiness threatening to make my chest explode. Things are fucking perfect.

Well, almost. But I'm about to fix that.

"Are y'all having a good time tonight?!" I yell to the crowd while I fiddle with the tuning on my guitar. A hundred thousand voices scream back in answer and I grin. "Good, good. Now listen, I'm hoping y'all can help me out with something. See, my girl is a little shy, but I think if all of you ask *real* nice, she might just come out here." I turn to look offstage and she's shaking her head at me but smiling.

"Come on now, Laney, get on out here." I gesture to the crowd and start the chant. "Lane-y, Lane-y, Lane-y..." They pick it up immediately and her name stars echoing around the amphitheater. I look back at her again and she looks torn between wanting to strangle me and laughing her head off. The crowd chants louder and louder and I give Laney a look that says *they aren't gonna stop, you better get out here.* She rolls her eyes but heads towards me. It's not the first time I've dragged her on stage with me, so she's gotten over her initial stage fright, and is usually good natured about it.

The crowd cheers and she gives them a little wave. I spin my guitar so that it rests against my back, and pull Laney in for a quick hug.

"Say hey to everyone, Lanes."

"Hey, everyone," she says into the mic and the crowd goes wild again, making us both laugh.

"Listen, I just have one quick question and then I'll let you get back to watching me shake my ass all over this stage." *Whoos* and screams ripple through the crowd and I throw out a wink. Laney huffs out a laugh, but it dies off quickly as I sink down to one knee, pulling the ring out of my back pocket. Laney's eyes fly wide just as the crowd absolutely loses their minds.

The craziest part is that I'd planned to propose *tomorrow*, when we had a rare night off. Kelly had helped me plan a whole thing with a romantic dinner on the beach and fairy lights and the works, but as great as it would have been, it didn't quite feel right.

But this does.

She's the reason I'm here, really. Every single song that got me on this stage, with all these people screaming and cheering and singing along, came from Laney in one way or another. She's my endless inspiration and I wouldn't be here without her, so this seems like the perfect place to ask her the most important question.

"Bowe?" she whispers as I take her hand. It's trembling slightly, or hell, maybe it's mine that's shaking like a leaf, actually. I don't have any doubt what her answer will be, not really, but I'm still nervous as hell all of a sudden. Maybe she won't think this was the right place.

Maybe she'll hate that I did it in front of all these strangers…but no, I don't see any of that in her eyes. I only see pure, unadulterated joy and love reflecting back at me.

"Laney Thorton, will you marry me?"

The crowd goes apeshit, but even with thousands upon thousands of eyes on us, the world narrows and it's just me and Laney and the future hanging in the air between us. Her eyes are watery and a single tear escapes down her cheek as she says the word that makes my chest feel as if it's going to burst:

"*Yes.*"

I slide the ring on her finger and leap up as the roar of the crowd hits us like a physical blow, so loud I think it shakes the very stage beneath our feet. I lift Laney into the air and spin her around, before kissing her deeply. I catch Kelly's eye and she's crying again, and I throw her a wink.

"I can't believe you just did that," Laney whisper-yells in my ear when I turn to smile back at the crowd, but I know she isn't mad. "How the hell did you have a ring??"

"Darlin', this has been in the works for a long time."

"A few months?" she asks.

"More like since the night we met." Her eyes shine and I turn to the microphone again. "Alright, y'all. This next song is one I wrote about this girl right here fifteen years ago. It's a little something about a weeping willow…"

The band starts playing and I lean in to kiss Laney one more time as the cheers continue to ring out around us. The stage lights shine down like stars, and happiness like I never could have imagined settles over every inch of me, down deep into my bones.

The girl who can make a weeping willow smile is going to be mine forever.

She's my heaven.

She always has been.

She always will be.

Acknowledgments

As usual, this book wouldn't have been possible without a whole host of people, so I need to thank:

- My husband, for always supporting me in this crazy hobby.
- Warren Zeiders for making incredible music that inspired this story.
- Lexie, Kayleigh, and Kala (forever funny) for being the best cheerleaders and bullies ever. Jeff beans. Get the pudding. Book Babes 4 life
- My amazing PA, Nancy, who I couldn't survive without!
- My awesome ARC readers.
- My Street Team for being the best hype team ever.
- All of you reading this right this second. I adore every single one of you! Thank you for taking a chance on a no-name indie author like me.

Also by K.D. Miller

Adult Contemporary Romance

- Carpe F*cking Diem
- Wrong Place. Wrong Time. Right Viscount.
- Puck the Holidays (Vipers Sin Bin - Book 1)
- Puck of the Irish (Vipers Sin Bin - Book 2)

Adult Paranormal Romance

- Red
- Dark Burning (Veracity of the Gods - Book 1)
- Sweet Tempest (Veracity of the Gods - Book 2)
- Vows Forged in Blood

Young Adult Sci-Fi/Fantasy

- Titan Rising (Outliers Series - Book 1)
- Titan Unleashed (Outliers Series - Book 2)
- Titan Reckoning (Outliers Series - Book 3)
- Evansfire